NOT A NORMAL FAMILY

A PSYCHOLOGICAL THRILLER

RACHEL HARGROVE

ISBN: 978-1-0881-8368-7

Imprint: Powerhouse Press, LLC

ONE
THE PRESENT

I can't stop killing.

I've tried, but there's a reason Washington State has a rich history of serial killers. Death is in the air. The whole state has a bleak smell. Moldy and damp. It turns putrid the longer it rains.

And it always rains.

It's mid-June and barely sixty-five degrees. A brooding sky frowns over the gritty landscape. Everywhere I look, darkness. This wasn't what I imagined when I packed for this family camping trip.

We're headed for the Mount Baker-Snoqualmie National Forest. Plenty of hiking, fishing, campfire songs, marshmallow roasting, and opportunities for me to *slip*. I've planned out how I'll do it. It won't be difficult. Scores of hikers go missing every year. Tragic, but it happens. Most people overestimate their abilities in the wild.

So far, it's just a fantasy. I can't promise it'll stay that way. I'll do my best not to relapse, but my hopes aren't high. My track record speaks for itself. I keep obsessing about how, when, and the expression on my victim's face when they realize it's me. I struggle to keep these violent thoughts at bay, but the closer we get to our destination... the more certain I am that something terrible will happen.

Seven of us are going on this vacation.

At least one of them will die.

TWO
AMBER

I hate my ex-husband.

I don't want to loathe the father of my child, but he makes it incredibly hard. My thumb hesitates over the message box as I stare at his infuriating text.

SCOTT

Are you bringing anything healthy to eat?

Halfway into packing for the trip, my phone chimed with his passive-aggressive question. I bristle at the glaring implication—that because I'm not skinny, I know nothing about eating healthy. Like I'm planning to feed us junk.

Twinkies and licorice rope.

SCOTT

Be serious.

More pings assault the air, but I close the screen and toss the phone on the king-sized bed. It lands on the linen sheets my husband bought for my birthday—one of his many thoughtful gifts since we married. I double-check my luggage for the bug spray, the camelbacks, and the brand-new hiking boots I've yet to break in. I should leave them here for a cast-iron excuse to stay behind at the cabin. But if I do, Scott will say I did it to avoid exercise. I can't stomach him being right about a single thing.

I would skip this vacation if it weren't for the mediation agreement Scott forced down my throat—a court-ordered annual family trip with both of us and Nicole. She turns eighteen next year, which means we'll never have to do this again. If I don't go, Scott *will* drag me into court. I'll have to pay a nasty fine *and* deal with my infuriating ex. I shouldn't have signed that contract, but guilt forced my hand.

Nicole took the divorce so hard. Poor girl. She always hoped we'd get back together. My chest still aches when I replay her heart-rending sobs, and later, her accusation that I broke apart our family. I hoped Scott and I would one day forgive each other and celebrate Nicole's milestones together. I wanted us to put aside the heartbreak and bitterness, but it never happened. Scott and I kept our contact limited to terse text messages. It worked out okay until I remarried. We could communicate without veiled insults or sarcasm, but things are much worse now. Nicole needs to see us getting along, but the way this morning is going, I'll have more success winning the Powerball.

SCOTT

Answer me.

Where are you?

Silence lulls, and then my cellphone shrieks with a request for a video call. Scott's face flashes over the screen. I groan. Dare I ignore him? No. I can't start on the wrong foot hours before the trip starts. Inhaling a deep breath, I accept the call.

Scott pops onto the rectangular screen. He has a broad hero's face with a chiseled jaw. A strong nose leads to hooded eyes so dark that staring into them tingles my spine with unease. Sweat clings to his fair skin that's dotted with freckles. The tight curls on his head spark like copper fire. A mechanical sound filters through the speaker. Is he on his treadmill? The camera pans to exercise equipment crammed in his cluttered garage. Through the mirror, Scott's athletic frame glides into view. It feels like another cheap taunt—*See what you left behind?*

"Hey, Scott."

"I'd appreciate it if you responded to my texts."

His clipped tone sends a wave of irritation through me, but I resist the urge to hurl an insult. *Keep the peace, Amber. Think of Nicole.*

I force my lips to smile. "I'm in the middle of packing. What's up?"

"I want an answer to my question."

A flood of blistering heat engulfs my cheeks. "I told you weeks ago. Hot dogs. Ground beef for tacos. Tomato. Lettuce. Cheese. All the fixings. I've got those microwavable bags for rice. I have plenty of meat for the barbecue. Fruit bowls. Yogurt. Oatmeal."

"I didn't *ask* for an itemized list."

"You blew up my phone to grill me about food."

"I asked if you were bringing anything that wasn't loaded with sugar and fat. A yes or no would've sufficed."

"If I say yes, you'll find something to criticize later. So get it out of your system now."

His sneer rakes a blazing line down my back. "I'm trying to teach our daughter healthy eating habits. I realize that's a foreign concept to you."

"A fat joke. Very original."

"It's not a joke to me, Amber."

A muscle jumps in my clenched jaw. "Scott, it's too early for me to deal with your bull—"

"Seriously? You can't last *one minute* into a conversation without profanity?"

I release a tense breath. "Because I'd rather put out a fire with my face than talk to you."

Scott sighs, rolling his eyes so obnoxiously that I wish I could stab him through the screen. "Look, I'm not letting you drag me into an argument. I only called to get an answer."

"Right, Scott."

"Don't be mad. You could've avoided this discussion with a simple text."

"Sure. It's all my fault."

"Yeah. You're already introducing drama into what's supposed to be a fun family event."

I will strangle this man.

I breathe in deeply and slowly let it out. Hours of therapy taught me how to talk to my ex without blowing an artery.

"Nicole has many options to choose from." I put him on speaker so that this phone call isn't a complete waste of time. "Is that all?"

I fold a swimsuit as Scott speaks in a halting voice. "No. I uh—need to know if we have enough food for one more person."

"Should be fine. Did you invite a friend?"

Scott steps off the treadmill and pats his neck with a white towel. "Fred is coming with us."

Fred is Scott's younger brother who suffers from schizophrenia. When we started dating, Scott regaled me with countless stories of his "crazy" brother. He warned me about him so often that I was shocked when I met Fred. He seemed…normal, and yet, his every comment was met by an eye roll or outright dismissed. His dad and stepmom never stopped treating him like a loser. I have no problem with Fred, but I have my reasons for not wanting him around.

I rub my head. "Okay."

Scott is silent for a few seconds. "I really would like him to come."

"I said it's fine."

"You say that, but you never mean it."

I slam another article of clothing into the suitcase. "Scott, I can't do this. I have to finish packing. I haven't had breakfast."

"Yeah, yeah, yeah. All right." Scott towels his chest as I try not to scream. "Oh, and don't mention Victoria. She broke up with him a few months ago. Left him a note and moved out."

"Weren't they together for, what, seven years?"

"Yeah. I guess she got fed up with him. Who wouldn't? He's back to living with Dad. It's...bad. He drives my stepmom nuts. I don't feel good about leaving him alone with them. He's a lot, you know?"

"If you say so."

Having never felt that way about Fred, I can't agree, and it's rich for Scott to call Fred high maintenance. My ex is not exactly low-key. Inviting his brother the morning of our trip is a prime example.

Scott rubs his forehead and grimaces. "You're mad."

I am. "Not at all."

He sighs heavily. "Amber, you don't have to lie. I get it. I don't want him there either, but he's family. I can't abandon him in a great time of need."

"*Scott.* Learn to take yes for an answer."

A lazy smile tiptoes across Scott's broad face. "I figured it'd be okay. You two have so much in common."

He layers his words with a heavy dose of sarcasm, spiking my blood pressure. I clench my mouth tighter. "Because we're both insane? Or are you making another fat joke?"

He rolls his eyes. "Geez, Amber. Lighten up."

"Funny how I'm always the butt of the joke."

He groans. "It was just a comment."

"I've had enough of your comments to last me a lifetime."

He throws his hand in the air. "I can't say anything without you jumping down my throat."

"No, you can't," I agree, heart pounding. "I have no interest in your unfiltered thoughts, and trust me, you don't want to hear mine."

"You have no sense of humor. Got it."

When we were married, he mocked my wardrobe. My reluctance to wear makeup. My friends. Day after day, he cracked "jokes" that ranged from innocuous to cruel. I chalked up the behavior to a personality quirk and shrugged it off. I still can't erase the heat climbing my neck whenever I replay him poking at my postpartum belly and saying *You feel like dough.*

Scott strolls into his tiny bathroom, where the mirror reflects the planes of muscle across his chest. He's an insecure jerk. He's jealous and fishing for compliments. I pity him. I should count my blessings, hang up, and do my best to ignore his taunts. But all I want to do is scream at him. I grit my teeth, barely able to hold back my temper, and force my tone into a neutral one.

"I have to get going."

His brow furrows. "You need to make more of an effort for our daughter's sake."

"Sounds good," I say, just to shut him up. "See you later."

I stab the red button, ending the call. I breathe deeply to disperse the rage swirling in my lungs. I have no outlet for this anger, and it sucks. I don't like myself when I'm around him. He brings out the worst in me, and I'm pretty sure I do the same to him. I'll go on this trip. I have to. But I won't be surprised if it ends in a murder-suicide.

THREE
AMBER

Zipping my suitcase shut, I drag it out of the bedroom and roll it down the hall. I push it, and it collides with the two other suitcases. Then I follow the savory scent luring me to the kitchen, where my husband and seventeen-year-old stepson are eating breakfast. As usual, my daughter is nowhere to be seen.

Cameron sits at the table I bought a few months ago, not realizing that his huge frame would dominate the Scandinavian furniture. My husband has the body of a linebacker. He's big, almost a head taller than Scott, but his size has never intimidated me. He doesn't raise his voice. His ability to stay calm no matter what the situation is what I admire most about him. And I love how he never rises to Scott's bait—not that he doesn't hate his guts.

Cameron ladles an extra helping of scrambled eggs onto David's plate. David eats like he's never had a full meal in his life. Flecks of egg land on the quartz counter. My husband clicks his tongue, his brow line furrowing.

"You're making a mess."

David mumbles an apology as he tears into a muffin. I squeeze his shoulder, and he beams at me.

"Morning, Mom."

I smile. "Morning."

David gulps down a glass of orange juice and attacks his food. In looks, he resembles his father. Tanned skin and thick, dark hair that's in desperate need of a trim. He's in that awkward phase of boyhood where his limbs look too thin and long.

I rumple his hair and approach the espresso machine, but my coffee mug is already filled. A brown leaf floats in white foam, wobbling as I bring it to my lips. The rich taste rolls over my tongue, and I groan.

"Thanks, Cam."

Cameron nudges his son. "The kid made it."

"You did?" I set the cup down on the table as David nods. "Wow, it's perfect. Thanks."

Pink stains David's golden cheeks. He gets flustered when I compliment him, which is an upgrade from him accusing me of lying. It took a few months to break through his sullen shell, for him to open up. When Cameron and his son first moved in, I thought I had my work cut out with two moody teenagers, but David turned out to be a sweetheart. He mows the lawn without being asked. He helps me with dinner. Whenever I go grocery shopping, he tags along. The average seventeen-year-old doesn't spend *this* much time with their stepmom, but I don't care. He's a good kid who's been through a lot.

"Did you pack everything?"

David bows his dark head, his eyes flicking to mine. "I think so. I got my clothes and stuff. The only thing left is my toothbrush."

"You don't sound excited."

"I am. I just…I dunno." He stabs at bits of egg, looking thoughtful. "I still haven't told Coach Scott I'm quitting football."

My ex is a software engineer at Amazon, but every Tuesday and Thursday, he helps coach football at the kids' high school. He's very enthusiastic about it.

"Scott will get over it."

David plays with his food. "Are you sure?"

"Yes, honey, and if he guilts you, tell me. I'll set him straight."

"He'll ask me why I'm leaving in senior year. He'll say I'm giving up athletic scholarships. What am I supposed to tell him?"

"You don't need a scholarship. We have plenty of money." I sit down beside him as Cameron ladles food onto a plate. "And he's not your dad. You don't have to explain yourself."

"I know. I'm being stupid."

I tap his wrist. "Don't call my son stupid. It hurts my feelings."

David snorts and looks away.

I eat the scrambled eggs mixed with bacon, biting back a groan. Cameron's cooking puts mine to shame. For a guy who works in tech, he's an amazing cook. Most men like him rely on delivery services. Not Cameron. He lives to eat. The other day he made homemade scones with raspberries from the farmer's market. *Delicious*.

Cameron sips his coffee. "Who were you on the phone with?"

I sigh. "Scott."

He makes a face. "How is the walking hemorrhoid?"

I raise my voice sharply. "*Cam*."

"Sorry, the tumor."

I wince. David laughs so hard he chokes on his juice. Cameron's cute nickname for my ex bothers me. Sort of. I only wish Cameron wouldn't disrespect him in front of the kids. Scott has enough ammunition against me these days. He'll accuse me of turning Nicole against him.

"He's being Scott, as usual." I dunk the buttered toast in my coffee, shrugging. "He called to hassle me about dumb stuff. Then he told me his brother's coming."

Cameron squints. "Fred, right?"

"Yeah. His girlfriend dumped him and his life is a mess, so Scott invited him along."

"Great," he grumbles. "Another Maxwell."

"I'm not happy about it either." I glance up to check if Nicole entered the kitchen, dipping into a whisper. "I tried to say no, but you know how he gets. He doesn't listen."

"Then make him."

"It's not that simple."

Cameron cocks his head. "Why not?"

I chew my lip, thinking about the drama bomb on the verge of exploding. It's almost like witnessing a violent car wreck. I want a front-row seat to the inevitable collision, but now is not the time. Not when we're about to go on this stressful trip.

"I'm trying to keep the peace."

Cameron puts down his mug. Liquid spills over the sides. "Babe, you can't let him walk all over you."

"I'm not." Although I didn't stop him from bringing his brother, which I'm not thrilled about. "I just want *one* family event that doesn't go up in flames."

Cameron grabs a napkin from the stack and wipes the table. "Once Nicole turns eighteen, we won't have to do this anymore."

"It didn't used to be so bad. He's been...different since we married."

"By that, you mean an unbelievable pain in our—"

"*Cam*," I bark, whipping around to check that Nicole hasn't joined us. Cameron does not attempt to disguise his contempt as he cuts his eggs with the edge of his fork.

"Sorry, not sorry. You'll never have one big happy family with him in the picture."

"As long as he's alive, he'll be a familiar face at every Christmas."

"Then I won't give up hope that a bear mauls him."

"Cam. *Stop.*"

Cameron loops my waist with his arm, yanking me onto his lap. My butt collides with his strong thighs and I fall against his chest, my gaze crashing with his fiery blues. My heart throbs. Even with his wrinkled shirt and rumpled black hair, my husband is attractive. Dark stubble clings to his sharp jawline. He grasps my neck, fingers digging into my hair, and pulls me into a hard kiss. Heat climbs my face. I slide my palms over his pecs, trying not to respond with the same enthusiasm as I would if we were alone.

I'm so dizzy with the sensation of his lips devouring mine, that I don't notice Nicole until a chair shrieks across the tiles. I tear myself off Cameron and glimpse my seventeen-year-old daughter, still in her pajamas, sitting at the far end of the table.

"Do you have to do that in public?"

I disengage from Cameron and return to my chair. "Eat and get dressed."

Nicole's glare drills into me. "Gee, what do you think I'm doing?"

"Being a brat, as usual," David deadpans, softening when he glances at me.

"You're such a jerk," she shoots back.

"Your face is a jerk."

Nicole's eyes sparkle with the love of a challenge. "Your dad's face is a jerk."

David laughs.

"Okay, *enough*." Cameron lowers his potent stare at my daughter, who wilts. "And stop talking to your mother like that."

"She started it," she says, patches of pink claiming her cheeks. "I can't even sit down without her barking orders like I'm a dog."

I set down my fork hard on the ceramic plate. "If you don't want me to be harsh, then stop giving me a reason."

She flails her arms. "What did I do now?"

I let out a long, frustrated breath. "You're late. You know how much I hate that."

Before I get another word in, she grabs a muffin from a bowl and charges out of the kitchen. A distant door slams. *Great.* She's in a mood.

We have a strict policy against slammed doors in this house, but I can't muster the energy to discipline her when I need to conserve it for the storm that's coming. I wash the dishes, praying for car trouble. A freak snowstorm. Anything to cancel this family vacation. Not only will I have to deal with my ex-husband and his brother, but I'll also have my pissed off daughter to manage.

What could go wrong?

FOUR
AMBER

SCOTT

I need you to pick up Fred.

We don't have space in our car and you're closer to his apartment.

My ex is trolling me. Either that, or he's trying to put me into an early grave with a rage-induced stroke.

I step outside as Cameron loads our SUV with our suitcases, and gaze into the lawn bursting with color. Lavender, moss, and ferns burst from the ground. Vines climb the porch posts. Roses twine across fences. Flowers spill over their beds, mingling with herbs. It's the only part of the house I didn't remodel. The previous owner had an eclectic taste that didn't jibe with my preference for neat, modern designs, but I like the garden. It's *organized* chaos.

Every morning, I sit out on the covered patio with my coffee and breathe in nature's gentle perfume. It's such an upgrade from the rambler in Shoreline. The colonial-style home with its cute white gables never fails to boost my mood. All I have to do is imagine Scott the day he visited my Queen Anne house, his discomfort when he shook hands with my more accomplished husband. I still remember the insulting amount of surprise in his lifted eyebrows as he glanced from me to Cameron—*you married this guy?*

He expected me to strike out with dating. I don't know why. I've never had a problem getting dates. Not to brag, but I'm not unattractive. It's like Scott couldn't conceive of a reality where I leveled up from our relationship. No doubt, he pictured me crawling to his doorstep, begging him to take me back. Instead I'm better off without him in every way imaginable. That must eat at him. I hope it does. He *deserves* the agony of rolling up in Laura's Crosstrek to drop off my daughter at a home he'll never have.

Nicole emerges from the front door, pink suitcase in tow, wearing a crop top and high-rise jeans with ripped holes in the knees. David follows close behind in a faded band T-shirt and dark denim, tendrils of hair curling on his forehead. He brushes them aside and seizes the handle of Nicole's luggage.

"Nicky, get inside. I'll load it up."

"Thanks." She smiles, climbing into the SUV.

My heart warms as David hauls the luggage into the trunk. I pat his back as he shuts the lid. Then I head to the front and slide into the passenger seat. Cameron's hand lands on my thigh as he turns, his steely gaze fixed on the children.

"We ready to go? Everybody's been to the bathroom?"

The kids nod, absorbed in their smartphones.

Cameron shifts the Range Rover into reverse and we roll backward, away from my sanctuary. I've over-prepared for this trip, so I'm not worried about food, but I'm very much a homebody. I spend at least fifty percent of my vacations longing for home.

My anxiety ramps up the moment we merge onto I-5. The ostentatious ringtone I've selected for Scott's calls pierces the quiet. *This better be an emergency.*

I answer the phone, my skin prickling. "What is it?"

"Sorry to *bother* you, but I need a response to my text."

"I'm not picking up your brother, Scott."

"Fred's coming?" pipes up David.

"Um, maybe." I return my attention to the phone, speaking firmly into the receiver. "He's *your* brother. *I* didn't invite him. *You* wanted him to come."

"I don't have a car big enough to transport him."

"That's *ridiculous*. You have Laura's Crosstrek that you use for mountain biking, paddle boarding, and whatever other sport you're currently into."

"Nice," he seethes. "Our daughter likes to do those things, too. It must've slipped your mind that I'm bringing all of her sporting equipment along with my wife's stuff. I guess you also forgot that we don't have a giant Range Rover. All those months in your hilltop mansion has made you forget what life is like for the regular folk. I'm not rich like your millionaire husband. I can't afford a gas-guzzling vehicle to schlep me to yoga class."

He just can't stop, can he?

I clench my mouth tighter. "Nobody asked you to bring all that. We're there for three days to do some hiking and cook s'mores. That's it. We're leaving early Monday morning."

"So I should give up my hobbies because you find them inconvenient?"

My God, he's impossible. "What's inconvenient is you surprising me with another guest, and then demanding that I pick him up."

"Well, you wanted us to be a close-knit family. Did you mean that...or were you lying?"

"You are such an insufferable pri—"

"There you go with the profanity!" he shouts, his tone inflamed and belligerent. "Classic Amber. Amping up the drama. My friend's kid has more self-control than you."

I chuckle, muttering under my breath, "Says the guy picking fights with me at every opportunity."

"What did you say?"

"Nothing."

He huffs. "You know what? Fine. Leave him behind. I'll let him know that you can't be *bothered* to swing by my dad's place. I hope Nicole sees how cold you are. So go ahead. Show the world how inconsiderate you are."

I stab the end call button and shove the phone into my purse. My hands shake as I fold them in my lap. I'm irritated at the current running through me. As Cameron's broad hand rolls over my clenched fist, the dam of emotion inside me almost breaks.

Am I inconsiderate?

"Are you okay?" asks David from the back seat.

I nod, not trusting myself to speak in front of the kids. Nicole's lips press into a whitened line. David's glare seems to dive into me. "He's so mean to you. I don't get it."

"His loss. My gain," Cameron mutters. "Whatever he said…ignore it."

My eyes mist. "He wants us to give his brother a ride."

The faintest sneer curls Cameron's mouth. "He's got some big cojones."

I chew my lip. "It would be on the way…he lives off Aurora."

"I don't care. It's the principle of it. He didn't even have the decency to *ask*. He just told you what to do, like he's your husband." Cameron shakes his head, his comforting hand still wrapped around mine. "You need to stop letting him steamroll you."

I sigh. "What if he gets upset?"

Cameron shrugs. "His problem."

I swallow my unspoken plea, aware that my dynamic with Scott needs to change. A sinking feeling bottoms out my stomach as we pass the exit we're supposed to take for his dad's place. I had my doubts at the beginning, but now I'm sure we're headed for certain disaster.

I'll be lucky if I come out alive.

FIVE
AMBER

We arrive at the campground with all limbs intact, but I'm not sure how long that'll last. Especially with the glares my ex hurls in Cameron's direction.

I stand in the driveway of our cabin rental, which lights up like a jewel against a fantastic backdrop of silhouetted trees and an orange sky. Seattle's brooding clouds seem to have followed us. Mist obscures a breathtaking view of Mount Rainier. The drive was worth it just to see the snow-tipped mountain peeking through the clouds, its blue glaciers dazzling in the sunlight.

Wow. I should've reserved more campsites this summer. It's nice out here. Cold, but nice. A rich smell saturates the humid air. A thick wall of green faces me in every direction, where tiny paths carve through the forest.

The kids race for the front door. Cameron rolls our luggage inside. Fred and Scott's wife, Laura, unpack bags of food in the kitchen, leaving Scott and I alone. His frayed T-shirt rides up his muscled back as he reaches for the bikes strapped to the roof. Scott yanks the bikes down. They crash onto the forest floor in a tangle of metal. He swears profusely as he bends over, examining a wheel.

I bite back a laugh. He's always been careless. He wrecked his car several times during our relationship and still insisted on driving Nicole and I everywhere. *Men are better drivers, Amber. It's science.* When I printed out a wealth of evidence proving otherwise, he called me a know-it-all.

Scott wheels the bikes into the garage and returns to the car, shaking his head. He gathers the rest of his things from the Crosstrek and shuts the door. I approach him tentatively, eager to dissolve the tension between us.

"Beautiful spot, huh?"

He grunts, sliding the keys into his pocket. "I guess."

"Good job picking the campsite. The kids will have a blast."

Scott leans against his car, staring into the woods with an apathy I almost admire. After a while, his frosty gaze swings to mine.

"Don't talk to me like I'm a child."

I gape at him. "What?"

"I don't need you to talk to me like I'm one of your first graders, okay? It's insulting."

"Geez, Scott. It's a compliment."

He sneers. I shake my head. Engaging with him while he's in a foul mood is a bad idea, especially when worse is around the corner.

In the kitchen, actually.

I seize a green-and-white bag from the trunk. Then I heave. It's heavy. The straps dig into my shoulders as I yank another bag clinking with beer bottles. Scott watches with a curled lip as I press the button, closing the trunk, and slowly begin my way up the steep driveway. A normal man would offer to help, but Scott isn't normal or a man. He's a child.

Scott whistles as he walks alongside me, oblivious to my struggle. My forearm trembles from the effort. After a few steps, it gives out. The bottles land on the concrete with a loud *clang*.

"Can you please help me?"

Scott's narrowed gaze finds mine, sliding up and down my body. I can practically hear the fat-shaming comments rattling in his brain. He takes an eternity to move. Dusts off his hands. He picks up the strap and eases it onto his shoulder.

"Typical."

He strides upward, and I struggle to keep up with his pace. "What is?"

"You asking *me* for a favor. It's fine when you need something." He lifts his free arm and lets it fall, slapping his hip. "But when it's important to me, forget it."

"Helping me carry food twenty feet does not compare with the major inconvenience of picking up your brother."

"Yes, it does."

I shake my head, fuming. "Should we go inside and put that to a vote?"

"Fred was on the way," he snarls. "God forbid you put off your precious schedule by five minutes."

My face flushes. I *like* schedules. Yeah, I run my house as tightly as a naval ship, but why is that a bad thing? Everybody needs structure. A morning routine. A ritual to set the tone for the day. I don't like it when my routines get disrupted, which was a constant source of tension during our marriage. Scott is very much an impulsive, flying by the seat of his pants kind of guy.

"Well, Fred's here. I guess fitting him in the car wasn't a big deal."

"I had to leave behind the paddleboard."

How horrible. I roll my eyes. "Scott, I don't want to fight. I don't expect to enjoy this weekend, but can we at least put up a good front for Nicole?" My thighs burn as I hurry to keep up. "Does she deserve to have yet another vacation ruined because of us?"

He halts, the strap slipping down his shoulder as his expression darkens. "You want me to lie to my daughter?"

"That's not—I'm saying we should make an effort to be polite."

"You said, let's 'put on a front.' That is *literally* lying."

"So what?" I hiss through clenched teeth. "Let's suck it up for one weekend so our daughter can have one memory of a time when her father didn't act like a belligerent fool."

"And now we're back to name-calling." He snorts, his stride increasing as he heads for the front door. "Why don't you take a good look at yourself?"

I clench my fists so hard, my nails bite into my palms. "I think we both need to step back and remember—"

The rest of my sentence is lost in a ripping sound. Cans of condensed milk roll down the driveway as the bag splits. Disdain fills his gaze, which falls on the marshmallows, graham crackers, red licorice, and Hershey's chocolate spilling over the ground. He lets out an agonized sigh.

"Jesus, Amber. Did you pack the whole candy aisle?" He unzips the insulated bag as I shove everything inside. He scowls at the can of condensed milk in my grip. "What is that for?"

"It's to make pumpkin pie," I snarl, zipping everything shut. "You'd know that if you'd ever helped me cook."

Scott flails his hands and gazes skyward, shouting, "There she goes again. Rewriting history. I was at work. I suppose I should've *quit my job* to cook pumpkin pie. *God.* For someone who's so obsessed with the facts, you have an awfully poor memory. I just can't win with you."

He yanks the bag onto his shoulder and storms inside the house. I scream at his retreating back.

"I also had a full-time job! It's called being a mother."

Scott's response is the front door slamming. My cheeks burn as I spot the kids gazing down at us from the second floor. This is bad. We need counseling. The way we treat each other can't continue, but I don't know how to make him stop. Nothing I say makes a difference, and this is turning into the vacation from hell.

My hands shake as I enter the kitchen, where Laura, Scott's fitness influencer wife, is lining up a camera shot. She's a twenty-something young woman with long, ebony hair and an artificial tan that stands out among the mostly pale Seattleites. The mermaid hair, shellacked nails, fake eyelashes, and overfilled lips paint a vapid persona, but she's a decent person. She's patient with Nicole. Affectionate. Loving. She reminds me of me when I was younger—ambitious, vibrant, and eager for life—before an unplanned pregnancy stripped away those ambitions. Laura is a radiant beam of positivity. She's one of those people you want to be around. I used to think she was perfect, but she's not.

Laura puts her camera aside and pulls me into a quick hug. "Thanks for bringing everything."

"Of course."

Laura unpacks the bag Scott dumped over the counter, a big smile blossoming over her face at the marshmallows and chocolate. "I know it's silly, but I *love* roasted marshmallows. Like, I can't get enough of them. Sometimes I roast them over my gas burner just to get that crispy outer layer."

I smile, warmed by that image. "It's not silly at all. I don't think we outgrow the things we like. I watch *Hocus Pocus* every year on Halloween and cry at the scene when the cat dies. And I'm still obsessed with coloring books. I have fifty of them in my office."

Scott makes an unkind sound.

"That's so cute. I love that you're so unapologetically you." Laura squeezes my shoulder as a good-natured grin flashes across her pretty face. She lights up when I take out the canned pumpkin. "What are you making with that?"

"Pumpkin pie."

"How did you know that's my favorite pie? Scott, did you tell her?" She beams at Scott, who shakes his head and walks outside. "I'll have to fight the kids for the last piece!"

I wink at her. "Don't worry. I brought enough piecrust for two. David can probably eat one on his own."

Her eyes sparkle with glee. "You're amazing."

"And Cam's making us raspberry scones in the morning."

"You're spoiling us, Amber!"

She hugs me again, squeezing hard. I'm not a touchy-feely person, but her affection warms me from the inside out. We'd be friends if it weren't for the baggage between me and Scott. She's not perfect, but she has a good heart. As far as I'm concerned, she's doing the world a service by marrying my ex. If Laura is as radiant as the sun, Scott is as gloomy as Seattle skies.

He reenters the kitchen. "Too much estrogen in here."

Laura socks his arm with a playful punch.

My mood nosedives as I spot a crossbow hanging over his shoulder. Why did he bring that thing? As if I don't have enough to worry about this weekend. I step around Laura, who puts the ground beef in the fridge.

"What's with the crossbow?" I ask. "Are you going to play target practice with bears?"

He snorts. "Don't be ridiculous."

"Then why did you bring a weapon on our family trip?" I demand, hands on my hips.

Scott's moody glare dives into me. "It's my hobby. Stop riding on me."

I grab his shoulder as he steps toward the garage. "I get a say in whether my children have access to weapons."

"They're teenagers, not children. They know this is dangerous." He shrugs out of my grip and steps through the side door into the garage. "And even if they did, *so what*? I've taught them how to handle it safely."

"David, too? *When?*"

"A long time ago. He came over with Nicole."

I bite the inside of my cheek. "You didn't tell me that."

"I wasn't aware I had to fill you in on every detail of my parenting, mein führer." He slides a finger over his upper lip and salutes the air.

"Scott, that's a disgusting joke."

"Well, I'm sorry, but you're turning into a real Nazi. We agreed not to get up in each other's business, but that's exactly what you're doing. Don't you trust me?"

I chew my lip, heart hammering. If I say otherwise, he'll stamp, scream, and make a scene. I keep my mouth shut, but he seems to gather the worst from my expression.

He shoves his crossbow onto an empty storage rack. "Well, I'm not an idiot. I know you think I am, but I'm perfectly capable of teaching kids safety. Do you think I'd hurt Nicole?"

"No, of course not. I just—" *I don't think it's a good idea for you to have a crossbow this weekend.* "You're a great dad. I've always said that. But I'm a mom. It's my job to worry."

He blows a gust of frustrated air. Then he heads back inside, where Fred sits beside Laura on a couch in the living room. The sight of my former brother-in-law and Laura with their heads bent together puts me on high alert. Scott still doesn't know about them.

How long until he finds out? And when he does, what will he do?

SIX
AMBER

Laura is cheating on Scott with his brother.

A few weeks ago, I walked in on Laura and Fred at the Majestic Bay Theatre in Ballard. It's a two-story building with three screens, the upper lobby revealing a dramatic view of downtown through the wall-to-wall glass. Large neon signs glow red and blue above the illuminated marquee, which hides a tiny box office. The brass-accented windows of its mahogany doors look like portholes, a nod to Ballard's maritime history. I love going there. It's a neighborhood gem.

I was on a mother-daughter outing with Nicole, watching the latest Jennifer Lawrence romantic comedy. I was following my daughter to the exit when I spotted Fred and Laura in the back row, making out in the dark like teenagers. The three of us locked eyes, but I never confronted them.

Awkward.

It doesn't help that for a month, Laura has left voice messages inviting me to coffee, pleading to "hear me out." She's a nice girl, but I have zero interest in listening to her relationship problems. It's inappropriate. Frankly, I don't understand why she's desperate to meet me. I'm not running to tell Scott about her affair. I'm just glad that Nicole didn't see them.

As though on cue, Fred enters the kitchen. He's heavyset, with darker hair than Scott but an auburn beard. He stands at a towering six-foot-something. Kind black eyes beam under a prominent brow ridge. He's a blue-collar guy. He used to work for a flooring contractor, then did tiling for another. His last job was at a hardware store.

He's quiet and a bit of a recluse. He spends every family event sitting near a window, staring outside, or strumming chords on his guitar. When he speaks, it's a whisper. He blends into the background, which makes his betrayal so surprising. *How* did this guy steal Scott's wife?

My palms sweat as I push a plate of charcuterie in front of him. "Hey, Fred. How are you?"

He ignores the side plates and grabs slices of roast beef, piling them in his hand. "Doing okay," he says, his tone stormy. "I'm in between jobs at the moment. Living with the parents is not exactly ideal. I'm sure *Scott* told you all about that."

"Um—not really."

"My shoulder's wonky from guitar playing. Maybe I pulled a muscle. I should stop busking. Feels pointless. It doesn't pay well, and no label will ever sign me. Look at me. I'm ugly. Nobody buys records from a male solo artist unless he's ripped, which I'm not."

Fred can be like this sometimes. It's best to let him vent. I plaster on a sympathetic smile. "That's not true."

"Trust me, it is. The music industry is full of crap. There's no artistry. It's all about algorithms." He stuffs the meat in his mouth and sucks the juices from his fingers. "*Scott* told you *about* my breakup with Victoria? Yeah, she left me a few months ago. Kicked me out. She's mad because I don't want kids. Who *wants* to bring a kid into this world? Everything is going to hell. All these wildfires. Crappy healthcare. Plus, I'd have to give up music and get a desk job somewhere. I'll die if I have to do that. Anyway, how are you?"

"Uh—I'm good." I struggle to find more words as he picks through the appetizer. "Have you written any new songs? I'd love to hear you play."

A bright gleam springs into his eyes, and his lips pull into a smirk. "I have, but I better not play it here, if you know what I mean."

He gives me a knowing smirk and a wink. Then he glances over his shoulder, his grin flashing at the group gathered around the coffee table, and *laughs*.

God, he's begging to get caught.

I push the plate of charcuterie forward. "Can you take this to the others?"

"Absolutely."

Whistling a merry tune, he waltzes into the living room. He wrote a song about *Laura*? A lead weight drops in my stomach. Coming here was a mistake. Fred has a chip on his shoulder the size of Texas. It's lucky that Scott is so self-absorbed, or he would've picked up on his brother's strange behavior.

"Mom, are you okay?"

I raise my attention from my chopping board to David's soft brown gaze, realizing that I've been stationary for too long. He's already chopped the tomatoes and scooped them into a bowl.

I sigh. "I just spaced out."

"You looked upset."

My heart warms at the concern weighing his voice. "I'm all right. Sometimes I'm lost in thought, like your dad."

"Is it...Coach Scott? Did he say something to you?"

This kid is too perceptive. I hate lying, I feel like it sets an awful example, but I don't have a choice. "I'm annoyed because he brought a crossbow. Someone could get hurt." I blow a tense stream of air. "Can you shred the lettuce?"

David opens his mouth and closes it, no doubt confused by the change in subject, but he nods and picks up the knife. Frowning, he bunches the romaine leaves and slices through them like I taught him.

Unfortunately, I can't confess where my anxiety is coming from. Fred. This is his fault. I can forgive Laura for a moment of weakness, considering she's married to a narcissist, but Fred? He has no excuse. He has no business messing around with his sister-in-law. Or taking her on dates. It's downright predatory.

I face the stove, where a stainless steel pot simmers with ground beef. I dump a can of crushed tomatoes into the browned meat and toss in the taco seasoning as the ventilation hood sucks the steam. David prepares the farmhouse table with place settings. He studies my face. "Is this okay?"

"Yes. Thank you so much. You're a big help."

He shrugs. "No problem."

"Why don't you play board games with the others? I've got it from here."

David glances at the living room echoing with Scott's boisterous tone. My husband is probably keeping the peace between Fred and Scott and could use backup.

"You sure?"

"Yeah. Go have fun."

David inclines his dark head in a tight nod, clearly reluctant to join them, but heads in their direction anyway. He's good about boundaries. Like his father, he respects me. I wish I could say the same about my ex-husband.

We weren't always at loggerheads. We met through a mutual friend in college, Jessica, who raved about Scott's genius in their organic chemistry class and claimed he was the smartest man she'd ever known. As a sapiosexual, that intrigued me. On our first date, he put in the effort to appear smart. He used words like *inertia* in casual conversation. He spoke as if reciting from the dictionary, but I saw it as quirky. One date turned into three and four. Hanging out with him was a blast. In the beginning, he made me feel incredible. So when he proposed after I got pregnant with Nicole, I said yes. It was a no-brainer.

The problems began after our shotgun wedding. He became distant and moody. My growing belly disgusted him. He told me he couldn't wait until I lost the weight. I had a difficult pregnancy fraught with complications. Preeclampsia. Mandated bed rest. I spent a week in the hospital. Once the baby arrived, I returned to a home covered in filth and unwashed dishes. Despite promises he would do the housework, Scott never picked up a vacuum. He didn't make me anything to eat. He's a great dad now, but it wasn't always that way. He left home for hours on various errands for his friends, seizing every excuse to leave me with a newborn, but posted pictures of him cradling Nicole on social media, often with anecdotes of his "hard but rewarding" journey to fatherhood. To me, he whined about how boring our lives had become.

Which made me hate his guts. While he enjoyed three square meals a day, courtesy of my useless in-laws who treated him like a prince, I scarfed down energy bars. While our friends lauded him for being an "amazing" father, Scott shamed me for not losing weight fast enough. I didn't have fifteen minutes to jog on the treadmill, let alone a shower, and I hadn't recovered from the C-section. I was glued with floss and tape, barely holding it together. I stayed with him for six agonizing years, until I found out about his affair through a text message.

Words cannot describe the gut-punching agony as I scrolled through a slew of graphic texts accompanied by nudes. The betrayal buckled my knees. I remember clutching his phone, shaking, as my heart was pulled apart by the seams. The messages dated back months. Slowly, it sank in that the life I knew was over. That my husband was a stranger. In a haze of messy tears, I confronted Scott. He admitted everything, crying. He begged me to go to marriage counseling. I refused. I was done with him.

Just like that.

I filed for divorce that week. It took a year to finalize, but I never shed another tear over our marriage's demise. I was better off without him, but Scott damaged me in a lot of ways I'm still not healed from. So do I feel a certain amount of schadenfreude that he married a cheater? Of course. I'm only human.

But I can't help but feel responsible for this powder-keg situation. I hate that Laura and Fred put me in this awkward position. Dread pits my stomach as I imagine breaking the news to him.

Do I tell my ex that his wife is cheating on him?

Will he believe me?

I waver back and forth, tortured by indecision. Maybe he suspects it already. Scott is in an extra prickly mood these days. He won't take me at my word, anyway. He's more likely to accuse me of jealousy.

I have to hold it together until Sunday. Then I'll never have to do this again. I can spend seventy-two hours in Scott's company without killing him. It's the others I'm worried about. I sigh, turning off the stove burners. Three more nights.

SEVEN
THE PRESENT

My father wanted me to kill.

Squirrels, that is. Long ago, he bought me a crossbow and took me hunting. The spring-loaded mechanism fires bolts at speeds as high as three hundred feet per second. It's deadly up to fifty yards, especially if you're shooting with a broadhead—an arrow point with two or more blades. They create the necessary blood loss to harvest animals. Some are designed to expand on impact to cause the greatest amount of injury possible. I've got a good aim. I can shoot a squirrel through its eye from a hundred yards, not that I care for murdering woodland critters.

I'm all for the big game.

The family tradition honed my technique. Years of practice have made me lethal. I'm not proud of it, but it's true.

I fire into trees, imagining neat holes in their skulls. I picture the bolts tearing through their eyes. Death will be quick—a mercy they haven't earned. I cock an arrow. Aim at the person who wronged me. My index finger touches the trigger. I inhale. I'm tight everywhere, wrapped in an invisible python's coils. My chest constricts.

Do it.

I want to so badly. The release of tension will be worth it. I will end them. I can only take so much disrespect before retaliating. They deserve it, a hundred times over.

Do it.

Heat climbs my neck as I battle myself. A sound distracts me—twigs snapping under the weight of a boot. Electricity jolts up my arm, and a bolt soars above the campfire, toward a bench. A single word howls through me. *No.*

EIGHT
AMBER

A *thud* slams into the wood above my head.

Jolted out of a nap, I open my eyes to a dying campfire. Glowing embers cast orange light on the empty bench, chairs, glasses smudged with handprints. I yawn, stretching out my legs toward the fading warmth. How long have I been out? The last thing I remember was slumping on Cameron's shoulder as Fred launched into a story from his college glory days.

A plaid throw slides down my shoulders as I stand, my nostrils filling with smoke and pine. I turn to pick up the blanket, spotting a thin stick jutting from the trunk. I run my fingers over the round shaft, caressing the yellow feathers. Is that a *crossbow* bolt?

I yank it from the bark, fuming. "Scott!"

I expect him to pop out, laughing, but nothing stirs except the sighing of trees. Gooseflesh rises in bumps down my arms as I grip the bolt and march in a random direction. I stare into the darkness, scanning for a bulky frame hidden in the brush.

This is so stupid.

Cupping my hands around my mouth, I shout his name. Leaves rustle. A shadow darts across my peripheral vision. My breathing hitches as a bush near me shakes. The tail end of something covered in fur escapes into another patch of forest.

I release a tense breath, annoyed with myself.

Scott isn't here. He took off. The drunken idiot must've panicked when his aim got a little too close. He realized I'd have a *huge* problem with this ridiculous stunt. Typical Scott. Act first, think later.

My sandals scuff on the uneven ground. I trip, catching myself on a tree as Cameron exits the house, making a beeline for the bench.

"Amber?"

I wave at him. "Over here."

He jogs over. Cameron is the picture of a man—broad-shouldered and powerful, furrowed brows, his eyes flashing with menace.

"What's wrong, babe?"

I hold up the arrow. "I woke up to *this* beside my head."

"What the hell? How'd that happen?"

"*Scott,*" I seethe. "He's the only idiot in this group who'd play a prank by firing at me."

His demeanor grows in severity. "You saw him do it?"

"Well, no. I was half asleep and heard a noise." I make a fist and strike my palm. "Like a thud. Splintering wood."

Cameron strolls forward, scanning the trees, the under-brush, the house. He holds me, his comforting weight falling on my shoulder.

"You sure?"

"Who else would do something so dumb?"

Doubt flickers in his gaze. "That seems reckless, even for Scott."

"Then—you think one of the kids?"

"No," he says quickly. "They're in bed."

"Then how did this happen?"

"I don't know," he murmurs, rubbing the back of his head. "It's really strange. Are you positive it wasn't there already? Scott was practicing with the crossbow earlier."

Am I?

I shuffle my feet, trying to remember. He was messing around with that stupid crossbow. It's possible I imagined it, I guess. Which means the bolt was there before I sat down. How did I not notice it? For God's sake, I'm the most detail-oriented person on earth. In my mind, I list an inventory of the scene: four logs on the fire. Laura sitting across from me. Sticks with charred marshmallows. A wine glass on my knee. David, peeling the blackened husk off a white blob before sliding it onto a graham cracker. Scott gazing at me with a bland half-grin.

Why am I doubting myself?

He did this.

I stalk into the house, peering in its windows. I wrench open the sliding door and charge through, the wall shaking as I slam it shut. "Scott. Where are you?"

"Babe, keep it down. The kids are asleep."

"I'm not letting this slide, Cam. This is so messed up." I fly through with the fury of a tornado, slamming doors. The last one reveals an empty room, and my frustration boils over. "Where the hell is he?"

"Outside, I bet," he murmurs, his fingers trailing down my arm before meeting my palm in a warm clasp. "Maybe I should handle this."

"No. I need to do this myself."

Cameron's smile tightens. "I'll back you up no matter what. I just think you'll regret it if you let your emotions get the better of you."

"That's his damn fault. He gaslights me, insults me, and all I'm asking for is some damned respect, but *no*. He refuses to act like a responsible adult. I've had it." I rip out of Cameron's comforting grip. "He probably drank too much. He does idiotic things when he's drunk, but it's no excuse. He needs to be held accountable."

"Okay. I believe you."

I scoff, annoyed with Cameron's pacifying tone. "Where is he, the feckless little..." I trail off, my body straightening like a hound on alert. I go rigid. I march to the backyard, heading toward sounds of laughter and splashing.

Rippling blue light plays on Cameron's tense face as we approach the hot tub.

A bikini-clad Laura sits on Scott's lap, taking a selfie as Scott flashes a peace sign. Empty beer bottles litter the ground. A rosy color blooms across Scott's cheeks and neck. He has rosacea, a skin condition that makes him flush easily. I used to tease him for looking wasted after one drink.

Laura disengages from Scott, her ebony hair tied up in a messy bun. She beams at me, beckoning.

"Hey, guys. You should join—"

"What is this?" I approach my ex, waving the arrow.

Scott's mouth twitches. *"What?"*

"I woke up with this right above my head." I lean over as Laura floats to Scott's side, looking solemn. "What's wrong with you?"

Scott inclines his head at Laura, speaking in a stage whisper. "I can never understand her when she's hysterical."

"Hey," warns Cameron. "Be civil."

"Remind *your wife* of that, too." Scott takes a long pull of his beer and frowns, his eyes tracking the arrow clutched in my grip. "Where'd you get that?"

"I was asleep on the bench when I heard something." I hurl the arrow into the foaming water. "When I turned around, I saw this."

"And?"

"You shot at me. I could've died. Is that what you want? Are these stupid pranks worth my life?"

Scott leans back, his elbows on the edge of the tub as he exchanges a bewildered expression with Laura. "So...you think I shot at you while you were asleep...and missed? Not to brag, but I've been doing this for a while. I wouldn't miss."

"Then how did this get five inches from my head?"

He plucks it from the swirling water, frowning. "I was practicing earlier. Must've forgotten this one."

Frustration gnaws at my stomach. "I can't believe you're gaslighting me about this."

"There's a simple explanation that doesn't involve attempted murder. It was there *before* you sat down. It might not even be mine. This is a popular vacation rental. People bring their crossbows all the time."

"Yeah, *sure*. There's a crossbow store in my local shopping mall, right next to the beekeeping and anarchist book shop."

Laura chuckles. Scott gives her a withering look before returning his attention to me. "Either someone is out to get you *or*—just putting this out there—you had too much to drink. It was a long day. You're tired. You imagined it."

"Damn it, Scott. I know what I heard."

He cocks his head, his lips curving. "People conjure up all kinds of things when they're in a dream state."

"I was awake."

Scott laughs. "Now she's saying she was awake. I thought the sound woke her up?"

"*She's* standing in front of you," I grit out, goaded past endurance. "And *she* would like to know why you're being ridiculous."

"Your theory is absurd. I didn't think there was *enough* drama this weekend? So I decided to add more by shooting at my baby momma?" Scott's hands fall into the water with a splash. "It makes no sense."

"I never said you had a sane mind."

"You'd rather believe that I'm a crazed murderer than admit that you're wrong. *Wow.* I'm amazed at how your brain works." He lets out an exaggerated sigh. "Fine. I'll prove it to you."

He steps out of the hot tub and wraps himself in a towel, gnashing his teeth. Then he leads us into the garage, pointing at the zipped case. He yanks on the lock, proving that it's shut. Cameron tries it. I do the same.

I bite the inside of my cheek. "Where do you keep the key?"

He pulls them out of his pocket. "Unless you're suggesting I unlocked the crossbow, started firing indiscriminately into camp, went back, locked it, and then jumped in the hot tub before you found me, I don't see how this is possible."

I cross my arms, my throat burning.

"Have I proved myself to you?" Scott takes an aggressive step forward, his tone belligerent. "Or do you want a written testimony, as well?"

Cameron palms his chest, stopping his advance. "Enough."

"Oh, please, it's not enough for this—*woman*," he spits out, his stare drilling me. "Accusing me of violence in front of my wife is screwed up. Why are you trying to ruin my marriage?"

I snort. "That's rich. You cross the line whenever it suits you."

"Really? Enlighten me."

"You invited your brother without asking me."

He makes a violent sound. "I did ask!"

"And speaking of ruining marriages, you're the one that cheated!"

"Here we go again," says Scott, throwing his hands up. "Invoking the sins of the past. I messed up once in seven years, and I'm the devil." He nudges Cameron with his elbow. "Better hope you're on your best behavior, pal, or she'll send you packing."

Cameron clenches his fists.

As usual, Scott doesn't take the hint. "You can hate me, but you know I'm not a psycho. I've never given you any reason to fear me. I guess that doesn't matter. When it comes to me, you aren't rational. But you can't admit that. Admitting that is like death for you. It's sad. I'm sorry you have this...toxic need to cause drama. I pity anyone who delights in bringing chaos to every moment." Scott's shoulder slams into Cameron's as he stomps out.

I hate him. I hate that he sounds so reasonable. That I'm jumping at shadows. That he's right—I can't stand being wrong when it concerns my ex. My pulse skyrockets. His explanation is the most plausible one. It's not like a crossbow bolt stands out in a forest. I could've missed it.

I allow my husband to pull me into our bedroom. Cameron cradles me in his arms, and I release a strangled sob.

"I'm sorry. He makes me crazy."

"Don't say that, babe."

"He's right, though. I have a hard time being objective around him. I always think he's up to something."

"Because he's an untrustworthy leech." He wipes my damp cheeks and plants a kiss on my head. "The court order expires soon. This is the last vacation we'll ever take with that idiot."

He angles his head and kisses me, his firm grip at my waist pushing me toward the bed. I let him undress me. Soon after, his hair-roughed chest glides over mine and I succumb to pleasure. The warmth of my husband's love almost makes me forget what happened. But as I lay in the haven of his embrace, the first thing I do is check my phone.

No cell service. Even if I wanted to, I can't call for help.

NINE
AMBER

I sleep poorly.

The flannel sheets and my husband's body turn the bed into a furnace. It's nearly three in the morning when I drift off. My dreams are a snarling tangle of images until rap music jars me awake. As my husband and I stumble out of our bedroom at six, Scott informs us we're going on a hike. He sends the group a link to the trail. Alpine Loop Trail —Strenuous.

Lovely.

Despite growing up in Washington, I'm not an outdoorsy person. For years, Scott tried to force me into becoming one. He was a man on a mission, determined to make me like hiking, camping, and kayaking like *everybody* in the Pacific Northwest. Outdoor sports never grew on me. I have a detached appreciation for natural beauty. I'm okay with observing it through my temperature-controlled cabin with an endless supply of hot cocoa and snacks. Sue

but I'd rather binge-watch a true crime documentary
ries than spend hours sweating in a forest.

That's why Cameron and I get along so well. He gets it.
He's a startup CEO and spends most days working, but
it's all remote. He takes meetings in the middle of Lake
Union while floating on his paddleboard. When he's not
taking short trips around Seattle, he's lifting weights in the
garage gym or listening to podcasts. It's probably killing
him that there's no Wi-Fi here.

I wrap the last croissant sandwich with plastic and pack
Ziplock bags with beef jerky for myself, the kids, and
Cameron. Nicole and David sit at the breakfast table,
digging into their oatmeal. She catches my gaze, murmur-
ing, "Are we sure it's safe out there?"

I cram energy bars into David's backpack. "What do you
mean, honey?"

"Aren't there bears and stuff?"

I barely suppress a shiver. I'm not the biggest fan of
wildlife, which is why I insisted on renting a house instead
of fabric tents that could be slashed open. I count being
eaten alive as the most horrific death. The woods we're
heading toward have plenty of predators, but my ex is
loud. He'll scare everything within five miles. Or maybe
I'll get lucky and he'll be killed.

"Oh, that's nothing to worry about. Bears tend to stay
away from people."

"Not necessarily." David scrapes at his bowl with his
spoon. "I watched this documentary about this crazy guy.

Timothy Something. I can't remember his whole name. Anyway, he was really into bears. He went up to Alaska with his girlfriend, and a bear ate them both."

Nicole scoffs. "Liar."

"Nope. A tripod set up at their camp recorded the entire attack. Werner Herzog even listened to the tape. Apparently, it was so graphic, they opted out of showing it."

Nicole stops eating, looking stricken. She's always been anxious. I try to build up her confidence, but it's hard. This world is designed to tear girls down or pit them against each other. The other month, I blocked her from accessing her social media accounts because she couldn't stop crying about Erica, her classmate who died by suicide.

I grab David's empty dish. "Nobody is getting eaten, sweetie. David, can you go upstairs and check if your dad's ready?"

"He is. He's waiting outside."

"Can you join him, please? And take these." I slide two backpacks on the counter, which David loops over his arm. "One's for your dad."

David slips off his stool and strolls into the living room, where Scott greets him with a hearty, "Morning, champ!"

Nicole makes a disgusted sound as oatmeal slides from her spoon to splatter her bowl. I'm not sure whether she's grossed out by the food or her father's attention to David.

"Everybody in this family is so weird."

I towel a dish dry. "Is that a bad thing?"

"You and Dad treat David like a little kid, but he's almost eighteen. Dad pretends David is his nephew because he's good at football. My *stepmother*," she bites out, still staring into her oatmeal. "I can't stand it."

I know you're supposed to cherish every moment of your kids' development, but I can't wait until the moody teenager phase is behind us.

I twist the dishtowel. "You know I love you very much."

"Yeah," she mumbles, her eyes misting. "I guess."

I stroke her hand. "You guess?"

Nicole flips her blond hair over her shoulder, her magenta lips matching her backpack's pink straps. "You're obsessed with David."

"No, I'm not."

"Yes, you are. You compliment him all the time. You praise ordinary stuff. It's bizarre."

"He's had a rough life, Nicole, and he doesn't have many friends. He lost his mom. I don't give him attention because I love him more, I do it because he needs it. Always help someone if you can. You might be the only one who does."

She nods morosely.

Scott's booming voice makes us flinch. "Okay, people! Time to go!"

I clean the last dish as Scott rallies everyone with his manic energy. My grim daughter drags herself outside. Scott thumps her back and pauses at the threshold, door half-open. He glances at me.

"Uh—are you coming?"

"I told you I would." Ignoring his condescending grin, I head to the foyer and shove my feet into the hiking boots. He frowns as I tighten the laces.

"Where'd you get those?"

I shrugged. "At a store in University Village. The staff recommended these."

"That's a walking shoe. You need boots with a thicker sole, or you'll twist an ankle." His eyes scan my body, lingering on the belly rolls highlighted by the Lululemon shirt that's a size too small. "We're going through very rough terrain."

"I'm well aware. The guy said these would be okay." I stand, reaching for the backpack on the floor. Scott grabs it, grimacing.

"What's in this thing? You realize we're only leaving for a few hours—not the whole day, right?" He lifts the bag. "This will only slow you down."

Always a critic. "I'll remember that when you're begging me for an energy bar."

He sneers. "Don't count on it."

I grab my backpack and slip it on my shoulders. "Where's yours?"

"I don't need one, Amber. I'm a CrossFit athlete. I can handle three hours of continuous exercise without overexerting myself. Can you?"

Probably not. But I'll be damned if I'll admit that to *him*.

I shrug. "I'll be fine."

He widens the door for me as I step out. "Your funeral."

TEN

AMBER

If his plan is to kill me, it's working.

I'm sweating profusely. Hunger gnaws at my insides. My heart hammers as I keep pace with the others. I breathe hard, pushed to the limit after an hour of hiking, but asking for a break isn't an option. My ears will bleed from Scott's *I-told-you-so's*. He'll berate me for not listening to him. I'll never hear the end of it. For the record, the shoes are fine. I'm just not used to walking this much or at such a steep incline.

Scott acts like the local tour guide, pointing out various flora and fauna as Fred takes point. Scott looks too much like Daryl from *The Walking Dead* with the crossbow on his back. Don't ask me why he brought it along.

The kids are glued to his side. Laura strolls ahead, pausing to take selfies. Cameron, in a show of solidarity, walks behind me. I suck down water from the reservoir's tube attached to my strap. I wipe my brow, and Cameron comes to a stop.

"You don't have to stick with me. If you want to go faster, I don't blame you."

"Why? So I can listen to the village idiot?" Cameron snorts, stopping a branch from hitting my face. "Nah. I'll stay with my wife."

I smile. "Well, if you're sure…"

"Oh, I am. The view from down here is nice."

I gaze at trees, frowning. Then he taps my butt as though to imply that's what's captured his attention. His fingers linger on my curves, and he fondles me. Suddenly, I feel gorgeous despite my sweaty armpits. As he grabs a handful of me and pinches, I laugh. "You're not helping me catch my breath."

His palm leaves my hip, but somehow his warmth lingers. "True. I need you to save your strength for later."

"What's later?"

"You're going to have a very challenging evening."

My cheeks warm as I continue walking uphill. "Tougher than this?"

Cameron lowers his voice to a growl. "Let's just say that by the end of the night, everybody in the cabin will be reaching for a cigarette."

I giggle, my cheeks burning. I bite my lip to keep from smiling before Nicole asks me why I'm laughing. I don't know why. Cameron's appetite for me is no joke. I'm hoping this hike doesn't make me too sore for later.

The hike is majestic; I'll give Scott that. Everything is coated in a thick, green moss. Dense ferns burst from the ground. The smell is unlike anything I've experienced. Earthy and fresh. I wish I could bottle it up and sell it to the masses. Visually, it's stunning. Flat orange discs grow from moss-ensnared trees with crimson bark. A family of deer strolls onto the dirt path. For a half mile, we follow the doe and her two fawns, the littlest one stopping every so often to stare at us. Laura spends way too long attempting to take a selfie with them before giving up.

The higher we climb, the more the elevation seems to thin out the vegetation until we reach a steep ridge facing Mount Rainier. Snow partially covers the ground. My hiking boot slips on the slick surface, and I stumble. My knee hits the ground hard. Pain splinters into my flesh as my husband's gentle hands haul me upright.

"You all right?"

"Yeah." I pat my throbbing knee, my finger brushing a nickel-sized hole over my track pants. Luckily, I wore double layers because I figured it would be cold at the top.

Cameron traces the inch of raw skin underneath the ripped legging. He grimaces and runs a hand through his dark waves. "Think you can keep going?"

"'Course. It's not a big deal."

As I put my weight on the leg, a sharp agony stabs into my muscle. I clench my teeth. I should've stayed at the cabin. This hike is doable for a couch potato, but I'll have wicked shin splints when it's over.

"You sure?" he whispers, stroking me. "There's still time for us to turn back."

And endure Scott's smug comments? His mocking smile when he waves me goodbye? No way. "I'm not giving up."

Cameron shakes his head. As I limp toward the others gathered around Scott, Cameron announces that he'd like a break. Scott's skeptical gaze seems to pierce my throbbing heart, and then his lips curve into a knowing smirk.

Everybody sits on a grassy meadow just before its steep decline into a bowl-shaped valley surrounded by thick pines. On one side of the ridge—snow and mist. The other glows with sunshine through dappled clouds. It's beautiful, but gazing down at the abrupt drop churns my stomach.

I tear into the croissant sandwich I meant to eat for lunch. It's only late morning, but I'm starving. Scott munches on Laura's energy bar. Cameron collapses beside me, slumping against a tree trunk. He wipes sweat from his forehead. Nicole rubs her shins. Fred inhales his sandwich and eyes the half-eaten croissant in Nicole's grip. Scott slings an arm around Laura's gleaming shoulders, his voice heavy with disdain.

"You guys need to do more cardio."

Cameron lifts his head. The fatigue disappears from his expression as he bristles like a pit bull in a fighting ring. "I hope you're not criticizing my wife."

Scott ignores Laura's hand on his thigh, his tone indignant. "Obviously, I want Nicole's mother to live a long, healthy life. Regular exercise is part of that. What's wrong with pointing that out?"

"I think what Scott means to say is that he's passionate about fitness." Laura pats Scott's leg, beaming with a smile so forced it looks painful. "And he wants to share that joy with everyone. That's why I quit nursing to become an influencer."

I grin, appreciating her valiant attempt to change the subject, which Scott blows up by opening his mouth.

"Yeah, but you also got tired of watching your patients wash down their metformin with Pepsi. It's frustrating when you've dedicated yourself to helping people and they don't listen to you. Am I right?"

"Shut up," I snap, cramming the garbage into my backpack. "I don't have diabetes."

"Not yet," he mutters.

I shake my head, laughing. "My God, you don't know when to stop."

"Rant at me all you want, but untreated diabetes is an epidemic." His assessing gaze pierces me, filling me with humiliation. "And you have a major risk factor."

"Yes. I'm big," I shout, ignoring Cameron's gentle squeeze on my arm. "Why don't you scream it into the mountains? There might be some people who haven't heard the news after years of you shouting it from the rooftops. So go ahead. Get it out of your system. Then do me a favor: Shut up about my weight."

An ugly crimson flush claims Scott's neck. "I never mentioned it. I said you had *one* risk factor."

Fred slaps Scott's shoulder, frowning. "Come on, man. It's not cool to bring up a woman's weight over and over. This isn't rocket science."

"That's not—you completely missed the point."

Nicole stands, righting her backpack. "Dad, I love you, but you're fatphobic."

Scott opens his mouth, his eyes bulging, but the sight of everyone's disapproval seems to silence him. Laura whispers something. He wrenches out of her grip and stomps off, the back of his neck flaming red. Laura watches him go, sighing. Fred gives her a sympathetic smile, and they share a look that's appropriate for lovers.

I grab a leaf from a bush and tear it to shreds. I don't care if my ex calls me fat a thousand times. As long as he never finds out about the affair or that I've known about it for months. Scott gets nasty when he's humiliated. He'll blame it on me. I know it. Watching Scott clench his fists tightens my throat.

I have to talk to Laura.

I have to stop this before it gets out of hand.

ELEVEN
AMBER

I think we're lost.

I hope to God we're not, but Scott has no idea where we are. He peers into the horizon, hand over his eyes. At some point the path disappeared, but he insisted we were on the right track. Now we can't even find the tail end of the trail.

For over an hour, we trek through forests with unforgiving terrain. Harsh sunlight eats through my sunblock. It's almost three. Scott and Laura have blown through their snacks and they're sharing three liters of water from Laura's reservoir, which doesn't seem to concern them.

They're more fixated on finding Cloudburst Ridge, which is famous among influencers for its picturesque view. Laura snaps photos of Scott with his boot on a rock, Scott without a shirt and flexing, and Scott wielding his cross-bow, which sends Cameron into a fit of hysterics. I can't spare any breath to laugh. I'm focused on not vomiting from sheer exhaustion.

A sharp whistle like a child's toy pierces the air. My heart skips as I search for the source of the whistling, hoping that we've stumbled on other hikers.

Scott waves the kids over as he points at an animal in the distance. "See that? That's a groundhog!"

"It's a hoary marmot," grumbles my husband. "They make those sounds when they feel threatened."

"A groundhog *is* a marmot, so I'm not wrong."

Cameron shakes his head, his mouth lifting in a condescending smirk that raises Scott's hackles. His face lights up, flaming red. Man, his ego is *touchy* these days. Thank God our daughter didn't inherit his narcissism. She marches beside him, tugging his sleeve.

"Dad, are we close? I'm exhausted."

"One more hour." He beckons her forward, down the rocks we climbed so Laura could film videos for her social media. "We'll be home soon."

Color me skeptical. "Is that another guess or a fact?"

"Fact," he snarls, holding up his phone. "I know where we are."

I've had enough of this. "No, you don't. First it was fifteen minutes, then thirty, and now it's an hour."

"Well, I didn't realize how much you'd slow us down." Scott swats at the air as flies land on his gleaming neck. "You ask for breaks every twenty minutes."

"That's not fair. You said this hike would take three, maybe four hours. It's been *six*. If I'm in rough shape, so are Cameron, Nicole, and your brother." I gesture toward Fred, who's hunched over on the ground. "Let's regroup and determine our location."

"No need. I'm following the app."

"Well, it's not working. We need to stop wandering in circles, pick a landmark, and get there before it's dark."

Cameron slides his hand over my back. "I agree. We're not on the trail anymore. I think we took a wrong turn. There was snow covering up part of the path."

Scott raises a brow, sliding his glassy stare to my husband. "I'm sorry, how often do you hike? A handful of times? You don't know what you're talking about. You can barely keep up with us."

"Scott, cut the crap. It's obvious to everyone that we're lost." I glare at Laura and Fred, who look down and fiddle with their clothing. "Right?"

Laura pats her husband's arm, beaming at him. "Don't worry, Amber. Scott's been in these situations before. He knows what he's doing."

"He says he knows what he's doing," says Fred.

I gape at Laura, annoyed with her unflinching belief in Scott. "Exactly. If he said the world was flat, would you believe that, too?"

Scott cocks his head and shakes it. Nicole clutches me, her eyes large and liquid with terror. "Mom, I want to go back to the cabin. I don't want to be stuck outside at night."

Scott waves her forward. "Then follow me."

I seize Nicole's shoulder, forcing her to stand still. "Hold on a second."

Scott wheels on me, shouting. "We don't have time for another break."

I grab the folded paper out of my backpack and thrust it in his face. "Show me where we are."

He glances at it, scoffing. "That's the wrong map. It's way too big. You got the one for the entire national forest. Alpine Loop Trail is right here." His finger jabs into a southeastern area marked by a tiny circular trail up Mount Rainier. "If you wanted more detail, you should have downloaded the offline map. Did any of you do that?"

"I didn't," I whisper, facing my husband. "You?"

Gritting his teeth, Cameron hisses a negative. I search for anyone who might've downloaded it, but everybody's wearing identical disappointed frowns.

"Of course not." Scott bunches the map in a careless ball and lobs it to me. "You people don't know the first thing about the outdoors. You're lucky I'm here."

"Then can you forward yours in case your battery dies?"

Scott thins his lips, the irritation in his voice growing. "We haven't had cell service since we drove to the cabin. Even if I could give you the map, it's a bad idea."

"What are you talking about?"

His nostrils flare. "If I give you the map, you'll divide the group. We can't afford to be separated."

My heart pounds. "Are you freaking kidding me? Who made *you* the leader?"

"I'm the only person here with experience, so I should lead everyone to safety. If you knew what you were doing, you would've brought a map we could use."

I gesture toward the thicket. "You're the one that got us lost!"

Scott tosses his head, growling. "For the last time. I'm in complete control of the situation."

"Are you sure?" asks Fred. "Because we've been marching around in circles on your hunch for a while."

"My God. Just open your eyes and look." He sweeps a broad arm at Mount Rainier. "We haven't gone very far. We're right on top of the trail. The GPS signal is just weak from the mountains and cloud cover. Let's stay positive and keep moving. If we hustle, we can make it back for dinner. Amber's grilling steak."

"If you think I'm cooking you dinner after what you put me through, you're delusional."

Fred laughs. Scott mutters something indistinct. He charges down the steep, thick forest, waving the kids forward. Fred follows suit with a heavy sigh.

I hang back. "Cam, what are your thoughts?"

My husband scratches his glistening neck. "He has the only detailed map."

"So we blindly do what he says? That's a recipe for disaster."

"Well, I haven't the faintest idea where to go."

"Me either," I whisper in a brittle voice. "Shouldn't we be searching for water?"

Cameron wipes his brow, studying my map. "According to this, there's a river south of here. He's headed in that direction, anyway."

My mind flutters away. I won't panic for the sake of the kids, who seem in good spirits despite the grueling hike, but I'm worried. David sticks by Nicole's side, catching her when she stumbles. I jog up to them and slide my hand up David's back.

"Are you okay? Do you need anything?"

David shakes his head, but Nicole clutches my elbow. "Can we stop for a bit? Please? My feet are killing me."

I bite my lip as Scott and Laura trudge down the precarious slope. "We can't slow down, honey."

Her eyes mist. "Are we lost?"

My honest opinion is *yes*. I exchange a glance with my husband, who lets out a tense stream of air. I'll feel much better when we get to a water source. If we ever find it.

TWELVE
THE PAST

I'm starving.

My insides feel like they're caving in. Rib bones stick out from my belly. I wish someone would take me away. Yesterday, my English teacher told me to see a doctor. I said I would, but that's a lie. Mom will never take me to a doctor. The last time I begged an adult for help, it didn't work. It made my life worse. I don't have any friends. Maybe if I did, they could bring me food, but the kids at school are disgusted by me. Everyone keeps a wide berth like I'm carrying something contagious.

I'm getting so thin, I'm in danger of disappearing. It's been a day since I ate. An apple, which is the only food I'm allowed besides lunch at school, and whenever Dad takes pity on me. I only have the energy for rereading Tolkien, gazing out the window, and fantasizing about life somewhere else.

A faint beeping echoes outside my room. I slip from the bed and tiptoe across the wooden floorboards. I hold the doorknob. Biting my lip, I twist. The door swings inward with a groan that stabs my empty stomach. As I peek my head out, I smell food. The sound of the microwave's hum ricochets upstairs, and I breathe in deeply. Cheese. It's one of those instant microwaveable bowls. I don't like them much, but I could inhale a case of mac and cheese.

I walk to the staircase, peering at the living room. My mom shuffles into view, holding a steaming bowl as she plops into the recliner. From this distance, the cheese practically melts on my tongue. My hand shakes as I grab the banister. I descend a step. Then another.

Pulse racing, I glance at Mom. She's still glued to the TV. I reach the bottom, turning right. I zip into the laundry room, which connects to a place that's forbidden to me— the kitchen. A tray of muffins sits on the counter. I grab one and sink my teeth into blueberries and wheat. Delicious. I could cry. The first goes down easily. My mouth is too dry for the second. I need milk to wash it down. Quickly, I move to the fridge. I yank the handle. It strains against a black wire. My heart falls when I study the lock on the door.

No.

"What do you think you're doing?"

Dad's voice is like a whip lashing my face. I release the handle as he takes my arm, shaking the muffin from my grip. It drops to the floor.

"I need to eat."

"Don't give me that crap," he thunders, glancing over his shoulder as though to check if Mom is listening. "You little thief. Your mom works so hard to provide for you, and this is how you pay her back?"

I lift my shirt, showing him the row of ribs sticking out, and my flat belly. "I'm hungry."

"Are you saying we starve you?" He points at Mom, who gets up out of her chair and waddles over. "Your mom changed her life to raise you. You owe her. And you've ruined her morning. Again! Now apologize to your mother before I put you downstairs."

"What's he doing?" she screams, moving to stand behind him. "Stealing?"

I shake my head.

Dad scoffs. "Tell her what you did, liar."

"I'm hungry," I whisper, too scared to look at Mom. "I haven't eaten since yesterday, and you only gave me an apple."

"You only gave me an apple," she mocks in a high-pitched tone. "What an ungrateful jerk."

Dad glances at Mom, his lip curving. "Maybe he can have a muffin."

"Absolutely not."

"Do you want him to faint?" he asks. "It's been a whole day."

She wheels on him, bristling. "Are you defending him again?"

"No, I just don't want to take him to the hospital."

Her gaze skims over me, and she makes a vomiting sound. Then she turns around and heads toward the recliner. She sinks into the cushions and digs into a bowl of chocolate-covered almonds.

Dad grabs me by the wrist and pulls me closer, seething. "Walk in that room and say you're sorry."

I nod. "But—"

"But what? You'll lie about being hungry?" he shouts, the loudness only for Mom's benefit. "You're a thieving, selfish little boy. And you're going to apologize."

Dad escorts me into the other room. Mom eats as I watch, my stomach gnawing. Then she puts down the bowl and stares at me, her hatred drilling into my heart.

"I'm sorry, Mom."

"Again," Dad orders. "And mean it."

"I'm sorry."

"You don't mean it," she growls in a low voice, reaching for the bowl. "You just want food. *Food*. That's all you care about. You're not sorry for what you've done to me. Are you?"

"No," I say.

A blur of white whirls past me and shatters on the wall. Almonds scatter across the floor. Mom jumps from the recliner, shrieking. "Look what you made me do!"

"I'll punish him," Dad says as he seizes my elbow. "You earned yourself a weekend in the basement."

No.

I lunge for the front door, but he jerks me back, dragging me along like a doll. I scream. I batter his chest. It's no use. He's too strong. His distant gaze pierces mine as he prods me down a flight of wooden steps into pitch-black darkness. He releases me when my bare feet touch concrete.

"Here you go," he booms, tossing the half-eaten muffin at my feet. "Since it matters so much to you."

"Dad, please. Don't go."

He climbs the staircase and shuts the door. The sliver of light underneath it disappears as he puts something in the gap. Blinded, I grope for the muffin. I bite into the buttery crust and slowly eat. When the last crumb passes my lips, I feel emptier, so I fill my head with dreams. I imagine a place where someone wants me.

THIRTEEN
AMBER

We're still lost.

Two desperate hours pass as we hike through treacherous terrain. As we step through thick vegetation on the steep slope, Scott rattles off a nonstop stream of dialogue that is probably meant to keep the kids entertained.

"We're pioneers," roars Scott as branches smack the crossbow on his back. "This is what frontiersmen did at the turn of the nineteenth century. Did Daniel Boone know where he was going when he set off into the wild? What about Lewis and Clark? *No.* They hitched up their wagons, traveled into uncharted territory, and hoped for the best. And that's what we're doing, kids. We'll be brave and put one foot after the other, like the American pioneers before us."

Fred scoffs, his voice layered with sarcasm. "Hopefully, we'll end up like the Lewis and Clark expedition and not the Donner Party."

"The Donner Party?" Nicole asks.

"I learned about it in fifth grade," David says, tying his jacket to his waist. "Bunch of pioneers got lost trying to get to California. They were trapped by an early snowfall. Things got so bad they had to eat each other."

Nicole's face blanches.

Scott frowns. "Yeah, well, that won't happen to us."

"They didn't just eat the dead," Fred says, stepping over a log. "They drew straws and sacrificed people. Then they mixed up the meat so that nobody would consume their family members—"

"What the hell is wrong with you?" demands Scott, whipping around. "My daughter is a little girl and you're describing how families butchered each other?"

A blush runs like a shadow across Nicole's cheeks. "I'm a grown woman."

"Sure you are," Scott deadpans without missing a beat. "But that's beside the point. I doubt anybody here needs a blow-by-blow of cannibalism." He gives Fred a meaningful stare.

"All right. I'll stop."

"I'd also appreciate it if you dropped the nasty attitude."

"You're the one talking everyone's ear off about American history. I guess the moment I contribute something, it's a *problem*." Fred lets out a contemptuous snort. "Hypocrite."

"I'm inspiring the group," Scott says, snapping a branch that caught his crossbow. "You're creeping everyone out."

"Sorry for scaring you. I didn't realize you were so sensitive." Fred marches ahead of Scott, who seethes with mounting rage. "I find it *interesting* how brothers and sisters turn on each other when resources get strained. Like, the relationships between family members last as long as everyone's basic needs are met. If not, it's every man for himself."

Scott halts, glaring at him. "*Shut up.*"

I'm grateful for Scott's ringing command, because it forces Fred into silence. Seconds later, Scott launches into another uplifting speech. Cameron and I roll our eyes, but we don't interrupt him. I'm content to allow Scott's BS wash over the kids if it keeps them calm…for now. Soon, the light will be gone. Unless we stumble upon a campground with all the amenities within the next hour, we'll have to hunker down for the night.

Scott crouches, his palms scooping away leaves and dirt. "Guys, come see this. This is an amazing discovery."

Thinking it's something useful like a lighter or a compass, I rush forward. His palm lies on the soil beside a large oak tree, where a cluster of wavy mushrooms grow from wood chips.

"Mushrooms?" I mutter, unable to keep the disappointment from my tone.

Scott grabs a stem. Then he twists and pulls, holding the mushroom close to his eye. "We can eat them. These are called hen of the woods. They're safe."

I lean over. "You don't know that for sure."

"I do. I dated a girl who forages for them and sells her haul at the farmer's market. This is hen of the woods. I'm positive."

"You've been confident of many things in your life. Like that weekend in Vegas with your buddies. Remember?" I bristle as Scott stares at me blankly. "You blew three hundred bucks on a craps table. Everybody told you to stop. You didn't listen. You kept getting more money from the ATM until you hit the withdrawal limit of *two thousand dollars*—"

"Don't boss me around. You're not my wife."

Yeah, thank God. "This is another *stupid* gamble, Scott. Don't be an idiot."

"I'll do whatever I want."

I grab his wrist as he lifts it to his mouth. "It could be poisonous."

Scott shakes from my grip and releases an impatient snort. "I appreciate the concern, but this isn't Vegas."

"Scott, don't be ridiculous."

"We're running low on sustenance," he says, derision and amusement filling his voice. "I hate to break it to you, but the chances of us stumbling into a five-star resort are slim. Sometimes you have to take risks. Like that French scientist who took lice from typhus-infected chimps, crushed them up, and tested the vaccine he made on himself. He could've died, but he didn't. He won a Nobel Prize."

I gape at him, wondering if he's lost his mind. "What the hell are you talking about? Nobody will give you a prize for picking up a random mushroom and eating it."

"I'm not delusional."

"Then why are you doing this?"

"Because," he huffs, "we need a food source."

Nicole grabs his elbow. "You'll get sick."

"You sound like your mother," he snaps, making my blood boil. "I know what I'm doing. Do I have to prove it to you, too?"

"For God's sake," I say, digging in my backpack. "There's no need for you to do this. I have plenty of food, if you'd just ask." I pull out the extra croissant he keeps turning down. He seizes it from me, glowering, and sticks mushrooms inside the sandwich. He tears it in half and gives the other to his wife, who turns it over, frowning.

"Honey, are you sure these are safe?"

"God, you too? Yes, I'm *freaking* sure," he explodes, his face beet red. "I spent hours foraging mushrooms with that chick. We had to hike off-trail to places that only she knew about. Some, like morels, only grow at higher elevations. Whenever we found hen of the woods, we popped them right into our mouths. They're good. Very savory."

I can't tell him he's wrong. My frequent trips to the farmer's market have taught me what morels and oysters look like, but I don't recognize the wavy caps on thin stems.

"Bad idea, bro," croaks Fred in his bullfrog voice. "Some mushrooms can destroy your liver. Even if you're ninety percent positive, it isn't worth the risk."

Scott waves him off. Then he bites into the sandwich.

"Dad!" Nicole shouts. "Spit it out."

Scott swallows. I'm stunned that he'd do something so stupid. Honestly, I shouldn't be surprised. It's a very Scott thing to do. Once he's finished, he wipes his fingers on his pants. He glowers at Laura, who still holds her uneaten half. "Eat up. You need the fuel."

Laura plasters on a brilliant smile. "That's okay. I'm not hungry."

"But you haven't eaten since that energy bar," he says, his demeanor growing in severity. "That was ages ago."

"I lost my appetite. I'm anxious."

Scott's face is a glowering mask of rage. "I get it. You don't believe me. You think the same as the others, I'm an idiot."

"No, I don't. I swear to God!"

"Nobody thinks that." My skin burns with the lie as Scott's heated gaze lingers on Laura. "We just don't want anyone to get hurt."

"Amber's right. Let's focus on getting home safe." Cameron offers a hand to help Scott up, which he ignores. "Laura doesn't have to eat them if she's not comfortable."

"Who are you loyal to?" Scott asks Laura in a low voice, taut with anger. "Them or me?"

Laura's eyes widen. "Honey, it's not about that."

She attempts to take his hand, but he wrenches out of her grip and stands up. "Why don't you believe me?"

"Of course I believe you! I love you. I just—"

"You just what?" he screams, spittle flying from his mouth. "You think I'm wrong? You think I'm a stupid, bumbling moron who picks up random plants and eats them?"

"How do you know it's safe?"

"For the love of—I *told* you." He flails his hands, his eyes dazzling with fury. "I'm experienced in mushroom gathering. Either you believe that, or you *don't*, and if trusting me is such a problem, why are we married? We might as well break up now. Pack your things. Leave."

He points at the clearing behind the forest. Laura wilts, emotion filling her gaze. I exchange an alarmed look with Cameron. I make a point of staying out of their fights, but this is too much. This is *abusive*.

I frown as a tear spills down her cheek. "Okay, this is getting too heated. Scott, back off."

A mottled flush claims Scott's cheeks as he bares his teeth. "You're not in charge. I am."

"I must've missed the election where everybody voted you as leader." Scott says something in response, but I talk over him. "Laura isn't going anywhere."

"I didn't *say* she had to leave."

"You *did* say that. That's no way to treat your wife."

Scott balls his fists. "Shut your fat mouth about my relationship."

"No," I shout, struggling to keep the quiver from my voice. "I've had enough of you bullying Laura. You're out of line. You don't threaten your marriage whenever you need an ego boost."

Suddenly, Fred lunges at Laura, dislodging the croissant from her grip. It tumbles to the ground, soiling the bread and cheese.

"What is everyone's problem?" bellows Scott. "We barely have anything to eat."

Laura picks it up and brushes off the dirt. "Honey, relax. It's fine."

"You'll get your wife killed," Fred says hoarsely. "This is so insane. You can't make her—Laura!"

She stuffs the sandwich in her mouth. There's a moment of silence before Nicole wails, bursting into tears.

Fred faces off his brother as Scott launches upright. He collides into Laura, who jumps in between them. She grasps his shoulders, shaking him. "Scott, Jesus. Stop it! I don't want any fighting."

Scott takes her arms, as though preparing to hurl her aside. "The miserable jerk deserves a beating."

Fred stands a foot away, his nostrils flaring. "Try it. I've got sixty pounds on you."

Laura balls her fists in Scott's shirt and yanks hard. "I ate it. Okay?"

Scott rips his gaze off Fred. "Good."

"Don't fight. I'm on your side."

He rewards Laura with a wintry smile. "We should keep moving."

FOURTEEN
AMBER

It's been an hour. How long before a poisonous mushroom takes effect? I watch Laura closely. Her subdued presence worries me, but Scott seems okay. He's more manic than ever. He talks nonstop as the forest grows more grim. We head downhill in an effort to escape the chill biting into our bodies. We're not dressed for the plunging temperatures at high elevation. It's chilly, but we'll be fine as long as we stay dry. When the darkness makes it impossible to keep going, we settle down for the night.

"It'll be like camping," Scott bellows, throwing an arm around an unenthusiastic Nicole. "We're roughing it, but that's fine. It's mid-June. We won't freeze to death."

"How are you feeling?" I ask him.

"For the *fifth* time, I'm great," he storms, his voice carrying across the clearing. "I know what I'm doing. We can survive on cow's parsnip, mushrooms, and any berries we find for a while. The land will provide for us. Think of what our predecessors went through to map this country.

Hostile natives. Starvation. Dysentery. We won't deal with *any* of that. We have radar, satellites, and little tablets that purify water."

"We don't have those with us," I snap, unable to bear it any longer. "And we're not pioneers. We're lost hikers. This is an emergency."

Scott groans. "If you'd rather be a Negative Nancy, be my guest."

"There's a thin line between positive and delusional," I say, spreading a blanket of leaves on the ground. "This is serious. You're filling their heads with nonsense."

"Ignore her, Nicole." Scott talks over me, patting her back. "Just ignore her. Your mother makes *everything* dra-ma-tic. First, I'm poisoning myself. Next, I'm getting everybody killed. Bad attitudes won't help our situation. You need to imbibe your soul with the pioneering spirit of our ances-tors. Would they have survived if they panicked every time they hit a rough spot? Heck no."

"We have no idea where we are," I insist.

"So?" he says, stunning me. "That's a normal problem in any expedition."

My patience with Scott frays as he prattles on with increas-ingly outrageous claims. Thankfully, he and the kids leave to collect wood. Nobody has tools to start a fire, but Fred fashions a bow drill with a branch and his shoelace. He coaxes a flame from the billowing smoke as Laura makes a rock circle. Once bright orange flames consume the logs, Fred and Cameron excuse themselves to scout the area. I slump against a tree trunk, my thighs aching from all the activity. I'm not looking forward to sleeping outside.

This is such a disaster. What if it takes longer than a day to get back? Two days? How long before the owners of the cabin rental report us missing?

My head pounds as I wrap my cardigan around me. I'm so happy I forced the kids to wear extra layers. My spine tingles with unease as Scott's loud voice filters through the trees. I'm used to Scott deflecting, but he's never been this irrational. Or mean. I hate the way he bullies Laura.

She stares into the crackling fire. Devastation craters her pretty face, sinking in my stomach. I know that look well. It lived in me during those sleepless nights of taking care of a newborn while my husband was AWOL. He pouted when I said he needed to step up his duties as a father. I hope Nicole never finds out how absent her dad was in the beginning.

I peel my sore body from the ground and join Laura by the fire. "Are you all right?"

She smiles weakly. "I think so."

"Laura, what he did to you was crazy." I gnaw my lip, choosing my words carefully. "I'm glad you're okay, but bullying you into eating those mushrooms was messed up."

She waves me off. "It's fine. Scott gets frustrated when his intelligence is challenged. I mean, he's a literal genius. He's so much smarter than us, but he's not the best at handling conflict. He doesn't understand that his brain works differently than ours. That he needs to be patient and explain things."

Why is she clinging to the whole Scott-is-a-genius thing? He's proven himself to be a moron. I shrug it off. Whatever. Arguing with Laura won't get us home faster.

"I don't know why I was so worried," she says in an undertone. "It was silly of me to pick a fight."

"You didn't."

"I was being stubborn."

"For good reason," I say, incredulous. "You refused to eat a wild mushroom. Then he threatened to leave you. That's wrong."

"He's been challenging to deal with since…" She trails off, gnawing her lip, and continues in a low voice. "I'm not supposed to tell you, but he lost his job."

"What?"

"Yeah. His boss gave him a bullshit excuse, and he's had a tough time getting in somewhere. He feels inadequate. Especially because Nicky prefers your house. Not that I blame her—Queen Anne beats Shoreline by a mile—but still, he's hurt. He needs my support. He can be sensitive."

"Trust me, I know. I lived with the guy for almost a decade. Have you tried counseling?"

She purses her lips as though tasting something sour. "We don't need that. Our relationship has hills and valleys like any other couple."

"I caught you making out with your brother-in-law." I hold up my hands as her cheeks smolder. "It's none of my business, but come on. You need counseling."

"We're fine," she says with a glazed-over look. "We're in love."

Whatever you say. "Then you need to end it with Fred. Sooner rather than later."

She buries her face in her palms, rubbing at her skin. "Please don't mention this conversation. He'll kill me."

"I won't." I reach into my backpack and grab an energy bar because she seems on the verge of tears. "Want one?"

"I'm good, thanks. That sandwich perked me up." Her bowed lips pull into a wide smile, the earnest beauty of her warmth stunning me for a moment. "I've been wanting to talk to you for a while."

"I don't want to hear about your affair, Laura."

"It's not about that." Laura toys with her phone, flicking the screen. "I found something."

"What?"

She glances at her phone, her eyes widening. Her gasp stabs my heart. "Oh my God. My face! It's all…*grotesque*. What the hell?"

I gape at her. "Um—I see nothing."

She wails as she stares into her reflection, her fingers prodding her cheeks. "It's all swollen! Oh my God. The *mushrooms*. Something's wrong. I'm having an allergic reaction!"

"Does it hurt anywhere?"

She bursts into sobs. "No, no, no. This can't be happening!"

"Is your throat closing up?"

"No, but I have hives. Damn it, they're everywhere."

"Where?" I hold her tear-stained jaw, scanning her flaw-less skin. "I don't see anything."

"What are you talking about?" she shrieks, her hysteria rising to a new fever pitch. "Just look at me."

I do. "I have no idea why you're acting like this. You look great."

"Giant bumps all over. My nose is distorted. I-I'm like a monster. Oh God. I need an ambulance." She seizes my jacket and shakes me, crying hysterically. "Do you have an EpiPen?"

"N-no, but—"

She wrenches at her hair, hyperventilating. I grab her chin and examine it from all angles. "Laura, stop. You're fine."

"Liar," she growls. "You're just saying that to make me feel better."

"Stop freaking out and *listen* to me. I'm telling you the truth. Aside from the red marks from clawing at yourself, *you look normal.*"

Laura tears out of my grip, sobbing. "I've ruined my life... my career. My marriage. It's all over."

I rub her shoulder, but she shrugs me off. I'm thrown by her behavior. What's happening? I spot the mushrooms Scott picked, strewn on a handkerchief next to his backpack. I walk over and pick one. Dark blue stains the bottoms of the stems. A memory from college flickers in my brain.

"This isn't hen of the woods. It's a psychedelic mushroom." I laugh, which is the wrong reaction, but our circumstances are so insane that I can't help it. "No wonder Scott was acting so weird."

"I poisoned myself," she moans, bolting upright. "I'm dying."

"You're fine, for God's sake."

She wheels around, screaming. "I have the face of a monster, and it's fine? Maybe looks don't matter to you, but my career is over."

"There's nothing wrong with you."

"He'll leave me if I look like this," she babbles, clutching at her chest. "No. No, I've screwed up everything."

I seize her arm, but her fist makes a violent swing at me. I let her go, backing off.

"Laura, you ate psychedelic mushrooms. You're high."

"S-stop. Stop it. Leave me alone."

Nothing sinks in. She doesn't believe me. Shaking her head, she mutters indistinct words. She tears away from me, in the grips of a hallucination.

My stomach hardens. Where the hell is Scott? Oh yeah. He ate them, too. Great. Just perfect. He's out there with the kids, no doubt grappling with his visions. This is bad. I have to find him.

I grab her wrist, attempting to steer her toward the ground. "I'm getting Scott. Stay put."

She rubs her face, hard. "It's not coming off. I have to get it off, Amber."

"We will. Promise. But I need you to stay here."

She nods, tears spilling onto her cheeks.

I feel terrible about leaving her, but my kids won't be able to handle Scott in this state. I wish Cameron or Fred would hurry back. I stand, trying to approximate Scott's location. As I stumble into the thicket where Scott disappeared, a branch snaps behind me. I whirl around.

Laura is wavering on her feet.

"Laura!" I roar across the clearing. "Don't move!"

Her wailing breaks with a deranged shout. "I'm a monster...I *deserve* this."

My chest tightens. "Laura, don't!"

She sprints into the woods, as though outrunning her visions.

FIFTEEN
AMBER

Now what?

I stare after Laura, my thighs tensing. A war rages inside me. Run after her or find my kids? Precious seconds tick by, my heart torn by worry over Laura's distress and the fact that my kids are alone in the woods with an adult who is tripping major balls.

"Mom!"

Nicole's scream pierces my chest like an arrow. Turning my back on Laura, I crash through bushes toward Nicole's voice. It's hard. I can barely see anything. Sunlight is a flicker over the trees. Darkness shrouds the woods in nightmarish shadows. "Nicky?"

"Mom, get over here!"

Her panicked shriek echoes to my left. I plunge in that direction and my foot catches on a root. The world swings, and my elbows slam into the ground. Swearing, I claw to a standing position and spot Nicole's young face hidden behind a light beam.

It illuminates a cross-legged Scott, who seems to be obsessed with his phone. His mouth agape, he stares at the screen. Nicole sighs, like a parent at her limit with a high-maintenance toddler.

"Dad's gone screwy. Like, way more than usual."

"I'm not surprised. Where's David?"

She shrugs. "Dunno. He went to look for help."

Great. I blow a tense stream of air through my teeth, and then I crouch beside my ex. "Scott?"

He gapes at his phone. "All the lines...they're moving. Wow. This is so weird."

I clap my hands in his face.

His narrowed gaze snaps to mine. He flinches. "*Jesus*. You too? Why is everyone's face so messed up?"

I clutch his shoulder, shaking it. "Because you ate *shrooms*. You're high."

His brow furrows. "What?"

"Psychedelic mushrooms. You're hallucinating. You and Laura took them with nothing in your stomach but those sandwiches, so the effects are very potent."

Scott glances at me. "How do I know this isn't a hallucination?"

"I don't have time for this. Up." I take his arm and tug him upright. "We need to get back to camp. Where's David?"

"You asked me that already." Nicole gives her dad an exhausted look. "I had to distract Dad. He was freaking out. I told David he should find you."

"Oh, Nicole. I wish you hadn't done that." My heart pounds at the thought of David stumbling around in the forest. "It's too easy to get lost."

Nicole's eyes widen under furrowed brows. "And that's *my fault*?"

"I didn't say that, honey." I seize Scott, leading us to the flickering orange glow. "Adults responsible for you should've known better."

"Great," she grinds out. "Blame it all on Dad."

"He did shove wild mushrooms down his throat after being warned not to, but you're right. Why should your father accept responsibility for anything?"

"He's being brave," she says hotly. "He's trying to help."

"Sweetheart, he's put us in more danger."

Nicole bristles. "You're always criticizing him."

I stop myself from snapping at my daughter. It won't do any good. Scott's always been her favorite. He's the Disney dad. He does all the fun things with our daughter. I'm the one dragging her out of bed in the morning, hounding her to finish her homework, and grounding her when she acts out at school, so I get that I'll never be her first choice. But it still hurts.

Scott stumbles behind me, obeying the pressure on his wrist. For once, he's quiet. The mushrooms are worth their weight in gold if they keep him silent. I haul him along, the darkness so thick that I wouldn't make out the ground if it weren't for Nicole's phone. Finally, we squeeze through trees and enter the clearing. I speak, but my voice is like a frail whimper. I clear my throat and try again.

"Cameron? *David?*"

A flashlight beams across leaves, Scott exclaiming, "So pretty!" with an awed gasp. The phone's light sweeps over our heads, and a tall form emerges.

"What the hell is going on? I returned and the camp was empty. I thought—" Cameron breaks off, frowning as Scott kneels beside the fire and stares into the flames. "Um... what is he doing?"

"Hallucinating." I sigh roughly, gesturing toward Scott. "The genius ate psychedelic mushrooms."

"You're kidding me."

"I wish."

Cameron glances at Scott, whose fascination with fire is getting dangerous. "How is that even possible?"

I shrug. "They grow all over Washington. I guess I should be glad they're not poisonous."

Cameron wipes his face, sighing. "For the love of God. As if we don't have enough problems."

"Did you run into David? Or Laura?"

"Yeah." He illuminates the parting bushes, revealing my stepson as he shoves through, followed by Fred. "Wait—where's Laura?"

"She disappeared in the woods."

My heart hammers as I whirl around, searching for another shape in the dark.

Scott tears his attention from the campfire. He stands up and approaches us, his pupils blown, clearly struggling to pull himself together. "Where's Laura?"

"She's not here," I tell him. "She ran away."

Scott steps into the light beam from Cameron's phone, fracturing it in two. "What? Why?"

"She was tripping hard on the mushrooms. She took a photo of herself. Started to panic. She was upset. Kept saying that her face was swollen. That her career was ruined."

Clarity swims in his widened gaze, and then he explodes, his tone blistering. *"And you let her believe that?* Jesus."

"She wouldn't listen to me."

"Why the hell didn't you *make* her?" he bellows, spittle flying from his mouth. "You never hold back on your opinion. The one time someone could benefit from it, you let her down? Did you even tell her it was a hallucination?"

"Of course I did. How can you say that?" My chest hitches as I replay what happened. "I told her she was high. I repeated it over and *over.* I brought her to the fire and made her sit. But she wouldn't stay. She vanished after I said I was going to get you."

"Oh my God." Scott faces the darkness, hollering. "Laura! Baby, where are you? Come back."

The kids' voices chime in, shouting for Laura, and then Scott hushes everybody with windmill arms. "Let's see if we can hear her."

I hold my breath. My ears strain for the slightest rustling of leaves, a shrill cry, anything, but there's nothing. Scott's panicked voice cleaves through the grim silence. "She's not responding. We have to find her. Let's fan out."

"Absolutely not," says Cameron, switching his flashlight off. "We can't go tearing off into the woods after dark."

Scott wheels on him, screaming. "Screw you, man. This is my wife we're talking about!"

"None of us have flashlights except for our phones, and they're not that great." Cameron turns his back on, the meager light landing on the ground. "We won't be able to see, which means someone will end up with a broken ankle. Then we'll be in even worse shape."

"I'm not abandoning Laura," Scott bellows, veins standing out from his flushed neck. "If you're *that* much of a coward, give your phone to me. I'll use both to navigate."

I shake my head, sighing. "Scott, you're high. You're no good to Laura right now."

"Fine, then. Who will look for her?"

Nobody volunteers.

Scott faces me, his eyes misting. "Amber, please."

"I'm sorry, Scott. It's too dangerous."

"Really?" he snarls, bunching his hands into fists. "Then why did you abandon her when she needed you?"

"I don't know," I roar, restrained by Cameron's hand on my shoulder. "Maybe because my *daughter* screamed, and you're her father."

"I'm supposed to believe you care about me?" Scott launches into a tirade that seems years in the making. "You are a passive-aggressive ice queen. You did the bare minimum in our marriage, and then blamed it on me when it fell apart. But at least you can tell people that you're superior."

Heat steals into my neck as I imagine Nicole's face, rigid with shock. It's so selfish of him to do this. We agreed never to fight in front of her. He's breaking the rules, but if I point that out he'll call me a frigid bitch. I open my mouth, but Cameron's gentle baritone breaks the silence.

"Guys, this doesn't help Laura."

Her name is like a wave of frigid water, drowning my rage. Poor Laura. Stuck in the woods, alone. My lips tremble as I picture her huddled in a ball, grappling with terrible visions. David glares at Scott as he stalks off, slumping near the fire.

Fred approaches Scott, hands deep in his pocket. "Hey… I'll look for her."

"That's not a good idea," says Cameron.

"I'll tie off pieces of fabric to the trees to mark my path so I don't get lost. Does anyone have something I can use?"

I search in my bag, yanking out a fluorescent-pink brewery shirt, and hand it to him. Fred takes it and wastes zero time stripping it with his hunting knife. Then he heads off with his backpack, the darkness swallowing him.

Please find her.

I couldn't bear it if he doesn't. I feel responsible for what happened. Maybe it's the schoolteacher in me that needs to corral everyone to safety, but I can't escape the feeling that I failed Laura.

Scott sits by the fire as Nicole frets over him, his arms wrapped around his knees. Cameron crouches beside Scott, talking in soothing tones, saying Laura will be fine. Just fine. That she's a strong woman who's survived worse, and that one day we'll laugh about this. Scott nods, his glazed-over eyes boring into mine. The malice in them alarms me.

Tears blind my vision as David approaches, pulling me into a fierce hug. "Mom, none of this is your fault."

I nod, biting back a sob. I know that. *Scott* doesn't. If Laura's hurt, he won't just blame me.

He'll want revenge.

SIXTEEN
THE PAST

I killed my mom.

It happened an hour ago, I think. I glance down at my clenched, bloody hands. They're shaking. I'm at the police station, sitting in a hard chair in a small room with a gray desk pushed against the wall. The cops said they'd be back, but they must be behind that glass, watching me. My insides ache. I'm cold. I want to go home.

Do I even have one after this?

Dad will send me away. He hates me. He'll give me up for adoption, and I'll have to live with a new family. If someone adopts me. My eyes sting as I try not to cry.

The door opens. Two policemen step inside. They're really big, but both look friendly. The silver-haired grandpa offers me his hand, grinning like a fox.

"Hello. I'm Detective Cobane and this is Detective Nunes." He shakes my hand and sits beside me as the other man stands by the door. "We want to discuss some things.

Maybe ask you some questions, and you can ask us questions. I want to make sure everybody's comfortable with what's going on and go from there."

He takes out a sheet of paper and reads me my rights, line by line. He's nicer than I thought he'd be.

"Do you understand everything? If you want an attorney, say the word. If my questions are too uncomfortable, we'll stop. You're in control. That sound good?" He makes me sign the waiver and sticks it in a folder. "Can we get you anything to drink?"

I lick my lips. "Coke."

Detective Nunes leaves, returning with the can. He flicks the tab. It opens with a hiss. Then he drops the Coke in front of me. I gulp down my first soda in months, the sugary fizz popping on my tongue. Before I'm finished, Detective Nunes gives me another. Then he returns to his spot near the door.

"All right," murmurs the kindly detective with gray hair. "So, I got thrown into this. I hoped that you could go back to the very beginning and tell me what happened."

My hands tremble as details flash in my head—the screaming, the rosewood ornament, the dark hole where her skull used to be.

"She's dead. It wasn't my fault. I-I just wanted her to *stop*."

"So you were fighting?"

I nod. "She hit me. She was mad at me for losing my keys to the house."

"Did she have a weapon?"

"No."

"Was she punching you with a fist, or was it a slap?"

"Slapping," I say.

"And what were you doing?"

"Nothing. I stood there and let her do it, like I've done before."

"Your mother hits you a lot?"

I shrug. "Sometimes."

"Why would she do that?"

"She hates me. She says she's a goddess from heaven trapped in a human body, and that she's stuck here because of me. She's forced to watch me, so I *deserve* to be punished."

"Your mom thinks she's a god?"

"Yeah."

"Wow. Okay." The detective taps a pen on the table, frowning. "And do you believe her? Do you think you're a god, too?"

I shake my head. "My mother is…not normal."

"Can you explain what you mean by that?"

"She's not like other kids' moms. She gags when I walk into the room. Screams when I sing or hum. She forces me to wear clothes that are too small. She banned me from the kitchen until I started breaking the locks. They took them down, but I used to be hungry unless I stole food."

"That sounds awful. I'm sorry to hear that. Did your dad do this to you, too?"

"My dad is okay. He only pretends to punish me in front of Mom. He'll raise his voice so that she hears him, but if she's not around he doesn't do anything bad to me."

"How long has this been going on?"

I shrug. "Since I can remember."

"Then it became too much, didn't it?"

"Yes." I wipe my face. "I was angry."

"She was hurting you. You wanted to make her stop for good."

I did. "I didn't want to hurt anyone."

The detective smiles. "Of course not. Sometimes people fight and things get out of hand. It could've happened to anybody, especially if you've been dealing with abuse for years. Can you tell us how you planned it?"

The can buckles under my grip. "There was no plan."

"Look, I'm going to be honest with you. There are a bunch of forensic people at your house right now. They're down there getting fingerprints and hair samples. Taking pictures of everything. If what they find doesn't match up to what you've said, you'll be in trouble. They're looking in your computer. They will figure out exactly what happened. This is your last chance to be honest."

Tears squeeze out of my eyes.

"I don't want anyone to think bad of you, but this isn't like you stole a bicycle. What you did is a big deal. Honesty is

NOT A NORMAL FAMILY   107

important. How you handle yourself will make a difference in what happens to you. To me, you seem like a normal kid. An honest kid. Do you want to make this right?"

"I-I do. I know it was wrong."

"So after she slapped you, what happened?"

"I grabbed that eagle thing on the table and hit her head. She fell, and I kept hitting her."

"How many times?"

"I-I don't know."

The detective sighs through his nose. "How did you feel as you were beating your mother?"

I blink, and a tear rolls down my cheek. "Angry. Really angry."

"How about now?"

"I can't think about it."

"Why did you kill her?"

"I told you," I say, my voice breaking. "She was hurting me."

"*Slapping* you. Which would get on anybody's nerves, but...your life wasn't at risk. Was it?"

He didn't understand, and I had no idea how to explain it. "She was killing...my soul. She was trying to erase me."

His brows furrow. "But you said she didn't have a weapon. You didn't *have* to kill her. You wanted to. Why?"

"I never wanted to hurt her. I wanted her to love me, but I screwed up everything. Now I've done it. I don't want to go to jail." My throat tightens. "Is my dad coming?"

"He's on his way."

He's going to kill me. My heart feels like it's bursting. I clutch my chest, crying. "I didn't—I didn't want—" I burst into tears, pain exploding from my empty belly. "I didn't mean to."

"All right. Take a deep breath."

Detective Nunes pats my back. I wipe my face, but it keeps pouring out of me. She's gone. I'm sad. I'm scared. Will I be homeless? Fear crashes into me like ocean waves. I collapse on the floor. People come and go. They murmur and walk around me as though behind fogged glass. I'm rolled onto a stretcher. It's not until a ray of sunlight strokes my cheek that the world focuses. An older woman with a ponytail leans over me, her pale, freckled face shining. A white tag swings from a lanyard around her neck. She has a friendly smile.

"My name is Doctor Jessica Jefferson. I'm taking care of you from now on."

SEVENTEEN
AMBER

I don't sleep.

Laura's terrified sobbing haunts me as I fight to remain alert. Nicole curls up with her dad, who sits upright against a tree. The euphoric side effects must've worn off, because Scott spends the night glaring at me, like *I'm* the reason Laura ate dodgy mushrooms, panicked, and ran into the woods.

Could I have done more?

If I followed her, she would've been fine. She'd be wrapped up in Scott's arms right now. I keep replaying my last conversation with her. She was in distress. I left her. I made a decision, but I didn't know it'd lead to this. *I didn't think.* It's killing me. Guilt eats at me as hours pass with no sign of Fred.

I shiver in Cameron's protective embrace despite the smoldering campfire. I face a thick wall of silhouetted trees. The forest plays its music: singing crickets, owls hooting, the rustle of small creatures darting into bushes. It needles my skin. Laura's out there, by herself. What a *nightmare*.

I close my eyes. When I open them, a grayish dawn is chasing the darkness. We'll leave as soon as we can. Laura will turn up. She couldn't have wandered far in her condition. Scott scrambles up as heavy footsteps approach, tramping through branches.

My stomach knots.

Fred bursts into camp, shaking his head. "I walked everywhere."

Disappointment laces Scott's tone as he shoulders his backpack. "Come on. Everybody up."

The kids stagger to their feet. Nicole and David wear identical horrified expressions. David slaps himself awake and grabs an energy bar. Nicole refuses hers.

"You need the calories," I tell her.

She purses her lips. "I don't feel like eating."

"I don't care," I grate out, my patience wearing very thin. "Eat."

"*Dad* isn't," she mumbles, staring at her father. "What are the chances she's still alive?"

"She'll be fine. It's not cold enough for that." David rubs her back, his smile crooked. "I've never done shrooms, but I hear they make people sleepy. I bet she hunkered down for the night under a blanket of leaves."

"Really?"

David nods.

A muscle tenses in Scott's jaw, but he doesn't comment. I give David a grateful pat. His gentle nature pairs well with Nicole, who scares easily. She beams at him before joining Scott, who seems on the verge of tears.

"Thanks for that," I whisper to David, who falls into step beside me. "You're very patient with her."

"I figure with Coach Scott riding your case all the time, you could use the help." Worry fractures his soft, brown gaze. "Will she be okay?"

I swallow hard. "I hope so."

We spend the entire morning searching for Laura as we fan out in equal distance of each other. Scott screams until his voice breaks. I can't look at him. I don't want to be infected with the same terror, even though it's bubbling in my lungs. We've lost two hours. Minimal water. Dwindling food. My phone has no service.

By nine, everybody is desperate to find Laura. Fred bellows her name, sounding almost as broken as Scott. My clumsy feet can barely keep up with them, and at eleven, we take a break. Scott smashes his fist into the tree bearing a fluorescent pink tie. "Damn it. We're going in circles!"

From my limited knowledge of backpacking, that doesn't surprise me. Everything looks the same. We don't have a compass. Or a map. Scott let Cameron glance at his, but the lack of visibility from heavy fog makes it impossible to identify landmarks and the GPS signal is still weak.

We pick another direction, and we march out of the thick forest and onto a ridge. Below lies an inviting meadow sprinkled with cosmos flowers. It's gorgeous, but so steep that one slip could seriously injure a person. I wouldn't trust my hiking boots to stop my fall. My gaze narrows on a bluish lump at rest under a massive oak.

A *body*.

A knot forms in my throat. "Is that her?"

Scott charges to my side as I point at the splayed figure underneath a tree. David blanches. Fred and Scott scramble down the hill, screaming her name. Cameron and I follow at a less brisk pace.

Please let her be alive.

The kids stay behind as we rush toward Laura, sliding on our backs. It's dangerous and scary. Little rocks cut into my palms as I make the descent, sprinting at the tree when the hill bottoms out. Fred gets there first. His panicked scream jolts my heart with adrenaline. I dash to the group, my lungs burning.

It's a scene out of a movie. Laura's face, as white as bleached paper, her limbs akimbo, her neck bent at a strange angle. My heart races from the utter lack of movement. Cameron jumps on her and starts compressions. Fred begs Laura to *wake up. Wake up. Please wake up.* Scott looks on, his expression as lifeless as the woman at his feet. The kids climb down.

"Mom, what's going on?"

I move my lips, but the words won't come. Nicole's gaze centers on Laura, and then she screams. David slides an arm around her waist. She dives into his arms, sobbing.

Cameron stops his compressions. Fred takes over, pounding her chest for ten minutes before he gives up, too. Cameron turns, mouth set in a grim line. Fred lets out a loud wail, collapsing beside Laura. Tears sliding down his face, Scott cups her cheek and murmurs something. It sounds like an apology. I'm trying not to listen. It's too awful. So is the sight of Laura on her back, her unblinking stare crystallized with pain.

I touch her ankle. She's ice-cold.

Dead.

EIGHTEEN

THE PRESENT

Another dead body lies under my feet.

I've played my part well. Nobody suspects anything, but this is my fault. I fight the urge to rifle through her things and collect a trinket—something to remember her by. I enjoy possessing my victims. Even in death, they're mine.

I'll add a symbol of her to my collection. An earring, maybe, because the vapid idiot couldn't stop yammering about how she'd been gifted them by a designer brand for her fitspo Instagram. As though it's an accomplishment to be beautiful.

Everybody likes Laura, but that woman is more plastic than the Mean Girls. I hate her. Everything about her screams fake. Her sugary smiles. Her dumb laugh. Laura is one of those revolting people you instantly loathe. She has no goals besides wanting to be rich and successful, has the personality of a cardboard box, and is a giant hypocrite. Laura makes money judging people's lifestyles. Her social medias are all about forcing a high standard of living down ordinary people's throats. Telling us plebs how we should live. Meanwhile, she's cheating on her husband.

With his *brother*.

Who does that?

Insecure, desperate girls like Laura. She's the type that has a library full of self-help books but is incapable of absorbing the material. Sadly, she lacks insight. If she did, she'd realize she was more toxic than Chernobyl. Maybe she would've removed herself from the world long before this day.

The world is kinder without Laura Maxwell. Her industry is why girls these days are overly obsessed with their self-image. She was problematic. She needed to do better. Now she'll only be remembered as a two-timing influencer who killed herself trying to get a selfie.

I need to take something. A strand of her glossy black hair? A ring? A glittering case peeks out from under her thigh. I lean forward, palm outstretched, but the flickering candle of my conscience makes me pause. My therapist wouldn't want me doing this. It's triggering my compulsion.

While the others sob and carry on, I steal the phone. It's warm, somehow. As though it absorbed Laura's life force. She was more attached to this thing than her husband. A hairline crack splits the screen, but it works fine.

I snap a photo of her body.

NINETEEN
AMBER

David is such a good kid.

I swear, he makes the rest of us look uncivilized. While I deal with Laura's death by having a panic attack, David and Nicole gather flowers. Through a haze of tears, I watch my daughter lay a wildflower bouquet on Laura's crossed arms. It's awful. How could this happen?

Nicole's a wreck. I tried to comfort her, but she shoved me away. A painful reminder that she's absorbing my ex's behaviors.

The kids gaze at Laura, hands clasped. After a while, Nicole's sweet voice breaks the silence.

"Do you think she's in Heaven?"

Worry pinches David's brow. "Dunno."

"*Do* you?"

"I don't know," he says roughly. "What does it matter?"

Nicole flinches. "I was just asking."

"You're right. Sorry."

Her pout trembles. "It's okay. Everybody's tense."

Not Laura.

I peer down at the body. I've been to funerals, but I've never seen a fresh corpse. Nobody ever talks about how eyelids stay open after death. It's unnerving. According to Fred, who is a true crime enthusiast, they're glued shut as part of the embalming process.

I study her serene expression. Is she blaming herself for letting her husband poison her? Or did she find peace? I hope she's in a better place.

Nicole pokes David's side. "Don't stare at her."

"Why not?" he murmurs. "She doesn't mind."

"Don't be morbid!"

"When you die, will you give a crap about what you look like? Or whether people are gawking at you? No, you'll be living it up in Heaven. Playing guitar with a chorus of angels. Rocking it out with Jesus."

Nicole giggles and makes a face. "I can't believe I'm laughing. What's wrong with me?"

His lip curls. "You're a psycho, like me."

She snorts. "Stop."

"I'm serious. It runs in the family."

"We're not blood-related."

"Doesn't matter. It's contagious." David slides an arm around her shoulders. "You and Mom are my family. I won't let anything happen to you."

Her eyes mist. "I'm glad you're here."

He smiles. "Me too."

My chest warms with a glowing ball of pride. Nicole's expression lightens as she walks away from the body. I wipe my cheeks and approach my stepson. He faces me, his expression tight.

"Thanks for taking care of her," I whisper, pulling him into my arms. "I'm so happy you're getting along."

"Both of you mean everything to me."

I squeeze him hard. "You're an angel."

He grins. "I don't know about that."

"You'll be an amazing father one day."

David lights up with the compliment. His warmth is like a blast of sunlight over snow. His watery gaze meets mine, and suddenly, he's as vulnerable as my daughter. "I love you, Mom."

"Love you, too," I say, my throat thickening. "I'll get us home. I promise."

"I'm not worried about that."

A smile trembles over his lips, his face shining with trust. This kid has a bigger heart than most adults. He'll be a fantastic role model for his future children, if he has them, but he'll never have the chance if I don't save us.

I disengage from him. "Can you keep a close eye on Nicole? We can't have anybody wandering off."

"I will, Mom."

I pat him on the back.

He turns, heading toward Nicole. Fred and Cameron stand under a towering spruce, heads bent together. It seems like a tense conversation. Fred's stiff posture recoils.

"What are we doing with her?" asks Cameron, hand on his hip. "There's not much we can do without tools, but we should at least talk about it."

Fred shakes his head. "I'm not good with bodies, man."

The tension rippling Cameron's forehead smooths over as I join his side.

"Hey, uh...we have to do something about...Laura." Cameron bites his lip, his gaze darting at the lifeless form under the tree. "We've lingered here too long, but Scott is refusing to take part in the discussion and we're running out of time."

"What discussion?"

"What to do with the body. Leave it. Bury it. *Burn* it," he whispers, his face blanching. "We also need to go through her things. I would've done it already, but I don't want to upset him."

"Where is he?"

Cameron points to an oak in the distance. Scott sits with his back against the trunk, head in his hands.

I swallow hard. "He's in no condition to do anything."

"None of us are. We still need to get his vote in."

Right. "Who should approach him?"

Cameron and Fred stare at me pointedly. I'm a woman, therefore I'm inclined to be Scott's emotional crutch. My jaw clenches. I can't do this. I'm barely hanging on as it is, but I nod and turn around. Someone has to do it. It might as well be me.

I march through the meadow, my feet stalling when I reach Scott's rigid frame. A gentle breeze plays with his tousled curls.

I lick my lips. "Scott?"

He doesn't move.

"Um, we need to talk. All of us, I mean. We…we have to decide what we're doing with her. Laura."

He gazes at me. "Do with her?"

"The body," I whisper. "You know…bury it or leave it—"

"Her," he explodes, his cheeks flushing. "Bury *her*. She's not an 'it,' for God's sake."

"Sorry, yes, bury *her*." I toy with my jacket's zipper, heart pounding. "And…they want…to search through her things. She could have something on her that can help us."

Scott lurches upright, glaring at the kids, who've joined Fred and Cameron. "What are they doing? Are they touching her?"

"No," I say, my hand falling on his shoulder. "Nobody will do anything without your approval."

Scott rips off my touch and charges toward the group, but when we're close enough to see Laura's features, he halts. The awful sight seems to kill his outrage. He clenches his teeth, his eyes misting. He trembles.

I avert my gaze. I should comfort him, but the shock of her death paralyzes me. I can't look at him. The judgment in his stare hurts, so I turn my attention to the others.

"How did this happen?" asks David, dismayed.

"She fell. Broke her neck." Cameron hunches on the ground, examining Laura's head. A moment later, he pulls the jacket back over her face. "This is why we shouldn't hike at night. This could've been avoided. It's a damn shame."

Nicole lets out a strangled sob. "Yeah, but how did she fall?"

Cameron shrugs. "She was stumbling in the dark."

"That's assuming this happened last night." I'm not an expert on the decomposition of bodies. "Or was it this morning?"

"She could've stroked out on the mushrooms, for all we know." A black look adds to the contempt in Fred's voice.

"No, I felt the break in her neck. She died from the fall," says Cameron, hauling himself upright.

Fred makes a choking sound. "I can't believe she's gone. Just like that."

I can't, either. I never would've imagined this outcome from a three-hour hike. Laura's death is a harsh reminder of the stakes. We have to get out of here.

Cameron seems to arrive at the same conclusion as he speaks briskly. "We have several options. One. Burn the body. I'm not a fan of that, for obvious reasons. It'll take forever to assemble all the wood we need, hours to start a fire, and we can't afford to waste the whole day. So that's out."

"Does everybody agree?" I glance at Scott, who is silent as the others murmur agreement. "Okay, what's next?"

"It's not really a choice, but I'll throw it in anyway," breezes Cameron, crossing his arms. "Burying her. That would be my vote, but we don't have the tools to dig a grave. Anything we can manage will be too shallow. Animals will get to the body, which leads me to the last option. Leaving her here."

I shift in place uneasily. It's a dreadful fate. Fred swears, raking his hair. The kids stare at Cameron, horrified. Scott glowers at him.

"You can't be serious."

"It won't be forever," says Cameron in a low voice. "Just until we can send park rangers to retrieve Laura and give her the burial she deserves."

"This shouldn't have happened. I would've stopped her." Scott gestures at me, shouting. "You left her alone. Why? Is this *punishment* because I cheated? I screwed you over, so now you're screwing *me* over?"

My throat tightens. "I did what I could."

"*Bullshit.* She's dead and you don't even care."

"Yes, I do—"

"You don't. If you did, you wouldn't let her become carrion, for God's sake." He glances around, his sharp eyes blazing. "We're civilized people. We don't let our loved ones rot in the open. Hell, we don't even do that to our dogs."

Fred shouts back. "We don't have shovels."

"We'll use our hands. It'll take a while, but it's doable."

"No," Cameron snaps. "We don't have time for this. A, our water is running low. B, we're almost out of food."

"Cam's right," I say. "This is an emergency. We have to make tough decisions."

"Yeah, yeah. I get it," Scott yells, his voice thick with tears. "Everything is more important than the love of my life."

"Scott, come on. None of us *wants* to do this." I palm his shoulder, quailing under his acidic glare. "Sh-she's gone, and that's horrible, but there's nothing we can do to help her."

"You always hated her."

I flinch. "That's not true."

"You did," he seethes, slapping my hand off him. "You despised her. You moved on, but God forbid I try to find happiness. You let her die to spite me. *Didn't you?* Don't shake your head, you disgusting liar. You left her! You knew this would happen—"

Scott's head whips back with Cameron's vicious back-hand. A loud thwack echoes through the meadow. Scott staggers, a bright patch glowing on his cheek.

"You hit me."

"Yes, I did," says Cameron in a measured tone, squaring his shoulders. "I'm happy to do it again if you keep blaming my wife. If Amber wasn't an overprepared saint, we'd be in bigger trouble than we're already in."

I touch his forearm. "Cam, don't. He's upset."

Scott balls his hands into fists, screaming. *"How can you be so heartless?"*

"I'm done talking to you," Cameron says, his indifferent stare flicking to the group as he pulls out the map I brought. "Let's put our heads together." He points at the sliver of blue snaking through my map, which intersects the Alpine Loop Trail. "We need to find this river."

"Should we head downhill?" I ask.

Cameron nods. "Yeah."

"What about Laura?" Fred asks, choking on her name.

"Unless anyone comes up with something better, we can't do much. We can't give her a proper burial. The best we can do is cover her with some branches and hang some fabric to mark the location of the body, which we've already done."

"Assuming park rangers *can* find it."

"One crisis at a time," mutters Cameron, rolling up the map. "Everyone, get your stuff."

"I'm not going," declares Scott. "You're nuts if you think I'm abandoning her."

"Dude, we just had this discussion—"

"*Laura's freaking dead.* I lost my wife. I can't brush it off like the rest of you. Are we really leaving her here?" Scott smacks the branch bearing the pink tie. "Like this stupid thing will be useful after she's been eviscerated and dragged off by whatever lives in these woods."

Nicole whitens.

"She'll be pulled apart and scattered. She'll be *desecrated*. Rodents. Small bugs. Feasting on her flesh out in the open!"

Nicole slides her hands over her ears, whimpering. "*Stop*. I don't want to hear any more."

"You want to let that happen to her?" bellows Scott, pointing at each of us.

He seems to be searching for an ally among the group, someone who will take his side. When nobody does, he faces me.

"You know how important her looks were to her, for God's sake. You can't do this. Please. You failed her, Amber. The least you can do—the very least—is bury her."

That nails me in the gut.

Cameron shoves him. "Enough."

Scott wipes his face and stalks off. Cameron and David disappear in the forest to get something to cover Laura. Nicole runs after her father. My stomach sinks as I replay Laura's last words, the screaming, the horrible visions she endured.

Fred shoulders his pack, eyes glistening. "Don't mind him. Scott, I mean. He's...well, he's grieving. He did the same thing when our mother passed. I want you to know that I don't blame you in the slightest. I just wish I'd come back sooner to help with Laura." He pats my arm, but the gesture fails to warm me. "It's his fault. What kind of idiot picks up a mushroom off the ground and eats it?"

I shrug.

"Laura knew better," he continues, his lip curling in a contemptuous sneer. "What the hell was she thinking? She'd rather join her husband in death?"

I say nothing. Anger is part of the process, and I'm the only one who knows about Laura's infidelity. He feels safe confiding in me. Maybe he's glad she's gone. One less person can share his awful secret. My body flushes.

What is wrong with me?

Fred slides his hands under his backpack's straps and grips them, his knuckles turning white. "She was planning to leave him. Did you know that?"

My insides clench. "No, I didn't."

"He was nasty to her, Amber. He abused her. That's why she came to me. At first, she wanted advice on how to make him...less of a jerk. Then it turned into more. I can't believe it—"

"Stop right there, Fred. I feel for you, I do, but this isn't the time or the place. I can't handle your feelings on top of everything that's going on right now."

"All right. Geez," he says, echoing his brother. "I was venting."

Vent on someone else.

I march past Fred, rage fueling my steps. Laura was using Fred. Dumping her emotional pain onto him. Fred and Laura wouldn't have been a couple. How would she explain herself to the family? It never would've worked. They must've known that.

I'm sorry. I should've done more.

My throat tightens as I face her, preparing to go. Leaving her feels wrong. I scan her body, clutching my backpack like it's a shield. Something is off. What's missing? It hits me as Cameron checks his phone for signal. I search the ground for the pink case that protects her phone, but it's nowhere.

"Where's her phone?"

Cameron blinks. "No idea."

"Do you think she dropped it?" I glance up the steep slope, biting my lip. "That's what happened, right?"

Cameron frowns. "Where else could it be?"

My scalp pricks with a needling sensation.

Laura loved the darn thing. She was never without her phone. Did someone take it? No, that's crazy. I'm searching for an explanation beyond the obvious because I'm upset.

She fell. It was a tragic accident, and that's all there is to it.

TWENTY
AMBER

One of us is gone.

Morale is low as we camp beside a dry creek. Spending another night outside is the last thing anybody wants. I've had enough of the great outdoors for a lifetime, but the setting sun cuts short our search for water.

My husband pores over my map by the firelight. My daughter lies on the ground and stares at the canopy of trees. David draws something in the dirt. Fred strolls back and forth, dropping dead limbs onto a pile. I think of Laura's body, lying under pine needles and branches, a feast for scavengers.

I'm drained. An ache pounds in my parched throat. My eyes burn, but no tears form. I can't afford to lose any water right now. We're down to a third of a liter each, aside from Scott, who has less than a cup in his reservoir.

A stony-faced Scott tosses a fresh log onto the fire. Sparks fly in all directions as flames creep up the bark, blackening the wood. His accusatory glare stabs at me behind the smoky veil.

"How are you hanging in, Scott?"

Judging by the tear trembling on his eyelid, not well. He inhales a deep breath and speaks in a low, tormented voice. "How do you *think*?"

I bow my head. "I'm so sorry."

"Don't. Nothing you say can make this better."

I swallow an exasperated sigh. "We're all upset over Laura."

"No kidding," he scoffs. "You left her there to rot like roadkill."

"Stop it." Cameron folds the map and tucks it into his backpack. "We have no tools. Barely any food and water. Digging a six-foot hole in our condition would be reckless."

Scott's posture crumbles. "I-I think we should have a f-funeral."

Fred dumps the rest of the logs beside the fire, the orange light dancing over his narrowed brows. He needs to keep his emotions in check. We don't need Scott finding out that Laura wasn't faithful. Heat climbs my cheeks.

"Do you want to start?"

Scott nods. "Laura, the world is crueler now that you're gone. You were my safety. You always knew when to reach out. When things got…too dark, you were there to tell me that I belonged. You were one of the few that believed in me. I'll miss you so much. I d-don't understand w-why you were taken from me. What did I do to deserve this? It's like God *hates* me."

Nicole wraps her father in a giant hug. "Nobody hates you, Dad."

I do.

"She was my everything. Now I feel this void inside me because she's dead and I don't have anywhere to put all this love." He breaks down, sobbing. "Why did this happen to me?"

Typical. He's made this funeral all about him.

Fred shakes his head and gazes up at the sky.

"I'd like to say a few things," I say. "You know, to honor *her* memory." I'm probably coming off like a jerk, but I'm having a difficult time reining in my annoyance.

Scott's enraged hiss cuts me off. "I'm sorry to interrupt what's most likely a savage attack on my dead wife, but I don't want to hear it. I'm barely holding it together as it is. I will not sit here and listen to your negativity."

My mouth gapes open. "This isn't about you. Or *us*. Or that *you* led us into this stupid forest and got Laura killed by acting like an idiot. This is about honoring a woman's life."

A bright mockery invades his stare. "That ship has sailed, crashed, and sunk to the bottom."

"Guys," warns Cameron. "Both of you. Cool it."

Several minutes pass in which the only sounds are Scott's quiet weeping and the crackling fire.

"I have something to say."

Everybody's attention snaps to David, who sits on the ground with his legs stretched out in front of him, his long sleeves rolled up to his elbows. "I didn't know Laura as well as the rest of you, but the few times I met her, she was gracious and positive. That's a rare thing these days. She seemed like the kind of person who gave genuine compliments."

"And she made those amazing chocolate cupcakes. The ones with the vanilla swirl on top," Nicole adds, and a smile flickers on Scott's face. "They were incredible."

Scott nods. "They were."

"She was so talented with photography. Did any of you follow her TikTok? She has one point three million followers. I-I bet they're wondering why she hasn't p-posted in days." A tear slides down her cheek.

They'll never hear from Laura again. With the phone missing, Scott won't be able to update them. I searched for the phone on the way up the hill, but I didn't spot Laura's glittering pink case, which seems odd. It's possible she dropped it in the forest, but she was clinging to it when she ran off.

Something else is bothering me. How did she make it to the ridge in the dark? It's more plausible that she spent the night in the woods, sobering up. Then she woke up, wandered to that dangerous cliff, posed for a selfie, and *slipped*.

And her phone evaporated?

I lick my lips. "Does anyone have service?"

My gaze wanders over the group as everybody pulls out their cellphones, switching them on before shaking their heads and stowing them. Nobody is hiding Laura's phone. I'm paranoid. Seeing things that aren't there.

"Tomorrow, finding water is our priority."

Scott stops weeping. "My map says there's a creek east of here. We should head there."

"You don't even know where we are."

"I know…the general location of our area."

Snorting, I toss a stick into the flames. "We're heading downhill."

"But that's the wrong direction," he snaps, his body stiffening. "I'm telling you. I have wilderness training."

"From what?" I scoff, tossing another branch in the fire. "*Man vs. Wild*? *YouTube*? You couldn't find your way out of a telephone booth, let alone this forest."

Fred lets out a low whistle. Cameron strokes my back in a gesture that seems to say *be careful*. I'm painfully aware that Scott is in a volatile mood and he's lugging around a weapon. That stupid crossbow.

Scott's ears burn flaming red, a danger sign. He stands, his nostrils flaring.

I inhale a ragged breath as he approaches me. His charged expression mangles my nerves. Every fiber in my body urges me to run. I scramble to my feet.

Cameron springs up, shoving Scott hard.

Scott holds up his hands, his tone cold and lashing. "You people are so jumpy. I just need to take a leak."

Doubt and fear congest my mind as he moves past me and disappears into the forest. I breathe in shallow gasps. He blames me for Laura's death. He's not likely to let that go.

What if he loses his temper again? And what if Cameron's not around to stop him?

TWENTY-ONE
AMBER

I wake up to enraged shouting.

I brush aside the blanket of leaves and bolt upright. Blackness overtakes my vision. I sway, stumbling in place. I'm running on zero calories since last night's meager supper. Conserving what little energy we have is a no-brainer, but Scott's never had much foresight, which is why I'm not surprised to find him locked in battle with Fred.

Oh no. Did Fred tell Scott about the affair?

My heart pounds relentlessly.

Behind the smoldering campfire, a red-faced Fred yells at Scott, who responds in mocking drawl. Fred brings up his fists. So does Scott, who hops around his brother like a fighting bird. Fred corners Scott against a tree and swings. The blow lands on Scott's cheek with a meaty thud. His head rips to the side. He stumbles.

If only I had a bucket of water to dump on them. Where's Cameron? I spot Nicole beside an enormous pine tree with David and rush toward them.

"What the hell is going on?"

David shrugs. "When I woke up, Uncle Fred had Scott in a headlock."

"Fred started it?"

"Yeah. He keeps screaming at Scott to give it back."

I frown. "Give *what* back?"

David yawns, stretching his arms. "Who knows."

A petty squabble among siblings is better than Scott learning what his wife did with Fred. My gaze scans the forest. "Where's your dad?"

"Dunno."

"Should we...do something?" asks Nicole in a tentative whisper. "Throw rocks at them?"

David waves his arm in a flippant gesture. "Let them duke it out."

"I can't just stand here," I say, appalled.

"Nothing else you can do." David laughs as Scott's wild kick misses and he falls on his butt. "Half my energy bar says that Fred wins. Any takers?"

Nicole raises her hand. "I'll take that action."

David turns to me. "What about you?"

Scott's guttural moan drags my attention to the two idiots. They're still swinging at each other. I should intervene. As a teacher, stopping fights is part of my job, but that usually involves me texting the resource officer.

A muscle tics in my jaw as I approach them. Then I shout in my best schoolmarm tone, "Stop fighting!"

Scott jabs Fred in the throat. He stumbles, choking. "Stay out of this, Amber. We're settling this like men."

"Like *children*, you mean. A fine example you're setting for your daughter," I roar, gesturing to Nicole, who glowers at me. "We don't have enough to worry about without you ripping each other's throats out?"

"Fred started it," he snarls.

"You sound like a five-year-old."

"Go away. This doesn't concern you."

Putting myself in harm's way is ill-advised, but I can't stand by. Someone will get seriously hurt, and then we'll have an injury to deal with on top of everything else. I shove myself in between both men. "I'm not letting you two murder each other."

Fred screams, making my eardrums pulse, "You will when you find out what he's done."

Scott lets out a scoffing laugh. "I'm saving us, you idiot."

Fred pushes me aside and launches at his brother. He shoves Scott and holds a fist upright, trembling. "Give them back, or you'll get another one."

"*No.*"

Fred swings, but Scott yanks out of his grip and his knuckles sink into the trunk. Pain shatters Fred's expression. They clash like wolverines, tearing at each other. Fred throws a punch. Scott seizes his wrist and gives it a sharp yank, throwing Fred's balance off, and lands a blow on his side.

I order them to stop, but it's as useful as screaming into the wind. Both seem determined to kill. Fred forces Scott on the ground, kneeling on his chest. He grabs Scott's throat and squeezes. A dark red flush claims Scott. He sputters protests. Jesus. He looks like he's about to pass out.

"For God's sake!" thunders Cameron, as he charges into the campsite. His dispassionate gaze centers on a struggling Scott. He grabs the scruff of Fred's neck and wrenches hard. Fred flies off Scott's body, landing in a thicket of brambles. Gasping, Scott scrambles upright. He lunges for his crossbow and cocks an arrow. He aims at Fred.

My lungs tighten.

Cameron approaches Scott, hands raised. "Hey, man, there's no need for that."

Blood trickles down Scott's temple as he heaves in breaths. "He's—a—freaking *maniac.*"

Fred makes a threatening move toward Scott, but Cameron shoves him back. "Tell them what you did, *coward,*" Fred demands.

Scott's Adam's apple bobs, but he stays silent. He wipes his face. Winces at the blood staining his palm. The arrow cocked in the crossbow trembles, but he keeps the bolt trained on Fred's chest.

"What did he do?" I ask.

"The idiot stole the food."

Appalled, I stare at Scott, who shakes his head.

"No, I *gathered* our resources. To make an inventory. The first step in wilderness survival is establishing a comprehensive list of our supplies. You said it yourself, Amber. This is an emergency. We need to take this seriously."

"Did I tell you to steal everyone's food?"

"It's not stealing," he barks, louder than ever. "I'm reallocating resources. There's a difference."

"Oh, and I suppose you're in charge of that, too?"

"Yes. I'm the only person here qualified to command a rescue mission."

Yeah, we'll see about that. I stalk to the bedroll I assembled out of branches and grab my bag. I unzip it and shove aside empty bottles and suntan lotion, searching for the eight bars I'd packed, the trail mix, and the beef jerky I'd been saving. All of it's gone.

"You took my family's food while we were asleep?" I say in a taut voice trembling with rage. "That's a new low for you."

"I made a tough decision. That's what leaders do." Scott lowers the crossbow and sticks the arrow in his quiver, his jaw set firmly. "I made rations with the remaining supply. Don't worry, I've divided everything fairly."

My teeth hurt from clenching my jaw, but he's right. We have to be very frugal about our remaining stores. Scott wipes an invisible tear from his cheek as he passes out energy bars, launching into another motivational speech.

"This is just a setback. I know it's hard, but we have to keep our spirits up. We have to shake off our grief and hunger, just as our pioneer forefathers did before us. They also suffered unspeakable tragedies in pursuit of their goals."

Amazingly, Scott's speech works. Not on me, of course, but the kids nod solemnly. My husband snorts, "Well, he sells a great line of bullshit. I'll give him that."

Cameron seizes the bar handed to him, tears it open, and stuffs it in his mouth. Then he returns into the woods to gather more kindling.

Stomach growling, I hold out my hand for my portion. Scott's fierce gaze pierces mine. Then he shoves an unwrapped energy bar in my palm. I roll down the wrapper, expecting to find more in the packaging, but I don't.

"What's this?" I glance up, finding Scott standing in front of the fire.

"Your ration for the day."

"I see that. Why is it smaller than everyone else's?"

Scott heaves a long-suffering sigh, as though I'm reacting how he expected. "We have to make sacrifices. We don't have a lot left, and frankly, you can handle not eating for a while."

"Oh, so the fat girl doesn't get to eat?"

Scott shrugs. "You said it, not me."

Fred groans, wincing.

Nicole marches up to her father. "Dad, that's *not* okay. You can't fat-shame Mom."

Scott makes a frustrated sound. "Look, I'm sorry if it's not politically correct, but you are extremely overweight. You have more than enough to spare. The rest of us...not so much. Therefore, you don't need full rations. It's not rocket science. You'll be fine. It'll be like bears when they nest for winter. Whatever."

Nicole's appalled gasp cuts into Fred's awkward laugh.

I seethe with mounting rage. "Now I'm a goddamn bear? Am I going to crawl into a cave and hibernate?"

"Amber, I don't need to hear the profanity."

"I don't give a—you're not in control of the food. Nobody voted for this."

His mouth settles into a grim line. "This isn't a democracy. I'm in charge."

My insides chill as he refuses to yield. He's gone insane. The death of his wife has clearly altered something in his brain if he thinks this is fair.

"Like hell you are. I want my food. Now."

He smirks. "And I want a medium-rare ribeye with garlic mashed potatoes."

"Give me the other half."

Nicole glowers at him. "Do what she says, Dad."

Scott shakes his head.

I launch at his backpack, clawing at the zipper. Scott shoves me off, but my fingers dig into the fabric. We play a maddening game of tug-of-war. I grit my teeth, pulling hard. Scott yanks. The bag rips out of my hands. I fall backward, slamming into the ground. Pain jolts up my spine, coinciding with Cameron's sharp yell.

"Jesus, what now?"

"It's not my fault," Scott blurts.

Groaning, I push myself upright. Cameron drops the wood in his arms and kneels beside me, scooping my back. He helps me to my feet, sighing. "What did he do?"

"Scott is giving me half-rations because I'm carrying extra weight."

Anger lights up my husband's face. Denials spill from Scott's lips.

"Dude, I swear, that's not how I said it."

Cameron glares at Scott and inches closer, which is enough to crack his resolve. Scott reaches in his pocket and slaps an energy bar in Cameron's hand. "Fine. Do whatever you want. I'm trying to save us."

"By starving my wife?"

"She would've been okay," he says, his hostile stare drilling into me. "I had everything under control."

"Sure, Scott. It looked like that when I found you high in the forest," I deadpan, sliding my hands to my hips. "If there's anyone who *shouldn't* be in charge, it's you. You got us lost. You bullied Laura into eating wild mushrooms. You created this whole mess."

"Laura's death wasn't my damn fault. She was pushed off a cliff."

My mouth drops open. He can't seriously believe that, can he? Maybe he has to.

Scott's eyes are burning orbs of denial and hysteria as he shifts from foot to foot. "My wife wasn't a careless idiot. Someone in this camp killed her."

A strained silence follows my ex-husband's dramatic claim. Unbelievable. Whenever I think he can't get any crazier, he ups the ante. Fury builds in my chest as the kids glance at him, then each other. He's so toxic. I can't have him poisoning their minds.

I point at the forest. "See the trees producing oxygen for you? Go to them and apologize."

"It was probably you," he says in a low voice, stunning me. "You were jealous of her. She's everything you're not. Pretty. Thin. Nice. She tried so hard to win you over. You never gave her a chance."

Cameron takes a threatening step forward and knocks Scott to the ground. My husband stands over him, fists clenched.

"Back off. Or I'll throw you over a mountain."

Scott storms off after grabbing his crossbow. Always loaded for his deadly aim. Cameron's threat wasn't serious, but Scott picked up his weapon. And, for the first time, I wish I had my own.

TWENTY-TWO
AMBER

Cameron takes control of the supplies.

Though I'm relieved they're in his infinitely more capable hands, my guts churn as Scott trudges behind, staring daggers at an unsuspecting Cameron. Every time I glimpse the feathered tips of his crossbow bolts, I feel sick. I imagine horrible scenarios—Scott killing my husband, killing his *brother*.

At Fred's suggestion, we head down the slanted forest. An hour after tripping over fallen boughs, we find a raging river. It's too unsafe to forge, but satisfying our thirst is a tremendous morale boost. Nicole lets out an excited squeal. Fred and David set to work on building a fire to purify the water. Cameron and I crack jokes as we pick salmonberries from a bush. Everybody is ecstatic.

Except Scott.

He sits at the riverbank, tossing stones into the water. He's in a bad mood after losing one of his three arrows in an attempt to shoot down a squirrel. Scott can't handle being wrong. He cannot accept blame. For anything. Ever. When he sideswiped a car on the freeway, it was *their* fault for driving in his blind spot. He's careless and crazy.

I should let him stew, but his accusation nags at me. I was too stunned to tell him off at the time. Chewing my tongue, I march forward until I'm behind him. He hurls a rock into the water like a petulant child. The pent-up ball of rage in my throat nearly explodes. *How dare you accuse me of that? Why do you hate me?* I don't give voice to my thoughts. I sit beside him, fists clenched as I struggle to mend us back together.

"I didn't push Laura. I would never hurt another person. Even if you don't believe that, I was at camp the whole night. There's no way I could've done what you're suggesting. I—" I break off, bewildered that I'm having this conversation. "I know you're grieving and lashing out, but you need to drop this 'Laura was murdered' nonsense. She fell."

He hisses a response.

"What?"

"I said, it wasn't an accident." He turns to me, his raw eyes welling with emotion. "She fell because *someone* wanted her to."

"And you think that's me?" My glare bores into Scott, who blinks and looks away.

"I might have...jumped to conclusions."

"Scott, you called me a killer in front of our daughter."

His lips whiten. "No, I didn't."

"Are you for real? You blamed her accident on me. You implied to everyone that *I* shoved her. How is that not calling me a murderer?"

"I was angry, okay? Everybody keeps dismissing me, but I'm telling you, something's off about Laura's death."

"You didn't see her. She was freaked out, not herself, I-I don't know." My head pounds as I picture her tearstained face. "Part of me wonders whether she threw herself off."

"She wouldn't. She had so much to live for."

"She was *high.*"

A tear slides down his cheek. He wipes it off, his voice hardening. "Laura was pushed. There's no doubt in my mind."

"You need to eat something."

"I need to find out who killed my wife." His glances over his shoulder, whispering even though the others are well out of earshot. "Fred was out there all night. He could've done it. I just don't understand why."

"Scott, drop it."

He laughs bitterly.

I'm fighting the urge to smack him as a chill spider-crawls down my spine. Nobody murdered Laura. Why would they? It makes no sense...and yet, fear needles my insides as Fred fills a water bottle downstream. *Fred* had a motive. He's the jilted lover of a woman who couldn't choose between him and his brother.

Hell, Scott is a prime suspect. Blaming me might've been a clumsy attempt at covering his tracks. I cycle through the last twenty-four hours. His performance at the memorial. His hostility toward me. His brother. Perhaps he knows about the affair. My body grows cold as I consider the possibility. This trip is an *opportunity* for him to dispose of everyone who wronged him. Starting with his cheating wife.

Stop it.

God, listen to me. I'm ridiculous. I've watched too many true crime documentaries. Scott doesn't have the stomach for murder. I can't let myself get carried away with these fantasies. It's the lack of food. It's making me erratic.

"Scott, nobody killed Laura."

"Then who stole her cellphone?" Scott's gaze narrows with suspicion. "Oh, you thought I didn't notice? I did. I just kept my mouth shut because I don't know who to trust."

I clear my throat. "It fell off when she was rolling down the hill."

"Where? We looked everywhere. She was found at the bottom of that cliff. It couldn't have been far."

"In the forest, then."

He sneers. "Or someone grabbed it off her corpse."

"Why would they do that?"

"Because they want a memento...because they need to delete evidence. Who knows. Maybe she took a photo of her murderer before he pushed her off."

"Then why not delete it and leave the phone beside her?"

"We're not dealing with a logical person, Amber."

"Okay, Scott."

His glare bores into me. "You think I'm crazy, don't you?"

"Honestly? I'm worried you're still under the influence of those mushrooms." I pat his back as his mood darkens like the clouds rolling in the distance. "I don't blame you. Laura died. We're all a little messed up right now."

"I know exactly what happened."

"Fine, Scott. If you want to sit here and brood, be my guest. But there's work to do." I point at the navy clouds spilling down steep cliffs, billowing toward us. "We have a storm coming in. If we don't build a shelter, we'll be caught in the rain."

"What do you expect me to do about it?"

"Help Nicole with the shelter. It'll take your mind off things."

He shoots me a withering look as he stands, heading off in her direction. Talking to him is like trying to engage with a brick wall. There's no use. Shaking my head, I approach the guys gathered around the firepit. David builds a circle of stones as Fred uses the bow drill to start a fire. Smoke streams from the rotating stick of wood, which is coaxed into a tiny flame with kindling. Cameron digs into the earth.

I kneel beside him and roll up my sleeves. "What's that for?"

"We need to sanitize the water, and we don't have a pot... so I'm digging a hole. I figure if we drop hot coals inside, the water will boil."

"Genius." I widen the hole with my palms. "I feel so much better now that we've found a way to do that. All we have to do is stay here. They'll find us."

"That could be a long time. Soon, the Airbnb host will know something's off. Your mom will notice the empty driveway. She'll blow up our phones and get voicemails. I think by early Monday, she'll report us missing. If she doesn't, the host will."

"Don't you have to be gone a full seventy-two hours before that?"

"Tuesday, then. She'll call every ranger station. You know how she gets. She'll insist on getting a team. There will be an intense search party for a couple of weeks. Still, it's like trying to find an honest politician."

"I don't know, Cam. We're not wilderness experts."

"Another thing. We should consider leaving Scott behind. He's a huge liability. He's lost his mind. Losing his wife messed him up. I don't trust Scott or his brother."

I draw in a breath and release it. "What's wrong with Fred?"

"He was acting weird with Laura's body. Crying. Touching her face. I don't know. It seemed overly emotional for a brother-in-law. I thought maybe I was seeing things, but I could've sworn he took something."

My stomach clenches. "Her phone?"

"Not sure."

I chew my lip. I never told Cameron about their affair because I didn't want to rope him into the secret as well, but with Laura dead...perhaps circumstances warrant the truth. Am I keeping silent out of fear, or because I want to do right by Laura?

I watch Scott yank felled trees from the forest, leaning them in an A-frame. He dusts off his hands and places them on his hips. Then a wave of grief seems to slam into him. His look of quiet contemplation breaks.

I can never tell Scott the truth. It'll break him.

He's Nicole's father. For better or worse.

TWENTY-THREE

AMBER

We are never getting out.

My cellphone battery dies, along with the last of my hope. At least we erected a flimsy shelter before it started raining. An A-frame of felled trees surrounds us, thick pine branches and their needles insulating the sides. Fred had the bright idea of tacking on strips of bark like roof shingles. It worked until the downpour began.

I huddle in Cameron's arms. David and Nicole shiver side by side, wrapped in Cameron's jacket. Fred alternates between shivering and rubbing his hands. My ex does neither, twisting the wedding band on his finger. With everyone gathered in one room, Laura's absence has never been louder.

"I'd give anything for bourbon right about now," Cameron mutters, his voice booming through my back. "Or a ribeye, charred almost black, the fat melting in my mouth."

"Heck, yeah. I'd devour a steak. I had this incredible one at a restaurant in Greenwood. I went there a few weeks ago. Prime filet mignon aged twenty-three days." Fred shuts his eyes and sighs. "I can still taste it."

Scott gives him a look. "Which place?"

"FlintCreek Cattle Company."

I've been there once with Cameron. Their cheapest steak is forty-six dollars, and while it is amazing, there's no way a chronically jobless Fred shelled out that cash for dinner. Not unless someone else was paying. I avoid eye contact with Scott, who blows a low whistle.

"Pricey. How'd you afford that?"

Fred examines his nails, shrugging. "I make some money."

Scott laughs. "Allowance from our dad isn't income."

Fred rolls his shoulders. "Maybe I didn't pay for it."

Treading dangerous waters there, Fred.

I pick at my skin as Scott grins, his interest apparently piqued. "You already have a new sugar momma?"

Shut up, Fred.

I expect him to deny it, but Fred releases a choked laugh. Ice spreads through my stomach as his eyes well with emotion.

"It's over. She's gone."

Scott tuts. "Too bad. I'm sure our stepmom would love to have the house to herself again."

A sob breaks from Fred's clenched lips. He raises his hands to his flushed face, hiding the tears. A brittle silence chokes the air, shattered by Scott's awkward chuckle.

"A stud like you will find another girl. You've got the Maxwell genes, after all."

My insides turn to stone as Scott pounds Fred's back with harsh slaps.

"There's no need to cry," Scott says. "At least *she's* not lying under an oak tree, dead."

Is it my imagination, or is Scott's pointed glare a little more than accusatory? The weight of Laura's secret is like poisoned lead, sinking in me like a giant ball. I can't stand watching Fred weep over his brother's wife while Scott, oblivious to their betrayal, comforts him. Laura's twisted neck flashes in my head. It's beyond sick. I'm going to throw up.

"I need some air," I announce, pulling from Cameron's embrace. "I-I think the berries didn't agree with me."

I sprint outside into the howling wind. The sky is a whirling black mass. My knees hit the ground as I bend over and purge everything in my stomach. Amid the semi-digested pink lumps and saliva, Laura's tormented eyes flash. Warmth touches my shoulders.

I jump, but it's only Cameron.

His gentle hand caresses me. "You okay?"

I break out into wild laughter. "None of us are."

Cameron stoops beside me, sliding his arm around my shoulders. "Get inside. You'll catch a cold."

I tremble as another wave of nausea rocks me. "There's something I've been keeping from you. From everyone.

Fred and Laura. T-they're having an affair. I spotted them at a movie theater months ago."

"Yeah. I know." Cameron strokes me slowly, my skin tingling. "David told me that Nicole walked in on them at Scott's house."

I blink. "Brazen."

"People like that *want* to get caught."

I bite my knuckle. "Then why did Laura beg me to keep it a secret?"

"Who knows? Maybe she wasn't ready to break up her marriage. Ending a relationship can be as traumatic as a death. It's not as simple as it seems. Speaking as someone who's suffered that kind of loss, I believe it. I'm sure she was dealing with a ton of conflicting emotions."

That's sad. I shake my head. "Why didn't Nicole tell me?"

"Easy. She's embarrassed. She sees David as a neutral confidant."

"Why didn't you mention this?"

"I was afraid the knowledge would twist up your insides with guilt, like it's doing right now." He kisses my temple. "It's not your fault, Amber."

"I-I know."

"Say it."

My eyes mist as he clutches me to his chest. "I-it's not my fault."

"Good. Let's get out of the cold."

We hobble inside the cramped A-frame, drenched. Scott peers at me, as though deciding whether the moisture on my face is tears or rain. I clench my fists as he rakes a hand through his auburn curls.

"We're wasting so much time sitting in this thing," Scott hisses, drumming his fingers on his knee. "We should be out there, trying to find our way home."

"We've been over this," reminds Cameron in his gentle baritone. "We can't do anything in the dark."

"I know. I'm just venting."

Cameron rubs his hands over my arms, warming me up. "Staying put is our best shot at rescue."

Scott shakes his head. "We won't survive. By tomorrow, we'll have no more rations. Which means our bodies will be in starvation mode. Fred and Amber can last a while without food, no problem, but the rest of us? We're goners."

The others flinch. Cameron tightens his grip on my arm.

I fume. "You just can't help yourself...can you?"

"I'm sorry if pointing out the obvious makes me insensitive, but facts are *facts*. You are excessively overweight. It gives you an advantage. When we run out of glucose, our cells break down fat, putting us in a state called ketoacidosis. Basically, your system gets loaded with ketones, which causes a host of life-threatening problems. I've watched all the *Survivor* shows. I know what I'm talking about."

I look around me. "We're in this together. What does it matter?"

"Because you're making decisions for everyone, but we don't have the same time you do."

"All the more reason to stay put. If we're exploring the wilderness with no idea where we're going, all we're doing is burning calories."

"It's worth the risk. Staying here is a death sentence." He gestures outside, where lightning flashes across the sky. "Unless you can magically summon sufficient calories for six people, every single day, hiking is our *only* option."

"Are you kidding?" I shout, my voice growing hoarse. "Getting more lost is not a solution."

"It's a gamble either way," Cameron mutters, stroking his bristled jaw. "Stay here…maybe we'll find berries to stretch out our survival for a couple weeks, but we won't be able to do anything. We can't survive off plants and the occasional squirrel shot down by the crossbow. We'll waste away."

"Let's vote on it," says Fred. "All in favor of staying?"

I raise my hand. After a second's hesitation, so does David.

Cameron glowers at him. "You're not an adult. Your vote doesn't count."

David scoffs. "Well, that's horseshit."

"Language," Scott snarls.

Cameron's scowl flashes in Scott's direction. "Don't lecture my kid."

"So Nicole and I don't get a say, but Boy Scout over here does? He got us lost." David points at Scott, who flushes deep red.

"He may have, but he's right about this," says Cameron.

"I don't care," David shouts, veins standing out on his neck. "He's a lunatic. I don't trust him."

"I'm your father. You'll do as I say."

I go rigid as father and son face off. David's clenched fist trembles. He looks like he wants to sock his father. I prepare myself to launch on him, but after a moment, he backs down. Cameron's hackles lower as he asks, "Who wants to set out in the morning?"

Scott, Cameron, Nicole, and Fred raise their hands.

David gapes at them. "You're all nuts."

"David."

David's voice trembles with gravitas. "I want to get home just as badly as you do, but you're making the wrong decision."

Nicole bursts into tears. I open my arms, and she dives into them, sobbing. I pat her back, my gaze lifting over her bare arm to the three men wearing identical guilty expressions.

"I hope you know what you're doing."

TWENTY-FOUR

AMBER

After a meager breakfast, we set out again.

I keep my distance from the men because I have serious misgivings about this idea. Leaving behind shelter, fire, water, *and* a reliable source of food makes no sense. Add in that we're bone-tired, weak, that our last square meal was three days ago, and it's downright reckless.

Why are we doing this?

This stupid hike is accelerating our demise. My feet stumble as we climb through salmonberry brambles that slice through my jacket. Five minutes in, and I'm already winded. I forced my portion of the berries onto Nicole, but she's still dragging. David, sweetheart that he is, stays glued to my side. My heartbeat thunders as I put one foot in front of the other, too drained to think. By now, the cabin owners and my family know we're in trouble. Mom is probably beside herself with worry. I'm not sure about Laura's people, but Scott's family isn't close-knit. They won't know about his disappearance unless my mother calls them. And Cameron doesn't have much family.

He turns his head, as though sensing his name in my thoughts. He smiles, his eyes pleading for an apology I'm not ready to accept.

I get it. He's desperate to go home. He's missing shareholder meetings and important emails. Sitting around and waiting for rescue doesn't appeal to men like Cameron. He's a man of action. So I understand his decision, even if I don't agree with it. I'm angry because he sided with my ex for the first time in our marriage.

Cameron holds a branch away from me as I step over a log. "You doing all right?"

My jaw tenses as he drops his arm, the branch snapping behind me. David takes a break from hacking at the underbrush with a long stick. He laughs with a scorned edge, "Such a dumb question."

Cameron pinches the bridge of his nose. "Your attitude isn't helping."

David tosses his stick aside and storms to his dad. My pulse races as father and son face off in a battle of wills that they seem to fight without moving. I want to defuse the tension, but I'm too tired to shout.

"Guys, please."

David gestures at me, his voice breaking. "She's not fine. She can barely walk and hasn't eaten today."

My husband frowns. "You haven't?"

I shake my head. "I'm not feeling great. It could be the low calories, all the activity, stress, or that I ate some berries without washing them yesterday."

Cameron rakes his damp locks, cursing.

"I'm okay." My hands tremble as I lean against a tree, so exhausted that the pile of leaves look like they'd make a good bed. "My stomach hurts, but I can keep going."

Cameron's protective arm draws me into his chest. Then he kisses my temple. Warmth sparks across my cheeks.

"I'm sorry, babe. We'll get out of here soon."

"You can't promise her that," David shouts.

Cameron pulls away, facing his son. "What is your problem?"

"We're all running ragged. Now we're hiking to God knows where, lost, draining our bodies of fuel. You don't know what the hell you're doing."

My ears ring with his harsh outburst. "Your dad's doing the best he can."

"He's not." Red-faced from shouting, David points at Scott and Fred, who silently watch us. "We're not getting home with *them* leading the way."

"You want to give it a shot?" asks Cameron.

"I do. We should be following the river." David jabs his thumb behind him. "Not stomping around the forest like idiots."

"We are," says Cameron. "It's twenty feet to the left."

"I want it in sight at all times."

Cameron and I exchange a glance, and he nods. "All right. I'll bring it up to the others."

As they change course, I summon the energy to head in their direction. Following the river proves more difficult than David's suggestion. Thick bushes block most of it, the shore filled with giant boulders that make navigating it a nightmare until we stumble upon a dry bed.

My aching feet sink into the wet sand blooming with tufts of grass. David strolls to the water's edge. He finds a large, dead hawk lying on the rocks and brings it over. "Look at what I found. It's not stiff or anything—probably just died."

Fred takes the bird and examines it, his eyebrows raised.

I'm as hungry as the rest of them, but eating dead animals that washed up on shore seems risky. Fred plucks its feathers and slices open its belly with his hunting knife, revealing a tangle of worms. Nicole scrunches her nose and steps away, gagging.

David stares at it eagerly. "We could still eat it."

Fred pokes at it with the knife, grimacing. "Not a great idea. Too easy to ingest a worm egg."

"We'll boil it for hours," I blurt, my stomach clenching. "And sear it on a hot rock...maybe with wild onions if we find any."

Fred licks his lips. "Oh man, that'd so hit the spot...but this is not safe to eat."

"We need all the calories we can get." David grabs it from him and finishes gutting the bird, his hands shaking. "If you don't want it, fine. More for us."

I lick my lips. Hunger pangs gnaw at me at the hint of barbecued fowl. It's barely enough meat for a snack, filled with parasites, and yet, my tongue pools with saliva. Good Lord. I'm craving a worm-infested bird. I have never been so hungry in my life.

David packs the hawk carcass in his backpack, and we keep going. We hike half a mile before the dry bed ends, and we're faced with roaring rapids. The only path is up the riverbank. Unfortunately, it's too steep to climb. David swears profusely.

Scott glances at them and shakes his head. "We can't scale that."

"I can do it," David says, examining the tight formation of rocks. "Yeah. I've got this."

I bite my lip as David approaches the riverbank. He scrambles up and slides down. He tries kicking footholds into the dirt. He jumps, swinging for the branch sticking out at the top. Missing it, he lands on the ground hard.

Cameron helps him upright. David dusts himself off and inhales a deep, centering breath. Then he tries again. Grabs it. Heaving himself up, David clambers and scurries to the top. His young face beams. Then shock stills his expression. He lets out a strangled cry and points behind us.

"There's a tent across the river."

I whirl around, but a thick wall of forest obscures my view.

"Where?" demands Scott.

"There," David insists, pointing at a patch of trees. "There's a campfire…a tent, a stove, and some other stuff I can't make out."

Cameron climbs up and stands beside his son. "Wow. We should check it out. Can you see anyone?"

"No, but they can't be far off." David drops down, grinning.

Cameron and Fred thump his back. I give David a high five. Nicole hugs him, sobbing, which seems to irritate Scott. His mouth twists as he utters a grudging, "Good job." Everybody's excitement is palpable, charging the air. Someone will be at the camp. They'll have food. They'll guide us to the nearest trail.

Thank God. Our nightmare is *over*.

Scott leads the way, singing "We Are the Champions" by Queen. Everyone joins in the chorus as we cross via the dry beds and move downstream to the tent.

"Hello? Anybody here?" David's voice carries through the forest. "Sorry to bother you, but we're lost. We need your help."

Nobody responds.

The tent's red sides ripple. My heart pounds. I wait for the flap to open. Someone's about to climb out and rescue us. We are *saved*.

I fight tangled branches to get to the campground. Various items scatter the clearing. A stove sits over the remains of a campfire. I touch the stone-cold logs. Frowning, David unzips the tent, peeks inside, and turns around. He blanches, shaking his head.

We're alone.

A knot in my belly grows as we search the camp. Everything's in disorder. I walk over the handle of a rusted knife. Scraps of fabric litter the ground, as though an animal ripped through a shirt.

My stomach churns. I follow the trail of clothing underneath a pile of leaves. *Don't do it. Don't look.* Ignoring the alarm pounding through my veins, I brush the leaves aside. *Oh my God.* Seconds pass as I process the horrible sight.

I cover my face.

Then I scream.

TWENTY-FIVE
THE PAST

My future stepmom yanks away my breakfast. Bits of scrambled eggs mixed with bacon scatter the table as she slams the plate onto the counter. I could easily take it, but her angry gaze swings over me. If I make a fuss, she'll get my father, who will instantly back her up.

I glower at her, undeterred. "Give it back."

Her withering glare rakes my skin. "Say the line to the camera, and I will."

Kim is a slip of a woman. Thin, reedy, and extremely blond. The brightness of her platinum hair rivals her whitened teeth. Heat flushes through my body and I clench my fists. I could stab the hand flashing with the pretty rock my dad gave her a month ago, but Kim would *love* an excuse to throw me in prison. I'm powerless to stop her.

"I'm not your pet monkey. I won't perform for you."

"You will or you won't eat," she says in that sugar-lined, Georgia accent. "You're almost an adult. That means you need to earn your way through life instead of leeching off others."

"You're the one using my dad like an ATM."

She purses her lips, raising her head. "Your dad left me in charge."

"You can't starve me forever."

"Try me."

This woman is a piece of work. My pulse speeds ahead as I imagine myself knocking her to the floor, throttling her. I force a smile. "At least in juvie, I had three square meals a day."

"I told your father they weren't being hard enough on you in there." She shoves my uneaten breakfast into the fridge. "If that judge had any sense, you'd still be locked up."

He gave me fifteen years, but suspended my sentence with conditions. Four years of probational officer visits, a stint in a juvenile facility, and when I got out, I had to stay with my father. Living here was tolerable until my dad started dating Kim.

She bends over, trying to plug in her ring light beside Meadow's dog bed. My golden Lab raises her head and utters a warning growl. Kim goes rigid. She doesn't like dogs and the feeling seems to be mutual. Kim makes a disgusted sound.

"Get that thing out of the kitchen."

Reaching under the table, I stroke Meadow's long, fluffy ears as her throat vibrates with an angry rumble. "Why? She's better behaved than you are."

"Take it out. *Now*."

Sighing, I grip Meadow's collar and lead her outside. Once the door closes, she stares at me through the small window, her breath fogging the glass.

Kim sets up her ring light. She's a social media monster. She makes her living hawking goop, snail cream, and whatever the latest trend is on her family vlog, *The Daily Grinds*. That means I have to be on camera fifty times a day. Sometimes she barges in my room to film me waking up. I hate it. I never consented to this crap, but Dad's all for it. Says it's making him a ton of money. Meanwhile, I'm an unpaid laborer who gets recognized by strangers on the street. They're always creepy men. One pretended to be my father and tried to pull me out of school.

My psychologists encouraged me to discuss my deepest desires, my darkest secrets, everything. It was freeing. They told me that Mom had narcissistic personality disorder. I was healing from what happened. Then Kim pulled me out of therapy, calling it a waste of money. I can't think or act freely in front of the camera. I can't be myself. I can't eat without her permission. She represses me more than the guards at juvie.

I clench the table's edge, my arms trembling from the effort of not throwing it over. Watching her die would be amazing.

Kim starts her video, speaking in a girlish whisper. "I've switched everyone to a keto program, which seems to help with inflammation. As you know, I have chronic bladder issues. It's something I talk a lot about on my channel. I just want to normalize talking about this condition because it's so debilitating. I'm so glad I have a supportive family. This kid has been such a trooper."

She wheels around and points the camera at my face.

I stare into the lens. "Blow yourselves."

Kim's bubbly attitude disappears faster than a Botox sale in L.A. She turns off the camera and slams it on the table. "That's it," she snarls, flecks of saliva flying from her mouth. "You're not eating breakfast, lunch, *or* dinner, you little jerk!"

"I don't need your permission."

"We had an agreement," she says hotly. "You'll eat when you say your lines."

"I wonder what your followers would think if I wrote a tell-all book describing how you starve children. I'm not sure they'd like it. You'll be canceled. You'll lose that sweet brand ambassador deal."

Swearing, Kim grabs the plate from the fridge, slamming it in front of me. Eggs spill over the wood and fall on the tile. I dig in as she pulls out a chair and sits beside me, her tone a sultry purr. "You know, I've been thinking."

"That's dangerous for you, isn't it?"

"You're so funny. Bless your heart." Her simpering laughter washes over me like acid. "You have one more year with us. Where are you going after you graduate high school?"

"Don't worry, I'm picking the college furthest away from here."

"Right. But I *could*—not saying I will—but I *could* leak the fact that you killed your mom in a viral TikTok that'll follow you for the rest of your life." Kim shrugs, wearing a lopsided smile. "Might make it tough to get into a writing program for grad school. And even if you're accepted, no decent agent will represent you."

"Someone represented OJ."

"Those were different times. People aren't as tolerant of murderers as they used to be."

I can practically feel her neck muscles straining under my skin. The vision of her choking tempts me, but I can't. I shovel food in my mouth, but she keeps talking, her words glazed with nauseating sweetness.

"I've read the case files. Pretty gruesome stuff. You bludgeoned her head."

My chest burns. "She abused me. Your husband, too, but you don't care about that."

"He denies it happened."

"He's lying."

"I don't believe you," she grinds out, and I fight the impulse to stab her with my fork. "I think you're a nasty boy who doesn't know what's best for him, and I want you out of here. Your father agrees."

"Get me an apartment, and I'm gone."

She giggles, showing me all of her pearly teeth. "Sweetheart. I'm not letting my fiancé spend a dime on you."

"Well, then you have a problem, because I'm not leaving until I graduate."

"Yes, you are. Get a job. In six months, I expect you to move out. During that time, you'll respect my business and stop sabotaging my vlogging. Oh, and you're not invited to our wedding."

"Like I want to be there."

She leans in, her glare diving into me. "Mess with me one more time, and I'll make sure this video goes viral. It'll follow you to every job. Girls you go on dates with. Your landlord. Your future wife's parents. Their children. Everybody will know what you've done."

"Your threats don't scare me."

Kim opens her phone, swiping to a photo album. It's a gallery of mutilated small animals. I recoil, heart pounding. My fork drops to the floor. She laughs at my reaction, flicking through the horrifying images.

"Look at all these poor things. So sad. I know how much you love Meadow. It'd be...so awful if something happened to her."

Nausea pits my stomach as I gape at this woman...this monster who is threatening my dog. Meadow is more family than my father will ever be. Kim will have no problem driving her to the shelter, poisoning her, putting her to sleep.

I can't let that happen.

Her manicured fingernails, little white blades, tap the camera's screen. "So, let's try again. And this time, smile real big. That's it. *Perfect.*"

She repeats her monologue and swoops to my side. She clutches my shoulder, her nauseating perfume invading my nostrils. As she leans over, she shoves the camera in my face. I glower at the lens. *Think of Meadow.* I pull my lips into a sneer and recite the lines. My expression is constipated, but she doesn't seem to care.

"Great," she says, the teasing laughter back in her eyes. "I'm glad we have an understanding."

We sure do.

When she leaves, I do some thinking of my own. I don't move for hours, playing out the scenarios. Then, once I've decided, I head to the master bedroom. I grab a bunch of Valium tablets from her medicine cabinet and return to the kitchen. Will six be enough? I crush them into a fine powder and stir them into an opened bottle of rosé in the fridge that only she drinks.

Later that night, I curl up with Meadow as Kim and Dad eat dinner. Their chatter drifts into my room. Kim says goodbye to my father, grabs her keys, and exits the house. And she doesn't come back.

TWENTY-SIX

AMBER

I scream until my voice breaks, pointing at the ground. I tremble and gasp for air, Scott's dry chuckle raking my skin. "What is it, a snake?"

It's a *human* leg.

Skeletal, but still attached to a woman's shoe. The horrible image brands my mind like a white-hot poker. I grip a tree for support and inhale deeply. Cameron trips over a root in his haste to reach me, swearing. Scott stomps over. My nausea sharpens with Scott's matter-of-fact comment, "A severed leg. That's what you're freaking out over?"

I stumble away, hit by a wave of dizziness. My knees slam into the earth. Acid burns my throat as I purge everything in my stomach.

Cameron's soothing hand glides over my hair. "It's okay."

Okay? We're not in the realm of okay. I make fists into the dirt. It's *hopeless*. We're doomed. Laura and this poor woman are dead, and we're no closer to home. I have no idea what to do. I can't take much more of this.

Fred kicks the stove across the campfire, scattering ashes everywhere. "This trip is cursed."

Scott's eyes blaze as he faces his brother. "Pipe down, for God's sake."

"I'm allowed to be pissed," Fred snarls.

"Do it quietly," Scott admonishes as he bends over, examining the woman's remains. "You sound like a prey animal. Whatever killed her will come running."

"We don't even know how she died," Cameron says, his arm wrapped around me. "It could've been anything. Exposure. Starvation. Infection."

"Really?" Scott says in a mocking drawl. "Exposure rips off your leg?"

Cameron rolls his eyes. "She was mauled after she died."

Scott pokes at the underbrush with a stick, revealing more remains. "Found the spine."

I moan, clamping my hands over my ears. Speculating about this woman's death is as appealing as studying her parts, but I can't help it. Who...or what...did this? A mountain lion? A bear? My throat tightens as I imagine her final moments. How is everyone so relaxed?

My daughter sits beside the blackened ring of stones, her expression wooden. I clasp her shoulder, but there's nothing to say. I have no words of comfort.

"Breathe, Amber. It's a dead body." Cameron's soothing baritone fails to calm me. "It can't hurt you."

"Whatever killed her can," interjects Scott, still prodding the dirt. "We need to search the camp thoroughly. Once we're done, we'll get out of here."

As much as I'd love to put a few miles between me and another corpse, I'm too weak. Days of little to no food have taken their toll, and I can barely sit upright, let alone walk.

"No," I grind out. "We're staying for the night."

"That's a terrible idea," Scott booms. "The leg was hidden under leaves. If it's a bear's kill site, he'll be back. Plus, every predator in Washington heard your shrieking. We shouldn't stay here."

"But she's badly decomposed," says Cameron, making me retch. "Which means she's been dead for a while."

"Yeah, but something chewed on her bones. See the marks from the teeth? *Look*." Scott points and Cameron obeys, his brows knitted.

"So? That doesn't mean she was killed by a bear."

"Well, I'm not willing to gamble my daughter's life on your hunch. Fred, Nicole, and I are leaving."

The hell you are.

I stand up, and my vision blackens. Dots of color burst through the darkness, revealing Scott's haggard face. I waver on my feet. "Absolutely not. Splitting up is a recipe for disaster. We have to stay here."

A hard line forms on Scott's shoulders. "You want to sleep near this deathtrap?"

"We're in no shape to keep going." I gesture toward a pale Nicole, who huddles on the ground next to David.

She props her head on her hand, sighing. "She's right. I can't, Dad. I'm exhausted."

"Nothing in here." Fred emerges from the tent. I gape at the rectangular impression in Fred's pocket. That's a phone, isn't it? Could it be Laura's?

I swallow my nerves, dismissing the thought. We *all* brought phones. Fred's life is hanging in the balance just as much as everyone else's. *Stop jumping to conclusions. I'm just upset.* For one brief shining moment, we were *saved*. Finding a corpse was a nasty shock.

Scott grabs a bright piece of fabric and rips it, tying it to the tree above the woman's remains. "The silver lining is we've found a missing hiker. I'm sure her family is beside themselves with worry. Think about the peace we're bringing them. They can finally lay her to rest because of *us*."

"Assuming we make it home," says Fred.

"I've had it with the negativity. Get to work." Scott tears the underbrush with his bare hands, clearing away the vegetation. "Everybody, search the camp. There might be a phone buried under the leaves. Matches. Flint. Whatever she used could help us survive."

"I'll start a fire," David mutters, heading into the forest. "This wood is too damp."

My spirits rise when Nicole finds a cache of food supplies —four cans of beans. Nobody finds the opener, but Fred digs a hole with his knife. We split it six ways without a single comment about my weight. I cradle the small pile of beans like gold. Slowly, I eat them. They explode with delicious savory flavor. I suck out the salt and lick the juices off my palm.

Cameron closes his eyes, sighing, "I never knew cold beans could taste so good."

"They say hunger is the best spice," says David.

It's odd. Somehow, I'm even hungrier. Three cans remain. According to the label, one can contains three hundred and sixty calories. That's sixty calories each. We're still in a massive calorie deficit.

After gutting the hawk he found on the shore, David spears it on a stick and roasts it over the fire. The ambrosial scent hooks me like live bait. My mouth waters despite the worms in its belly. Everybody takes a piece.

"Beans and meat," muses Scott as he nibbles on his portion. "Hey, it's almost a meal."

David eats his share, moaning with pleasure. "Everyone should experience the level of hunger that makes you gleefully suck the eyes out of a bird's skull."

Nicole winces.

Fred tosses a tiny bone into the dancing flames, his posture going rigid as though he's seen a predator. He stands, lumbering several feet away. His foot nudges something that rattles, and then he lets out a whoop of delight.

"Jackpot!" He seizes a small box, followed by a gun. "It's a Glock. Nine millimeters." Flipping open the barrel, he examines the chambers and whistles. "Loaded, too. Missing one round."

Scott glances at where I discovered the skeletal remains. "Wonder if she fired at whatever attacked her."

"For the *last time*, we don't know how she died."

"Something tore her to shreds."

A stick snaps in Cameron's hands. He's the cool head of the group, but a man can only be pushed so far. He hasn't had a square meal in days, and he gets in a mood without proper food.

Which makes me nervous, because now there's a gun. Its addition to the group has me on high alert. Now Scott has *two* weapons. Fred might be the more reasonable brother, but I wouldn't put it past Scott to steal it. He still doesn't know about the affair.

What if he finds out?

Scott's glare skewers me. "What's your problem?"

"I think we should take out the bullets and leave it behind," I grit out.

"Are you mental? We're not doing that." Scott exchanges an incredulous look with his brother, laughing. "Besides the crossbow, this is the only protection we've got against whatever's in these woods."

Bears don't scare me as much as you do. I turn my attention to Cameron, hoping to gain an ally in him at least. He grunts, running a hand through his scraggly hair.

"It could be useful for hunting game."

"Scott has a crossbow."

"I only have two arrows," Scott shoots back. "If I come across a deer, I want every weapon at my disposal."

"The idea of us stumbling on a deer, shooting it, and somehow processing the meat is a fantasy. And how do you expect to do that with a handgun? Is anybody here a hunter?"

Scott glances at Fred, who raises his hand. "We used to go with Dad when we were young. Our stepmom made us stop when we were teenagers."

That's right. Scott grew up without a maternal figure. His mother died when he was young, and he described his father as a player with a revolving door of women. One of them was a vegetarian. Scott called her cooking "rabbit food." During the brief time his dad dated her, she insisted on emptying the fridge of meat. She must've put her foot down on the hunting, as well. If I trusted everyone in this group, I'd keep the gun. But I don't.

"You still can't hunt with it," I argue.

"Sure you can. Just has to be at close range." Scott huffs out laughter. "*Leave it behind.* Wow, that's your worst suggestion yet."

"Let's vote on it," says Cameron.

David's aggravated tone cuts in. "Do seventeen-year-olds count, or will we be ignored?"

"You'll be ignored," Cameron deadpans.

David crosses his arms over his knees, frowning. The dirt smudging his round cheeks and the angry slash of his dark eyebrows tug at my heart. Tearing my attention from my stepson, I slide my hand over Cameron's bicep.

"Cam, they're almost eighteen."

"*I don't care.* They're not of age."

I bristle as Scott gives Cameron an approving nod. "Give me a good reason why two almost eighteen-year-olds can't vote."

"Gee, Amber, I don't know." Scott taps at his temple, squinting. "Maybe because teenagers are impulsive and make bad decisions."

"You got us lost," David snarls, rage twisting his face. "I found this camp. I'm why we have a meal. If anybody should lose their vote, it's *you.*"

"Yeah. We deserve a say in what's going on," says Nicole.

"Fine. They get a damned vote." Cameron's icy gaze sweeps the camp, but nobody protests. "All in favor of keeping the gun?"

Everyone raises their hands. Only my stepson takes my side. I glare at Nicole, who sides with her father. Well, that stings.

Scott's delighted smirk flashes in my direction. "It's settled, then."

Heat flares across my cheeks. Cameron grasps my ankle, wearing a sympathetic frown, but I yank from his grip. He's in the doghouse tonight, and frankly, every night he values Scott's opinion over mine. Nobody is using their brain. Everyone's worried about *food*, but it'll run out soon.

What then? What happens when six people are pushed beyond their limits, and there's a fight for the few resources we have?

I march out of camp, confronted by a wall of thick trees. Some are covered with moss and others have bark peeling, but they all look the same. My throat tightens. Mist clings to the air, mingling with the oppressive darkness. Monsters in the woods don't scare me as much as the devil inside us.

Anyone could be a killer.

TWENTY-SEVEN
AMBER

Dear God, if someone else has to die, please let it be Scott.

I inwardly recite my prayer as I rip pink berries from barbed vines, golden shafts of sunlight illuminating the dense forest. The next day, Scott, Fred, Cameron, *and* Nicole vote to leave.

My daughter's loyalty to her father stings less than my husband's betrayal, but it still hurts. I know he's doing his best, but I needed a moment alone, so I left to forage for food. Scott, unwilling to miss an opportunity to gloat, tagged along. All morning, he's been rubbing it in.

"That's *three* votes," he snorts, piling as many salmonberries as he can in the pouch made from his shirt. "Four if you count our kid. Even your husband doesn't agree with you. You lost."

"Jesus, Scott. This isn't a popularity contest."

"Never said it was. Nobody sides with you because you have poor judgment." His half-cocked smirk stabs my heart.

I stare at him. "What would you call poisoning yourself with mushrooms?"

That wipes the amusement from his face. His lips whiten. "Bravery," he says, finally. "I took a chance, and it didn't pay off. There's nothing wrong with that."

"Okay, Scott."

His ears glow red. "If you had your way, we'd be starving at the old camp."

"As opposed to starving here?"

"I keep telling you. *We* don't have the luxury of time. I'm definitely leaner." He pats his stomach and gestures to mine. "You've probably burned off some fat, but honestly, you have a lot more to go."

I barely stop myself from slapping him. He's an idiot. The obnoxious meathead *has* to put me down to feel better about himself. I know that, but it's hard to ignore the constant attacks. The stupidity. His refusal to acknowledge that this entire trip is his fault. I throw a couple berries in my mouth to spite him, swallowing them whole.

"No point getting mad over the group's decision," Scott drawls as he yanks berries from vines. "I didn't pitch a fit when you refused a proper burial for my wife."

"Shut up, Scott."

He clicks his tongue. "Why are you so hostile?"

"We have a perfectly good shelter. We have food. Water. You're forcing me to walk. *Again*."

He laughs. "God forbid you exercise."

"Every step we take, we're sweating out electrolytes. Sodium. Potassium. Without those, our hearts quit pumping. Our lungs stop absorbing air. I'm just as dead when those run out." When his lazy smirk doesn't disappear, my jaw tightens. "The point is, it doesn't matter how much fat I have, you fucking moron."

I make a fist, my fingers stained orange from picking. Scott finally shuts up, but I can't stifle the boiling feelings within me. My chest shakes. I breathe in and out through my mouth. Just when I've dampened the flames to a low smolder, Scott's exaggerated sigh brings them roaring back.

"I've tried and *tried* to explain things to you, to work together and make peace for our daughter's sake, but all I get is profanity. I'm disappointed in you."

"Laura would say the same about you," I snarl, enjoying the flash of pain on his face. "Too bad she isn't here."

"Nice. Were you saving that all day?"

"Don't taunt me about my weight, and I won't remind you that you're responsible for her death."

"I didn't. Kill. Laura."

He strides forward, his eyes wild. A bramble catches his arm, opening a long gash on his skin. Blood wells from the wound, but he hardly seems to notice. His glare hints that he's on to me, like I hated his wife. Like I've got a grudge against her for marrying him.

"Something was going on between you two. You were dodging her calls."

I break into nervous laughter. "Forgive me for being a busy mom."

His potent stare drills into me. "You're lying."

"Scott, back off."

"We should've found the trail by now, but it's been setback after setback. First Laura. Now this dead chick." He adopts a low, fevered tone. "Someone is messing with us."

"Who? Fred?"

"It's possible. He's always had a chip on his shoulder, plus, he's insane. Your husband is no fan of mine, that's for sure. And there's that stepson of yours."

"*David?* Are you out of your mind?"

"He's rough. That's why he's great at football, but he's overly aggressive in every defensive position. He focuses on the other players instead of the plays."

This is what I get for listening to my ex. "He sounds like a normal teenage boy."

"Yeah, right."

"You know what I think?" I wheel around as Scott slams to a halt, blanching. "The lack of food is getting to you. It's dawning on you how bad our situation is, and you can't handle that this is your fault. That would mean sentencing your wife, daughter, and four other innocent people to death. Accepting blame is too painful, so you're dreaming up this absurd fantasy of someone murdering your wife. It. Was. An. *Accident*."

Rage transforms Scott's face, rippling across his deep frown and the malice twisting his mouth. He takes a sudden step toward me. I'm not quick enough to dodge the hand flying to my nape. He grips my throat, snarling. "I'm not responsible for her death."

Sure you aren't.

His proximity pits my stomach with nausea. The weight of his hand and his freezing touch are too familiar. I square my shoulders at him, daring him to hit me. "Go ahead. Prove what a big, strong man you are. It's not like you haven't done it before."

His neck flushes with mottled red spots. Then he raises his hand. Pain bursts across my face. My head snaps to the right. I stumble, hitting a tree. My wide gaze collides with Scott's furious eyes. I hold my burning cheek, the sting swooping inside me, squeezing my heart.

Shaking, I march back to camp. Scott chases me. He grabs my elbow, a desperate edge in his tone.

"Wait."

I wrench out of his grip.

"I'm sorry, but what did you think would happen? You *provoked* me. Amber…Amber, what are you doing?" Scott bellows after me. I crash through the bushes, putting as much distance between us as I can. "Amber, *hold on!*"

That's it. No more placating Scott and pretending to be a united family. I'm getting Cameron and we're leaving. I don't know how we'll separate Nicole from Scott, but we must. This is too dangerous. I don't trust him.

I sprint into the camp. Logs tumble from Fred's arms. He gives me a searching look and sidesteps Scott. "What did you do?"

"Nothing. She slipped. She fell and wants to blame it on me, like usual. I can't take a dump without my ex-wife complaining about it. Always the bad guy."

He keeps babbling as Fred glances at me, a storm gathering in his expression as he connects the dots. "You hit her."

Scott flinches. "No."

Fred's tone darkens as he seeks me out. "Did he?"

I ball my fists, heart hammering. This is my cue to exile Scott, but if that happens, then what? Nicole will refuse to go with us. She'll stay with her father. I can't risk that.

Luckily, Scott's high-pitched gasp cuts off my response. He screams bloody murder and stalks to the campfire. He picks up an empty can of beans among two others, their contents spilled all over the fire.

All of it—*gone*.

Someone sabotaged the food.

TWENTY-EIGHT

AMBER

"Who did this?"

Scott's demand is met by ringing silence as everybody gathers around the smoldering campfire. Several piles of beans lay in the center of the ashes, dirt powdering them as though kicked up by a shoe. The empty cans sit by the fire like a punchline to a grim joke.

Scott clutches one of them, his fervent stare sweeping the camp. "Nicole?"

His attention zeroes on our daughter, whose blank, unhappy expression twists something in my heart. She sits on the ground, hugging her tattered leggings. Her unkempt blond ponytail swishes as she shakes her head. "I was by the river."

"Tell your father the truth," he says, hardening. "Was it David?"

Beside her, David scoffs. "Screw you, man."

"Was it?"

"We didn't do anything."

And yet, that seems to fuel Scott's suspicion. I can't exactly blame him. The angry tears and the pink patches burning high on Nicole's cheeks don't paint an innocent picture.

"Nicole, if you're covering up for your stepbrother—"

"She doesn't need to," David shoots back. "Why would I dump our food on the ground?"

Scott kicks the other empty can across the fire pit. "Only a kid would be this stupid."

My lips inch into a sneer. "You're the one winning the Darwin award, getting us lost, stuffing your face with shrooms."

Scott's lightning rod glare strikes my chest. He takes a furious step forward, but Cameron gets there first. He shoves him backward. "Don't you dare."

"Somebody sabotaged our food supply. This was all we had. It was supposed to buy us time. Now we're screwed. We'll starve within days." Scott's accusatory gaze jumps from David to his father, to Fred. "Which one of you was it? Fred?"

His brother flashes him the bird. "I was gathering firewood."

"A likely story," he sneers, wheeling around at my husband. "And you?"

"I was watching the kids."

Scott confirms that with a sullen nod from Nicole, which seems to aggravate him. He hurls the can at the ground. It lands at my feet. I pick it up, my insides gnawing as I study the jagged marks in the aluminum. Whoever it was worked hard to cut it open. Hunger pangs claw my gut.

"From now on, we use a buddy system." I dump the beans clinging to the sides into my hand and divvy them up. "Nobody will be left alone."

Scott waves off his portion. "Too late for that."

"What do you want us to do, Scott? Arrange a tribunal for spilled beans?" I would laugh if my stomach didn't feel like it was caving in. "Do you realize how insane you sound?"

He whirls at me. "Stop diminishing this."

"We don't even know what happened—"

"Then I'll tell you. This was a calculated attack," Scott says, earning an eye roll from Fred and stunned looks from the children. "Whoever did this wants to kill us. They've been messing with us since the beginning."

I stare at him, mouth agape.

"It's one of you." He points at each person, his finger trembling with gravitas like a hellfire preacher condemning his congregation. "One of you is a killer."

I burst into laughter. "I'm sorry, what? A killer among us? This isn't a *Law and Order* episode."

"They planned this. They brought us here...got us lost." He nudges the empty can with his boot. "Now they're starving us out. Killing us. One by one."

He's out of his mind.

"You're ridiculous."

Scott throws up his hands in a see-what-I-have-to-deal-with gesture. Then he shakes his head, sounding grave but so damned reasonable. "I'm not surprised you're not taking this seriously. You didn't believe me from the get-go. If you want to sweep attempted murder under the rug, fine. That's on you. But I won't do it."

I want so badly to shut him up, but I can't. Fear is mirrored on everybody's face. Nobody believes this was an accident. I don't like it, either. If it was one can, I'd accept it, but all three? Who would do such a thing?

"I can think of a million reasons this happened," says Fred. "The food was spoiled. The cans could've been breached. They emptied them so we wouldn't poison ourselves."

Scott flings his hand and makes a disgusted noise. "Without discussing it as a group?"

"Maybe they wanted to avoid a witch hunt."

Scott's vicious snarl is like a tennis volley. "Or they're guilty of much more than sabotage."

Cameron massages his temples, fatigue lining his handsome face. "We need to put a pin in this discussion. It's not helping."

"I hate to break it to you, but someone here wants us dead."

That word lands like an anvil, shattering me.

Scott fills the void left in the stunned silence with more venom. "There's a traitor in our midst. And I'll tell you something else. Laura didn't trip down a hill. She was pushed."

I grab his wrists. "I need a private conversation with you. Now."

Scott looks down at me, teeth bared. "I don't trust any of you." He yanks out of my grip, shaking. "You're all against me. You loathe me. Laura was the only one who didn't, and she's gone. You think that's a coincidence?"

"Scott, use your brain. There's nothing to suggest she was pushed."

"Except for her broken neck," he yells. "And her phone disappearing."

"You're crazy," mutters Fred.

"Fine. I'm nuts. Why didn't she have her phone? Why couldn't we find it?"

Fred shrugs. "She dropped it in the forest."

"That phone was her life. Why would she drop it?"

Fred's exasperated tone cuts the air. "She was high."

Scott gives an impatient jerk of his head. "You can't blame everything on the damned mushrooms."

"Yes, we can, Scott," I say. "She wasn't in her right mind."

"I ate them, and I was okay."

Fred laughs. "Yeah, sure."

"I'm tired of your attitude," Scott snarls, wheeling around. "All of you. This is a second attempt on our lives. How can you not see that? Even if you believe this is a one-off incident, what about Laura? She didn't fall off a cliff, for God's sake. This isn't a Road Runner cartoon. She was vulnerable. Whoever it is—probably Fred—took advantage."

Cameron murmurs something about not jumping to conclusions, but Scott powers on, his voice growing louder and more powerful. He smacks his open palm with a closed fist.

"Every time we make some progress, we hit a major roadblock. Every single time! It's supernatural at this point. And how do you explain Laura's phone vanishing? You can't."

"Uh-huh," says Fred, elongating the vowel. "And someone planted the shrooms, knowing you'd be dumb enough to eat them. If we're going by your logic, you killed her."

Scott points at Fred, his face alive with a "gotcha!" expression. "Or you're deflecting because *you* did it. Think about it. Who has been downplaying Laura's murder? Fred."

"I didn't hurt Laura, you idiot."

"Your behavior has been really weird. You didn't know her, and you were crying. For hours."

A ripple of anger runs through me. "So? Maybe he's an emotional guy. Nothing wrong with that."

"Sure. If that were true." Scott crosses his arms, facing his brother. "You didn't shed a tear when Mom died. I'm supposed to believe that my wife's death moved you? You've been around her for, like, five minutes."

Heat steals into my face. "Scott."

He holds up a hand, shutting me out. "We need to have this out. You've been ogling my wife during this whole vacation. Yeah, I noticed."

Fred stammers an inaudible response, gazing at his shoes. He might as well be waving a giant red flag. I want to rip out my hair.

"What did you do?" Scott bellows, advancing on him. "Did you try to do something, you creep? Feel her up? Then when she rejected you, you tossed her down a cliff?"

"Jesus, man. I would never."

A ball lodges in my throat. "Enough. You have zero evidence to prove what you're saying."

"Oh yeah? Look at him."

My stomach churns as I watch Fred stammer his defense like a bad witness on trial. His guilt couldn't be more obvious, but it's the affair eating at his conscience...not Laura's death.

Cameron puts a hand on my back and gives me an imperceptible shake of his head. As I swallow my confession, Cameron leaves my side. He strides forward, easing his body in between the two brothers. Hands on Scott's shoulder, he speaks softly.

"I'm paranoid?" erupts Scott. "Whoever did this had a knife. Who has one? Fred."

"I didn't have it on me," he shouts.

"Really?" Scott fires back. "Then how were you cutting branches for firewood?"

"I-I didn't. I picked them off the ground."

I stare at Fred. He's not the violent type, but I don't know him like Scott. He could've found Laura, had some kind of heart-to-heart where she rejected him, and he overreacted. Is that possible? Maybe. My breathing hitches as I picture Fred sawing at the cans while the rest of us foraged. I have no idea what to think anymore.

Fred angrily gestures toward the campfire. "I want to get out of here just as much as you."

"Do you?" says Scott, his voice inflamed and belligerent. "Or are you trying to drag us all down with you?"

Fred's black glare swims with tears. "I'd walk into that river and drown myself before I hurt someone."

"That's why you're moping all the time. You're consumed with guilt over what you did. Isn't that right? Tell me the truth!" Scott repeats the question in an enraged scream that makes Fred stumble backward.

"I-I don't know w-what you want me to s-say."

Fred trails off, his words dying in a whimper. His terrified eyes search the camp for an ally. His gaze clashes with mine.

I grimace. "We need to focus on getting home. We can't keep fighting amongst ourselves. Let's take a few minutes to cool down before we do anything rash."

Scott snaps his head in my direction, as though he feels the waves of shame wafting over me. "You think he did this, too."

"No, I don't. I swear—I want us home. Once we're safe, you can fight with your brother all you like. Until then, we're a family. A dysfunctional family, but we stick together." I grab his shoulders and Fred's, desperate to link some kind of connection. "I don't think anybody here would want to hurt us. Whoever did this must've had their reasons."

"Just because someone is related doesn't mean we tolerate lies, drama, manipulation, and murder." Scott faces me, seething. "Right?"

A bead of sweat rolls down my cheek.

Whatever he reads on my face seems to set him off. He stalks to Fred, who has already dashed across the camp. Scott seizes a stick off the ground, looking like he's out for blood.

My lungs tighten. "Cam, stop him!"

Cameron grabs Scott, yanking his elbows back. Scott attempts to break free, hurling obscenities, but my husband forces Scott down the slope leading to the rock beach. I ignore Scott's unhinged screaming and turn my attention to Fred.

My heart hammers. "You should probably leave."

He wipes his cheeks. "Where am I supposed to go?"

"I don't know. But you're not safe here anymore. I-I can't control him. I'm sorry. I'm so sorry." The guilt from Laura's death waylays me. I sink to my feet, gutted. I failed her, and now my family is falling apart. "Just go."

Fred nods, tears slipping down his long nose. "I guess this is goodbye."

I swallow hard.

Fred picks up his jacket, his backpack, and the crossbow, briefly touching Laura's black hiking bag. His eyes sparkle as he faces me. "He's going to get you all killed."

Then he leaves without a backward glance, his warning lingering like toxic smoke.

TWENTY-NINE

AMBER

Now we are five.

A strange feeling permeates the group as everyone settles down for bed like the dense mist that bites deep into my flesh. We're not a family anymore. We're survivors, clawing to the finish line of a winding maze.

We avoid his name, as though saying it out loud will invoke a vengeful ghost. Fred isn't dead, but it feels like it. He might be lost forever. How many days will he last? What if we make it out, but we can't find him? And if that happens, how will I live with myself, knowing that I condemned a man to death?

As night's dark curtain descends over the forest, my gaze bores into Scott's back. I follow his every move like it's my full-time job. It will be, as long as we're out here. Our lives depend on it.

In these woods, he's the only thing that scares me. My ex-husband is the *real* threat. Stirring up drama. Pointing fingers. Turning my daughter against me. He probably got greedy, opened up the cans, wolfed them down, and dumped the leftovers in the flames. Scott is that selfish.

My ex is the common denominator. He's pretending not to know about Laura's affair. Maybe *he* led us off trail and put Laura in a vulnerable state so he could kill her. He might've engineered this disaster. It makes sense. She cheated on him with his brother. Scott doesn't take rejection very well. I can attest to that...but that gives Scott too much credit. He lacks the brains to pull off something so Machiavellian.

Scott sits with his back to the campfire, orange light rippling up his T-shirt and ragged Lululemon pants. He spent the whole day pouting while the rest of us foraged, boiled water, and salvaged as many beans as possible. Wrapped in David's sweatshirt, Nicole plops down beside Scott. Even with her arms tucked in the fabric, she trembles like an autumn leaf.

Nicole budges up against him. "Dad, I'm *cold*."

Scott slides his moody glare from the fire and wraps an arm around her. Nicole tucks her head under his jaw. He sighs, tension melting from his brows.

A branch snaps.

"Dad, are you okay?"

Scott's eyes flare open, the haunted look returning to his hollowed gaze. "No."

"Do you think we'll get back?"

"What kind of question is that?"

She shrugs. "We might die out here."

He wipes his face. "That won't happen. I'll get you home."

"Are you sure?"

Her wavering tone seems to set him off. "I'm your damned father. That's my responsibility. Or is *Cameron* taking that job, too?"

I frown, straining to hear more, but their next words disappear in a murmured hush. Then Scott's angry retort bolts through the dark. "Did Amber find out?"

"Not sure. I mean, she doesn't talk about that stuff."

He scoffs.

She pats his knee. "Dad?"

Scott rubs his temple. "I'm fine. My stomach hurts, but I'm all right."

Orange light ripples across Nicole's round face as she seeks me out. "I'll ask Mom for berries. She has some left."

Scott catches her arm before she stands, pulling her down. "Don't bother. Your mother hates me."

I click my tongue, fuming.

Nicole frowns. "She's worried about us."

"You, maybe, but not me. She wouldn't care if I ended up like that skeleton in the bush. Hell, that husband of hers will throw a party."

"*Stop*. That's not true."

"It is," he hisses. "He can't stand me because I had her first. She hates me because I wasn't perfect. Because I'm a human being. I made *one* mistake, and she blew up my whole life. You know?"

Nicole nods dully.

"If she cared about our marriage, she would've fought harder. She didn't even try to make it work." Scott glances at Nicole. "Why not?"

Nicole bites her lip. "I dunno. I was, like, seven when you guys broke up. I'm used to it."

"But what's your opinion?"

Always a class act. Unload your baggage onto our daughter. She's starving and cold, but that's second to your problems.

He's so selfish. My rage peaks when his big frame shakes with the unmistakable sound of a sob. Nicole rubs his back, her face pinched with fatigue and pain. How many times has he done this to her?

I clench my jaw so hard that pain shoots into my teeth. When Scott pulled this crap with me, I comforted him. I sometimes felt like an unpaid therapist. Dealing with someone who constantly needs your validation is exhausting.

So I jumped at the chance to leave him. After he cheated on me, I spent a week in an Airbnb. It was fantastic. The first time I'd breathed in years. I was so happy to get away, I didn't fight for our marriage. The day Scott signed the divorce papers, I was elated. But it turns out, all I did was condemn our daughter. Now she's his emotional crutch.

Nicole fiddles with a strand of hair as her father waits for her answer. "Dad, I think I know who messed with the food."

Scott gives her a long, hard look. *"Who?"*

"Cameron," she whispers, her confession winding me. "He had the knife before...it happened. I saw him sharpening sticks for hunting fish."

"Does your mother know?"

Nicole shakes her head.

"Thanks for telling me, kid, but I'm positive we've gotten rid of the threat. Fred has every reason in the world to sabotage us." He scratches his beard, growling. "Maybe he teamed up with Cameron to torture me."

The staggering arrogance of this idiot.

I've had enough. I disengage from Cameron's arms and make a show out of waking up, stretching and yawning. Nicole scurries to the spot by the fire where David sleeps. I wait until she's settled, then I make a beeline for Scott.

"I heard everything."

Scott's unhappy gaze pierces me. "Eavesdropping?"

"You can't talk like that to her. Nicole is not your emotional sounding board. She's a person. She has needs, too."

"If our relationship has suffered, that's *your* fault. You turned her against me by involving her in our business."

"Like what you were just doing?"

"I was asking questions," he says, his curt voice lashing at me. "You fed my daughter a villainous narrative."

"A villainous narrative?"

His nostrils flare. "You told her I cheated."

"What was I supposed to do? I *had* to tell her about your affair. Anything else would've been a lie."

His lip curls. "You are such a hypocrite. You asked me to lie to Nicole a few days ago."

"For God's sake, Scott, let this go. We both moved on." *Or appeared to, at any rate.* "We need to focus on what's best for her."

Scott smiles. "You made me look like a fool in front of her. You must be so pleased with yourself."

"Yeah. I'm having the time of my life, watching you lose it. Having a front-row seat to your demise is all I want in this world. Wake the hell up. We're lost. We're out of food. We might not survive this."

His poisonous stare dives into me. "That's what you're hoping for, isn't it?"

I stand, my heart billowing with hatred. "Fred's right. You're crazy." I turn my back on him and head to the tent. It's a marvel I can even find it, given I'm blinded by rage. I stumble inside. Cameron turns off the flashlight on his phone, tossing a book aside.

"Hey, babe."

"Hey. What's that?"

He shrugs. "Some book I found."

I'm in no mood to chastise him about wasting batteries. I close the flap and sink into his warm lap, sighing. "I need to stop talking to Scott. He's driving me up the wall."

"You and me both."

"Scott won't be able to call me fat for much longer. I'll be a bag of bones soon." I chuckle, but there's nothing funny about the ache in my belly. "Tell me we're going home."

Cameron kisses my cheek, his face solemn. His lips fall on my mouth, light and teasing, and then he pulls me into a rough kiss. I cling to him like he's scaffolding, craving the safety of his arms. Something breaks free from my chest. Tears slide down my cheeks. I cry. He kisses me again and again, his lips burning a path down my neck. His hand slips under my shirt. He slides up my skin, cupping my breast. I bite back a groan, pulling his wrist away.

He breathes hard, eyes half-lidded with lust. "What?"

"We can't. Scott and the kids."

"And?" he whispers fiercely. "What, I can't make love to my wife because he lost his?"

"You can't because I haven't bathed in forever."

"Neither have I," he drawls, amusement softening his words. "Sorry. Got too worked up."

"Getting caught in the moment is one of your best quali-ties." My palm makes lazy circles on his chest, and he smiles. "You make me feel beautiful."

"You are." He gives me a sharp look, as though daring me to disagree. "I only tolerate your ex for Nicole's sake, but once we're home, I *never* want to see him again."

If we get out of here. I'm not negative, but my hope dwindles every day. I'm terrified for Nicole and David. Cameron strokes my back.

"I've been doing some thinking. I need to work less and spend more time with you. I've been self-centered." He nudges my jaw, forcing my gaze to collide with his ferocious stare. "You're my everything. I just...I want a do-over."

My throat tightens. "Cam."

Starvation must be messing with his mind. I stroke his frown until it softens. I press my lips into his. Then he cups my cheeks, making me feel like a dandelion blowing apart. For a while, my problems melt away. I'm weightless, riding a cloud, and then distant sobbing filters into the tent. My body goes rigid.

"What is that?"

I listen hard. "It's coming from the river."

Fred. His lonely voice echoes, strangling me. My nails dig into Cameron's shoulder.

What if Scott isn't crazy? What if there is a killer...and we made a mistake?

THIRTY
AMBER

How many days has it been?

Five? Seven? Our situation is bleak, but I refuse to die like this. I can't. I'm too weak to move, but I tear myself from the campfire's warmth. I stumble into the forest. My heart hammers. I'm starting to fear this place. The branches over my head are like a hollowed rib cage. *Imprisoning me.*

It rained last night, which made the colors darker and richer. Evergreens glisten with moisture. Ferns choke the ground. A fresh smell taints the air, which is so still. No birds. No animal calls. In this forest, nothing lives but the plants. When we die, our bodies will nourish this night-marish landscape. We will decompose. Our skeletons, too. Gnarled roots will drink the nitrogen released from our moldering flesh.

Get it together, Amber.

My vision blurs as I trek deeper, brambles snagging my clothes. Pink salmonberries cling to a bush. My aching fingers pluck them off. I drop them in the front pocket of my backpack. I pop a few in my mouth. The burst of sugar dissolves on my tongue. After a few minutes, I've stripped the bush of berries.

It's barely a handful.

My stomach clenches.

"Suck it up, Amber," I whisper, my teeth chattering. "You don't have time for a pity party. Laying down and dying isn't an option. Keep going. Don't give up."

My pep talk doesn't work. Berries are keeping us functional. Death closes in on us like a vulture circling a corpse. I'm constantly dizzy. My heartbeat thuds slowly. Nicole's more gaunt every day, and my poor daughter doesn't have any fat to lose. My husband and stepson stumble when they walk. God only knows what happened to Fred. Drops slide down my cheek before I realize that I'm crying.

A branch snaps ahead.

My pulse races as David steps into view, followed by Nicole. David's dark head swings from side to side. I hide behind a tree. I don't want them to see me like this.

Nicole clutches David's hand. "Are we alone?"

"We're good," he says, in a suggestive tone that piques my interest. "Doubt anybody cares what we're up to."

I frown, suddenly wide awake. My attention centers on their interlinked hands, their bodies too close together, and my daughter's foolish grin. It pulls into a full-blown smile when David kisses her temple.

What the hell?

Alarm bells ring as I gape at them, open-mouthed. That's more intimate than he should be with his stepsister, not that Nicole's complaining. David tugs her into an embrace. She leans into his touch, tucking her head under his.

"Is anyone looking for us?"

David caresses her arm. "Yes. Search parties are combing the forest by now. They'll give it their all for a few weeks."

Nicole frowns. "Will they find us, though?"

"Yes."

"What if they don't? We might be outside the radius, or whatever." Nicole slides out from his arms, her voice strained. "I-I'm not sure how much longer I can go without food."

"Stop worrying. I won't let anything happen to you."

He cups her face and brings her close. Nicole's adoring gaze falls on his mouth. They kiss. It's quick and hurried, but without hesitation. Like they've done it before.

My stomach drops.

David breaks off first, rubbing his neck. "I still feel strange about kissing you."

Nicole grins. "*I* don't."

"Yeah, well. You won't get in trouble. *I* will." David picks a large green leaf and shreds it, his cheeks pink. "Do you think Mom will approve?"

"Ew—why do you call her that?"

"Because Mom feels more accurate than Amber." He shifts to another foot, sounding uneasy. "You didn't answer my question."

"Since when do you care about her approval?"

He shrugs. "I just wanna know."

"She'll probably freak out and ground me. Anyway, don't call her Mom. You can't be my boyfriend *and* my step-brother. That's too weird."

"Sure I can." His tone turns defensive as Nicole flashes a playful grin. "It's frowned upon, but not illegal. Like taking more than one free sample from Costco."

"So *not* the same."

Nicole's laughter rings through the forest. She playfully shoves him. He pulls her into another hug. Nicole melts into him. I watch my not-so-innocent stepson stroke her back, a sweet gesture that makes my blood boil. Then they walk around a bush. The sound of their retreating foot-steps is strange, like it's coming from a can.

What the hell?

Nicole and David are dating? When did this happen? Does Cameron know? And what is David doing? Sneaking her away for…what? For God's sake. I can't believe this.

Determined to put an end to whatever is blossoming between them, I step out from behind the tree to confront them. Only, they've disappeared.

Shoot.

"Nicole?" I charge through the bushes where they last stood. "Nicole Elizabeth Maxwell. I saw you. Come out *now*."

They don't respond. Fuming, I scan the trees for movement. A swaying fern catches my attention. I run toward it, screaming their names. I reach it and sprint in another direction, blundering through the woods.

"This is ridiculous."

I whirl around, searching for them. They must've gone back. Where's the camp? A solid wall of green surrounds me. The vegetation is so thick that I can't tell where I am.

Oh my God. I'm lost.

Dad's home.

He arrives in a state of great agitation. Car tires squeal as he pulls into our driveway. He opens the door. From the open bedroom window, I watch him stagger out of the car. He holds onto the car door, doubled over as though he might puke. Clearly, he's having a bad day.

I can't *imagine* why.

A curve touches my lips as the neighbor greets him. My idiot father indulges her with a few sentences, even though he calls her a "boring cat mom" behind her back. He loves playing the family man. Pretending to give a crap about my schooling or sports. He lies about our close relationship. He lies, lies, and *lies* like it's his full-time job, and he's good at it. He's like a professional actor from Juilliard. All my life, he's fooled nurses, schoolteachers, and neighbors. Everybody thinks he's perfect.

Dad gives the neighbor a half-hearted wave, his voice drifting inside. "Hey, Nance. How's it going?"

"Good. I've been meaning to catch you. You have to tell me how your hydrangeas get so big," gushes Nancy from her porch. She's a sixty-something retiree who lost her husband a year ago. She loves my dad because he does handyman work around her home whenever she asks. Meanwhile, Dad complains about her the second he walks in.

"Oh. I'm not sure," he says in a booming voice. "They were here before I moved. I think, um, it depends on where you plant them. They like a lot of water, hence the name—*hydra*. Although, I never water them. You don't need to if they're well established."

He proceeds to give her terrible advice on the upkeep of hydrangeas, and even diagnoses a fungus on her plants before he's rid of her, fifteen minutes later. After saying goodbye, he approaches the door. Unlocks it. Steps inside. Slams it. The walls rock in the wake of his rage. He unleashes his fury in a scream, his energy zipping my spine. Then he thunders upstairs, shouting my name.

Here we go.

The door flies open. Dad crashes inside, reeking of booze and despair. He hurtles toward me, but Meadow's anxious bark catches him at the knees.

Dad glares at her. "That damned dog."

Meadow is my only ally in this house. I love her to death. If my father wanted to hurt me, he could easily do it, but he's never been the violent type. Today might change that.

"What is it?" I ask him, feigning boredom. "Does Nancy need something?"

Dad's shoulders curl forward. He folds in on himself, collapsing like a deck of cards. His pain is beautiful to witness.

"Dad, what's wrong?"

He palms his face as a name trembles from his mouth. *"It's Kim."*

I lick my lips, fighting a smile. "Is she…all right?"

He shakes his head. A sob racks from his chest as he rips the tie off his neck. He weeps in a nauseating display.

"Sh-she's dead. C-car crash."

"Wow," I deadpan, turning to my writing. "You're sure?"

He nods. "They found her car wrapped around a tree. I-I identified the body."

Hot damn. I could sing.

It worked. I'm shocked, but not regretful in the slightest. Hiding my glee is hard. "Gosh. That's awful, Dad. I'm so sorry."

He hangs an arm around my neck, boohooing. "She was going to be your mom."

He hugs me and cries. His tears soak my shirt and it's gross, and yet a confusing swirl of warmth battles the nausea pitting my stomach. A pathetic part of me still craves his affection. I just want to be loved. My old therapist told me that there's no shame in that desire, even after what he's done.

I pat his head.

He pulls back, teary-eyed. "I don't know why this keeps happening."

"Bad luck, I guess."

I stab my notebook harder than I intend, the dotted I on *slice* piercing through the paper. My heartbeat picks up as Dad moans about Kim, his babbling grating my nerves.

"She was so smart…a visionary. That vlog of hers was so brilliant. She helped people. She—"

"—was a fake, dumb bitch."

I resume writing. My dad's stare heats my face.

"What did you say?"

"I mean, I'm so sorry. What a loss," I say in a hollow voice, setting down my pen. "You're right, Dad. Heaven has gained an angel. She will be sorely missed."

"Don't be sarcastic," he snarls.

"She was a harpy from hell. I couldn't stand her." I slide his arm off me and sink to the floor beside Meadow. "At least I'll be able to eat whatever I want."

Dad's jaw goes slack. "*Jesus*. You had something to do with this."

I stroke Meadow's fur. "Interesting theory."

"*Did you?*"

I smile. He grabs my notebook and flings it at me. I deflect it, the metal rings crashing into my palm.

"Answer me, you little jerk," he growls.

"No. Yes. Does it matter?"

He leans in. "Did you do this?"

"You'll never know."

"Tell me what you did," he grits out, his identical gaze scanning mine.

"I'd rather not spend my life in handcuffs."

"What did you do to her?" he demands roughly, earning a growl from Meadow. "Did you mess with the car?"

"That sounds beyond my abilities." I pet Meadow's glossy fur, shushing her. "I find it easy to imagine someone drugging her. Finding a doctor that prescribes benzos isn't hard. Some give them out like Jolly Ranchers. A few crushed-up tablets would do the trick. Dissolving them in alcohol hides the gritty texture. Mixing benzos with wine is ill-advised. It causes people to become uncoordinated... they could easily lose control of their car."

Dad makes a violent sound. He throws my chair, and it crashes into the dresser. Meadow releases a throaty bark.

"You killed her! You little bastard."

"I wasn't even there," I say, relishing in his confusion. "Out of curiosity, was there anything left to identify her, or did they have to scrape her off the cement?"

He stands, red-faced, like a teakettle about to blow. "You're a sick *freak*."

"Not as sick as the woman you were about to marry. She was hurting me, not that you care." I pick up my notebook and catch his expression, which is disturbed. "Calm down. I didn't drug her rosé. That's a silly story I cooked up. A bit of improv."

"You will regret this."

"Regret what? Kim had a drug problem, and that's all there is to it. It's sad, but so common."

He rakes his hair, bewildered. *"Drugs?* She didn't do *drugs.*"

"That's crazy talk. She had them in her medicine cabinet." I throw the notebook onto my desk and right the chair. "She was very liberal about taking them. You're not around during the day, so you don't see her swallowing a million pills."

"I don't believe this."

"Okay, Dad. Continue to live in your fantasy land. But if you need to blame someone, blame yourself. She was barely coherent when she grabbed her keys, went outside, and got herself killed. You could've stopped her. You didn't."

Dad dissolves into tears, sinking to the floor. He slumps, sobbing like a baby until Meadow takes pity on him and licks his hand.

"I loved her," he moans, stroking my dog. "So much."

"Sorry, Dad. You'll have to find a new woman to make our lives terrible. I'm sure it won't take you long." I push Dad aside and sit behind my desk, my body trembling with adrenaline. "Leave my room."

He gets up and shuffles out the door. He moves to a different part of the house and cries. I slide on headphones to block out his whimpering. I hadn't planned on her slamming into a tree. She was supposed to die in her sleep. Still, it worked out. I got away with it.

I'll get away with the next one, too.

THIRTY-TWO
AMBER

This can't be happening.

I'm lost. If I don't find the others, I won't make it. I'll become a skeleton. They'll discover me months later, stripped of meat, embedded in the earth just like that poor hiker. My pulse races as I scream their names. Where should I go?

The faceless trees seem to mock me. Everything looks the *same*. And I didn't mark the way back. Stupid. I cup my hands around my mouth, hollering. It's pure hysteria. Panic. Bitter tears slide down my cheeks. Deep sobs rack my chest, then I remember what Scott said about screaming attracting predators. A bear will come out and savage me.

A bush in front of me parts.

My heart stops. I imagine a broad head emerging, revealing massive shoulders and a gaping maw filled with razor-sharp teeth. The immense frame rears up as it prepares to kill me...

My husband jumps out. "There you are. I heard you shouting. Are you hurt?"

"I-I got lost."

Cameron offers me a half-crooked smile. "Amber, you're fifty feet from camp."

I shake my head and let out a relieved whimper, falling into his arms. I'm sapped of strength. Cameron's gentle grip encircles my waist. Then he walks me a short distance, and suddenly, the smell of burning wood invades my nostrils. The playing of the river returns to my ears. My body shakes as the terror leaves my system, and I laugh.

"I thought I was lost."

Cameron kisses my temple, whispering sweet nothings in my ear. "It'll be okay. I'm not letting you out of my sight. Promise."

"Sorry. I-I'm going crazy."

"No, you're not. You're starving. That messes with anybody's mind."

Behind Cameron, Scott gives us a look of loathing.

Cameron's firm grasp on my forearm leads me to warmth. He makes tea from the water in the pot hanging over the fire. Then he pushes a steaming mug into my hands. Rose-hips and dandelion roots float in the water. Cameron divvies up the berries I found, and I dunk my share in the tea. If only this were broth. I'd feel so much better with more salt in my system. Saliva pools on my tongue as I imagine the savory scent. Great, now I'm hallucinating smells. If only I'd imagined that conversation in the woods.

I glance at Nicole, who sits with her stepbrother, hands clasped around her knees. What happened in the forest slams into my head, chasing away the residual panic as discomfort fills my heart. Nicole and David. My daughter and my stepson. They're together. When did this happen?

I assumed David was taking on a brotherly role. Now that I'm watching them, it's obvious. His hand on her back. Their secret smiles. Those stolen glances. Nicole's blush when he winks in her direction.

This is not okay. I need to talk to Cameron. I open my mouth to ask my husband for a private word, but I'm stopped by Scott's dark frown. He can't know. If he finds out, I'll never hear the end of it. He'll make all kinds of accusations. I can't handle complaints about my parenting right now. It'll set me off.

"Listen, everyone. We need to discuss our next steps," says Scott in an important-sounding voice that he's polished over the week. "This isn't working. We need a new plan."

"How about one that doesn't leave you in charge?" suggests David.

Scott lets out a rough sigh. "I'm getting a *little* fed up with the back talk, kids."

David rakes a hand through his hair in a devil-may-care gesture that Nicole seems to eat up. How did I not see this? I peer at my husband, but Cameron is more interested in warming his hands by the flames.

"We should hunt something," he grunts.

I grind my teeth. "We've barely seen any game."

"I might've been able to get something with a crossbow, but *someone* let Fred take it from camp." Scott's gaze flicks to meet mine in a silent accusation, and my blood boils.

"What was I supposed to do, tackle him?"

Cameron's smooth baritone railroads Scott's reply. "Let's try fishing. We need the protein."

Scott gives the pole that Cameron spent the afternoon sharpening a dubious glance. "I don't know. That means standing in the middle of those rapids."

"We don't have a choice—"

"We should make a fire." Nicole pokes at the log with a stick, showering the air with sparks. "A huge one. Burn a bunch of trees. Rangers are bound to notice."

Cameron shoots down that suggestion with a growl. "That could kill us, and we have to keep the skies clear for helicopters. They won't find us through the smoke."

"What if they're searching the wrong grid at this very moment? It could be weeks before they move on. A fire will bring them to us." David's gaunt stare seems to reflect the heat from the campfire. "It's time for drastic measures. We're on our last legs, here."

"Amber, what do you think?"

My attention snaps to Cameron. "We have no energy for hiking. So if we set the forest ablaze, we're stuck...which is dangerous. Then again, so is starvation."

David is undeterred. "What about a bigger fire that's contained?"

"No," says Scott. "We're not doing that."

"Why not?"

"Because I don't want to be responsible for millions of dollars in damage. And because I'm making the decisions." Scott gives the holster a tap. "I have the gun. Therefore, I'm in charge."

"I hate to break it to you, but this isn't *Lord of the Flies*." I shake off Cameron's biting grip and stand. "Holding that doesn't make you a leader."

"Yeah, well, this hasn't been a democracy since my wife's murder."

I scoff. "That makes you a tyrant."

"Call me whatever you like, but whoever planned this isn't screwing around."

"I thought we exiled the bad guy?" Judging by his clenched fists, Scott's not sure about that decision. "It makes me nervous when you touch your gun." I breathe a sigh of relief when Scott's hand drifts from his waist. "Maybe you should give it to Cameron."

"It's mine," he snarls. "If you want it, sweetheart, you can pry it from my cold hands."

He's nuts. "Why are you so paranoid?"

"Something isn't right," he says, voice growing with conviction. "We're lost because someone keeps nudging us in the wrong direction."

I blink, struggling to gather my bearings. "That was you."

"No, it wasn't. Not the whole way. Fred led us downhill. Then we followed the river until *your kid* suggested a detour."

Cameron's vitriol could peel paint from walls. "Which got us food."

Scott waves that off. "And then it disappeared."

"You're out of your mind."

"Am I? Nicole and I are leaving, then. Figure out how to survive on your own." Scott seizes his backpack, hurling it over his shoulder. "Nicole. Come on."

I smolder, not impressed by the joke, but Scott doesn't apologize. His eyes glow with a hard intensity.

My abdomen tenses. "Don't be like this."

Scott pats the holstered gun. "Don't make me defend myself."

I choke on my saliva, unable to accept this development. My pulse hammers. "What are you doing? *We're family.*"

"I should have left the second Laura died. Screw this. I'm out of here." Scott whirls on Nicole, who is wedged between David and me. "Let's go."

Nicole shakes her head rapidly.

He strides closer. "Get up!"

A sheer black fright sweeps through me. Then I step in between my daughter and Scott, who reacts as though I might tackle him. I'm not dealing with a rational man anymore. He's beyond reason.

"Scott, this won't be easier on your own."

"I'll take my chances," he growls. "Move."

"Fine. You win, but I'll be behind you. We'll follow you. That's what your whole tantrum is about, right? You need to be in charge, no matter who gets hurt?"

His smile is cold, flinty. "Step aside."

"We all want to go home."

"I wish that were true, but it's not."

"Splitting up doesn't accomplish anything!"

The corner of his mouth twists. He steps around me and approaches Nicole. He seizes her arm, and Nicole cries out. Cameron and David pull her, shouting. I grab onto Nicole's backpack, but he wrenches it from my grip.

I shove myself between her and Scott, growling, "If you want Nicole, you'll have to shoot me."

He blows out his cheeks, hissing. "Shoot you?"

"That's the only way you're getting her," I say in a low voice, gaze boring into his. "You'll have to kill me."

He laughs, his solemn expression cracking. When the chuckles subside, he grits out, "Sometimes I wish you didn't exist. That would be less painful."

Scott will never kill me. Before this trip, I would've agreed with that statement. But looking at him now, I'm not so sure. He's not the Scott I went to college with or the dad that helps Nicole with her physics homework. He's a feral version of himself, pushed to the brink.

I can't trust him.

My pulse gallops ahead. "Scott?"

He says nothing. The knot in my throat pulses. I glimpse something moving fast—a blur of motion at my waist— and for a moment I think he's drawn the gun. Then I'm ripped back.

Cameron throws me behind him and bellies up to Scott, shouting. Nicole screams. Cameron and Scott are face to face, trading insults and shoving each other. F-bombs burst in my ears. Dimly, a pair of footsteps registers through my panic.

I whirl around at the intruder as he speaks.

"I found a way out."

THIRTY-THREE
AMBER

A bright-eyed Fred stands behind his brother, chest puffed out, wearing a grin so smug it ought to be fined. He looks good, like he's had a few square meals. I glance around us, at the shrunken postures, and compare them with his straight-backed stance.

"I found a road." Fred drops the second bombshell as I'm processing his return. "And a cabin."

And just like that, the tension dissolves. David lets out a cry of relief. Scott slumps on a giant boulder, the backpack sliding from his shoulders. Cameron backs off, no longer looking like murdering Scott is a great option.

"Where?" I blurt, clawing to a seated position. "Did you bring anything?"

Scott dismisses him with a wave. "He's lying. He's trying to rejoin the group."

Fred shakes his head. "Nope. I'm here to save you."

"Are people on their way?" Nicole grabs my arm, emotion welling in her eyes. "Thank God."

"Well, not exactly—"

"You shouldn't be here," Scott seethes. "You're banned."

Fred shrugs. "Hey, if you'd rather starve, I'll turn around."

"How far is it?" asks David.

"The road? A couple miles, tops." Fred gestures behind him. "A game trail led me to it. From there, the cabin is a full day's walk."

David exchanges an excited glance with Nicole. Cameron picks up his bag. "Lead on."

"Hold on. What if he's lying? What—" Scott cuts off as Fred fishes something from his backpack and tosses it. A package sails in the air like a white dove. Scott snatches it, uttering a low moan as he tears it open and shoves a brown cake into his mouth.

Nicole socks him on the shoulder. "Da-ad, you're supposed to *share*!"

So much for putting Nicole above our needs. Scott's forehead ripples in a pinched expression. "I need the calories. I'm starving."

"We're all starving."

Nicole's outrage transforms into relief when Fred passes her one, then David, then Cameron and me. I blink at the cellophane-wrapped cake that lands beside my hand. A wildness grips me as I rip into the plastic. The dessert is in my mouth before I've processed that I'm holding food.

Twinkies. I've never been a huge fan, but it tastes like pure decadence. Chocolate and sugar explode over my tongue, flooding my brain with euphoria.

Groaning, I swallow it down.

Within seconds, everybody demolishes the cakes. David licks the wrapping. I do the same.

"Thank God these things never expire," Fred says, unpacking his backpack to pull out more staples. "Who knows how long they've been sitting on that shelf?"

Shelf? Meaning, he found a *house*?

That's right, he mentioned a cabin. It's over. Hope soars through my stomach. David dives at the canned Bolognese and claws it open while Nicole watches, licking her lips. They tip its contents into the blackened pot. Cameron congratulates Fred with a thump on his back. "How did you find it?"

Fred's lip curves. "After you guys kicked me out, I wandered around and stumbled on a game trail. It led me to a road. I kept going. For hours and hours. I was hoping I'd flag a passing car, but on the second day, I saw it, smack dab in the middle of the woods. A cabin."

"If you got out, why come back?" asks Scott.

"Because there's no cell reception. I wasn't able to contact anyone, so I hustled back. Good thing I did, considering the state you're in."

Scott scowls.

"Yeah, you saved our butts," says Cameron.

Fred smiles, soaking in all the attention. "The cabin is crudely made. There's moss between the logs. A rock chimney. No car, but there are tire tracks. Someone built it against park regulations. Whoever did this will get in a lot of trouble once forest officers see it."

That's strange.

I pick up the crinkled plastic as unease spreads through my limbs. "Was anyone inside?"

"Nope," says Fred, sliding his hands into his pockets. "Completely abandoned."

Alarm bells ring in my head.

Mouth full of another helping of Twinkies, Scott sits upright, adopting his commanding posture. "All right, Fred, you're back on the team. Here's what we're going to do. We'll have a big meal. Then we'll set out for this so-called cabin."

Fred nods along. "I agree."

"Well, I don't." I crumple the wrapping as everyone turns around to face me. "Sorry, but this is ridiculous. I've never heard of anything so far-fetched in my life. You're all buying that he stumbled on a cabin? Really?"

Fred flinches as though I slapped him. Scott stares at me. In a frightening imitation of her father, Nicole rolls her eyes at me. "Stop it, Mom. You don't know what you're talking about."

"This is a private park. Logging is *illegal*. You can't haul a bunch of equipment into a forest and build a cabin." I point at Scott, whose narrowed gaze verges on menacing.

"Yesterday, Fred was *persona non grata*. Today, you're welcoming him with open arms."

"This is an emergency," Scott says in a clipped tone. "You know, like you keep harping on about. We have to put aside personal squabbles."

"What about when he 'sabotaged our resources'?"

"Hey, that wasn't me," Fred shouts.

"Right. That could've happened for several reasons. My guess is *someone* with poor impulse control opened the cans, starting gorging themself, and felt guilty about it." Scott's raking glare slides up and down my body.

Cameron makes a furious sound, but Nicole responds first. *"Shut the hell up* about Mom's weight."

I ball my fists, trembling. "You know, I *can* go three, sometimes five minutes without stuffing myself."

"I don't trust you," Scott seethes. "But Fred is telling us he found food, and all you want to do is criticize."

"There *is* no log cabin."

Scott seizes the empty can of spaghetti Bolognese, snarling. "Then how did he get this? Do you think it grows on trees? He got it from somewhere."

I shake my head. "Maybe he stashed it ahead of time."

Scott rolls his eyes, slapping his thighs. "For God's sake, I can't even. You're not equipped for high-stress environments."

I give up on convincing Scott, addressing my husband and two kids. "Doesn't anybody find this weird? We're on the verge of death, and then he magically finds this place with exactly what we need? It's very *deus ex machina.*"

Nicole stalks in front of me, red-faced and furious. "Read the room, Mom, and *shut up*. Nobody wants to hear your opinion."

I flinch. "Don't talk to me like that."

She rolls her eyes. "What will you do, ground me?"

"*Hey.* I'm trying to keep you safe—"

"Safe?" Her harsh laughter sinks another dart in my heart. "You're arguing with the person who just fed you. Why do you have to ruin everything?"

Scott's hand glides on her shoulder. "It boils down to your mother's need for drama. She has to be the center of attention. That's why she keeps inventing reasons to scare us."

"You're not much better, *Dad*," she snarls, shrugging off his touch. "The way you talk about Mom is disgusting. Why do you hate fat people?"

Scott colors fiercely. "I don't *hate* them. I just disapprove of the lifestyle."

"You're not helping," she screams, pain squeezing my heart. "Did you *ever* get along? Was there a moment when you actually loved her? Sometimes, I wonder if you *forced* her into having me."

Scott bristles, turning toward me. "See what you're doing to our daughter?"

Nicole flips Scott the bird.

Scott gapes at her. Then he musters his shock into outrage. "Apologize right now!"

My mouth slackens as she snatches her pack and storms off, David sprinting after her. He grabs her. She rips out of his grasp. Their angry voices echo toward us.

Scott watches them, hands on his hips. "Amber, I can't have you dividing us. If you continue to be a problem, I'll have to make a hard decision. Understand?"

Meaning he'll get rid of me? Cameron palms my arm, his polite way of telling me to shut up.

I shrug him off. "Go to hell, Scott."

Scott nods as though this was the response he expected, and walks off, shaking his head.

We rest for an hour. Then we leave, following Fred into the wilderness. Scott and Fred take point with Nicole trailing close behind. Despite my stomach churning with calories, my aches and pains are magnified. Nicole's words burrow deep into my heart. As promised, we reach a stretch of graveled road and decide to stop. It should fill me with confidence, but my insides clench as though we're in the sights of some predator. I lie down, making a pillow with my backpack. Cameron turns to face me, his soft brown gaze filled with sympathy.

"Honey, she didn't mean it."

"She did," I whisper. "I don't blame the kids for latching onto hope, but Scott? He's acting like we're saved because his brother *says* we are. The same guy who messed around with his wife. It's insane."

"Scott doesn't know that," he reminds me. "And that doesn't mean he's a murderer."

"Something is off about him." I steal a glance in Fred's direction. He sits cross-legged, beating a tune on empty aluminum cans. "Is he still taking his meds?"

He shrugs.

"I don't like this, Cam. Maybe I'm crazy from lack of food or...but I don't trust them. I needed to believe this has been an accident, but my gut says it's not."

"I'll keep my eyes open." Cameron grabs my arm, his voice lowering. "At the first sign of trouble, grab the kids and *run*. Understand?"

"Agreed."

THIRTY-FOUR
AMBER

We reach the cabin early on the second day.

It's as Fred described. A rustic refuge tucked in the woods. Sawed off trees surround us, their stumps raw. Sawdust clings to ferns. An axe is mounted in the cabin. I study its construction, scanning for clues. Whoever built it has carpentry skills. A tarp lies over the rafters, weighed down by leafy branches and stripped pieces of bark. Moss is stuffed in every crevice. Inside the cabin, food staples fill the wall.

I pick up a can of spaghetti Bolognese. My stomach growls as I scan the expiration date, which isn't for another couple of years. "This is crazy. All this in the middle of nowhere."

"I know, right?"

Fred puts on a show of bemused astonishment, but it's obviously staged. Why would he lead us here? Apparently, nobody shares my concerns. Cameron and the kids are in good spirits. Even Scott warms up, giving his brother a grudging smile.

"Wow. This is a great find."

I cross my arms. "Came in just the nick of time, too."

Fred grins. "Yeah. I can't believe it. At first I was like, damn, I must be hallucinating this place. It's unreal."

I frown. "Did you see anyone when you got here?"

"Nope," he says, shaking his head. "Empty. I didn't stay here long, so maybe they'll come back."

Or they're already here.

Fred excuses himself to go hunting. I can't escape the hair-raising feeling that this is a trap. We've been guided into a false sense of security, but why would Fred do that? I rack my brain until Scott's sharp tone cleaves my thoughts.

He plucks a can out of my stepson's grip. "I know we're hungry, but we have to make an inventory. It won't last forever."

David raises his eyebrows but doesn't object. I search for someone, *anyone*, to challenge Scott, but my husband has taken the ignore-the-idiot route. He's scouting the campground for tools. Nicole shoots me a guilty look.

Fine. I'll do it.

I clear my throat. "Kids, can you excuse us for a second?"

Nicole sets out her chin stubbornly, but David obeys in an instant, taking her hand when she doesn't follow. When they're outside, I face Scott.

"We desperately need food and we happen upon a cabin filled with Chef Boyardee? Don't you think this is shady?"

A shadow crosses his eyes. "What are you suggesting?"

"I don't know. I'm trying to imagine scenarios where this is built, stocked with food, and left behind. Who made this? Why abandon it?"

He shrugs. "They were lost."

"Jesus, Scott. Use your head. There's a road right there. Nobody *gets lost* with an axe, dozens of canned peaches, and a tarp." I grasp the makeshift doorknob and twist it, marveling at the detail. "Whoever built this made several trips from wherever they're staying."

He makes a flippant gesture. "So he wanted a permanent spot for camping. Not everybody can afford fancy cabins, Amber. Spots are booked months in advance. He probably did it a long time ago."

"No, they didn't. Everything is brand-new. Check out the tree stumps. They're bright, which means the trees were chopped recently." I suck in my bottom lip as Scott stares daggers at me. "This is weird."

Scott sighs, returning to his inventory list. "Only you would look a gift horse in the mouth."

"And look what happened to the Trojans when they didn't. Am I the only person with a working brain?"

Scott snorts, making a hashmark in a book he found in the cabin. "I just saved your life, and all you want to do is criticize."

"I'm sorry. *What?*"

"Yeah. If I hadn't insisted on following my brother, you would've starved to death."

This man is unbelievable. "Fred found the cabin. Not you. Second, you accused him of killing Laura. You ran him off camp."

"And thank God I did, because he discovered this."

"Are you suggesting that *you're* our savior?"

"Of course I am," he drawls, his swaggering arrogance on full display. "Because of my decision, we have a shelter with food to last us a month or more."

I glower at him, my teeth grinding. "I'd admire the mental gymnastics you're doing to make yourself the hero, yet again, if our lives weren't at risk. I'm begging you. Put your ego aside and *think*. This isn't right."

Scott points at me. "Or you can't stand being wrong and you're looking for problems."

"No. My gut tells me that something's off."

"Then ignore it, because your instincts are wrong. You wanted us to sit tight, remember? If we had, we never would've stumbled upon that tent...or the road...or this. If we'd listened to you, we'd all be dead."

"Why is this food here?"

"For God's sake. *Who cares?* I don't give a rat's ass how it got here. What does it matter if it keeps us alive?" Scott throws down the book where he's been tallying his inventory and massages his temples. "I can't deal with you when you're hysterical."

"You're going to hear me out, damn it. We need to do what's best for the kids."

His accusatory glare dives into me. "Speaking of, we should discuss your stepson's relationship with our daughter."

Scott knows. Color me surprised.

My stomach caves in. "I just found out. What about you?"

"I had no idea until this trip," he says in a halting voice.

"It's recent, I think." I gnaw on my lip, avoiding his accusatory glare. "They're around each other a lot. I thought they were getting along."

Scott snorts. "They sure are."

I grimace. "Let's talk to them when we get back."

"This has to be stopped in its tracks. I don't approve. I've already warned the cheeky jerk."

I bristle. "What did you say to him?"

"That if I ever see his hand on my daughter again, I'll remove that hand." Scott grunts, picking up the book to flip to the page with his list. "You'd think a mother would be more vigilant. How long has this been a thing?"

My cheeks burn. "I have no idea."

He brings his hands together in a mock clap. "Parent of the year over here. Can we get a round of applause?"

"*Scott.*"

"How could you *not know?* They're under your roof most of the time. Are you so wrapped up in your husband that you don't notice them?" He shakes his head, tutting. "Nice parenting."

The hurt is swift and brutal. It rips open something vulnerable in my chest. My throat closes up as Scott disappears in a haze of unshed tears. My hand trembles with the need to slap him, hard, but if I do, I'll be the crazy one.

So I curl up on the floor. Faint cracks in the wall illuminate four dark corners. A pile of firewood sits beside the door, saturating the air with the smell of freshly cut wood. Our possessions are scattered everywhere. The insulation isn't perfect, but it's better than outside.

I lie on a mattress of dead leaves, crying. I'm sick of sleeping on the ground. I can't wait to dive into my bed at home, put my phone on mute, and go to sleep without the echo of Scott's voice.

The door opens as I close my eyes. Blinding outdoor light silhouettes my daughter's petite frame. She walks inside and sits beside me, frowning.

"Mom?" she whispers, tremulous. "Are you awake?"

I roll on my back. "What is it?"

"I wanted to say that I'm sorry. Earlier, I didn't mean what I said. I know you're doing your best."

She pats my arm, and my insides twist. More and more, it feels like she's channeling her father's disrespectful attitude. Like I'm a hysterical woman who can't be trusted. Rage grips my stomach. The urge to launch into a tirade against her father grows, but I swallow it down and force a smile.

"Thank you."

She nods. "Dad says we should treat you with compassion."

How wise of him. I grit my teeth, sitting up. "I'm not interested in my ex-husband's opinions."

"Don't be like that."

"Damn that court order." My breath comes out in a strangled sob. "I wanted you to have one nice memory of being together with your parents. But it was a disaster. I did my best...I wanted to make you happy, but I won't do this anymore. Scott and I don't get along and we never will. This is our last vacation with him. Once we're home, I'm done with him."

Nicole's lip trembles.

"I'm sorry," I whisper brokenly, my throat tightening. "I wanted to give you a perfect family. I did, but real life isn't perfect. It's messy."

"I know that," she grinds out. "I gave up on you getting back together when I was thirteen. I just wanted you to exist without killing each other."

What if that's his goal?

Tension grips my guts. My jaw clenches, but I don't dare voice my suspicion. "Nicole, about what you said earlier. I loved your father. I did. But people fall out of love."

"I know."

"And he never forced me to have you. Believe me, sweetie. We wanted you so badly."

I pull her into a hug. After a while, we disengage. Nicole wipes her face, gets up, and leaves. I'm left in the darkness, my pulse thundering. Now I'm definitely not falling asleep. I search the inside of the cabin. It's dark, so I can't see much, but I crawl on my hands and knees. My fingers brush a square object with a supple texture. Then I open the door to illuminate the room. Light spills over a leather-bound book with gilded trim.

I flip it to the first page.

THIRTY-FIVE
LAURA'S DIARY

I hate Amber Pierce.

I hate her perfect hair. Her stripper lips. Her stupidly gorgeous face. The fake way she welcomed me with open arms. How my husband can't stop talking about her. If I have to hear Scott whine about his ex-wife one more day, I'll geld him. What does he see in that know-it-all?

My therapist says I should express myself more, so here I am, airing my grievances. I'll use this diary to purge my negative thoughts. Hopefully, it'll prevent me from doing something crazy. She'd deserve it, though. She turned my husband against me. He used to be attentive and sweet. Now he's a bitter jerk.

It's Amber's fault.

She seduces every man she comes across. I'm sick of it. I can't stand watching Scott turn into a drooling moron when he's in Amber's orbit. Whenever there's a family event, they trade barbs like an old married couple, and he acts like a complete idiot. It embarrasses me. Then I blow up at him as soon as we're alone.

Fighting is *our* love language. When we're screaming at each other, our relationship is in a good place because we're fighting *for* us. Things are bad when he goes days without glancing in my direction, when we exchange pleasantries like roommates and fall into a mundane routine.

There's no passion anymore. I can loudly praise another man's looks over dinner, and Scott doesn't blink. But if *Amber* so much as *strokes* Cameron in front of Scott, he throws a tantrum. Scott should be indifferent toward his ex. He's not. He obviously has a thing for Amber.

She knows it, too. She provokes him all the time. Attention-seeking twat. Stop making eyes at my husband.

Scott is mine.

○

SCOTT IS RIDICULOUS AGAIN.

Now it's his leg. He injured it years ago and has nagging aches. Instead of visiting the physical therapist like I *told* him, he gripes about the pain. He complains. A lot.

My shrink says I'm his emotional dumping ground, which is right. He doesn't respect my feelings whatsoever. We barely have sex, and when we do, it's very one-sided. It's like I'm a doll he uses to get off, so I've been fulfilling that need somewhere else.

Yes, I'm cheating.

I'm sleeping with his brother, Fred. He's not my type, but he gives me attention. Blows up my phone constantly. He's written a song about me. He left a message the other day, playing it. It's nice. Fred is a gifted musician, and his voice is tender for a man his size.

I've set it as my ringtone. It blasted in the kitchen while Scott was zoned out in front of ESPN. He didn't recognize it. He will eventually, and this will explode in my face. Whatever. Scott *should* find out. Part of me wonders if that's why I'm writing about it in this diary. All he has to do is open the damned book, and he'll know why our marriage is in shambles. But he won't. That would require him to care, and he doesn't. I'm tempted to write "Laura's Diary" on the cover, but that's too desperate. I feel pathetic enough as is. I just want what's owed to me.

I'm his wife.

What must I do to make him notice me?

AMBER KNOWS.

I'm scribbling this in the scant lighting by the fireplace. My hands are shaking, but I have to get this out of me. *Amber saw Fred and I.* We were on a date at the movie theater. Fred had his paws all over me. She looked surprised, but there was no confusion. She knows what she saw.

Scott's asleep upstairs.

She'll notify him this weekend. I'm sure the sanctimonious prude can't wait to dish on my affair, which is ironic considering the skeletons in *her* family's closet. There's no way Scott will let this slide. He's always hated his brother. He'll flip out on me and hopefully, we'll have a long, messy fight and have amazing make-up sex. Or he'll be so irate that he'll demand a divorce, but if he brings up that word, I'll tell him what I told my therapist.

Over my dead body.

THIRTY-SIX
AMBER

The door swings open.

I stuff the diary under a backpack as Fred's grizzled face pokes inside, his gaze landing on me. His brows flicker. "Everything all right?"

My heart thumps madly. "Y-yeah."

"Can you lend me a hand?"

I swallow tightly, hoping like hell that the diary is hidden. Though I'm not sure why it matters. Whoever left it on the ground expected it would be read.

Fred widens the door, his brows furrowing. "Amber?"

My frayed nerves fire alarms in every direction. "What do you need me to do?"

"I'll tell you when we're there."

I stand, disoriented. A frustrated scream builds at the back of my throat, but I bury it and follow Fred outside. I have to leave this room and separate myself from the bilge in that diary.

Gorgeous shafts of sunlight beam through the canopy of oaks, heating up my skin. Fred picks up his sack, slings it over his shoulder, and gestures for me to follow. I stride past David and Nicole, who take turns chopping firewood. Everyone is involved in some sort of domestic task. Cameron is off somewhere, foraging. Scott is scouting. I stroll onto a worn path, not caring about our destination.

I'm reeling over the awful things Laura wrote about me. She hated me? *Why?* I cringe, imagining Scott griping about me over the dinner table. No wonder she felt unappreciated, but that's no excuse.

My God. So many red flags. She had problems. Big ones. I had no idea their relationship was so...toxic. All this time, I'd assumed Laura was finding comfort in Fred's arms, but she was just using him to make Scott jealous. I can't wrap my head around that logic.

Why was her diary on the floor? Someone must've fished it out of her bag, read it, and dumped it. Who would do that? Is Scott playing games with his brother? Laura used Fred. Perhaps Scott wants to rub it in his face. That could be...but Fred is the likely culprit. I'm sure reading that horrible entry hurt. He must feel betrayed.

Either he took the diary off Laura's corpse while the rest of us were distracted...or he's known about this for months. Does that mean that *he* killed Laura? Or was it Scott after demanding a divorce? That's extreme, but Laura seems like the type of person who pushes people toward extremes. *Over my dead body.*

A chill spider-crawls down my spine.

Hanging around with Fred in the middle of the woods is the last place I want to be. Disappearing into the forest with him was a monumentally bad decision. Panicking, I grope for my can of bear mace, but I left it behind. I force my voice into one of determined calm.

"Hey, Fred? I need to go back."

He turns, beckoning me. "We're almost there."

We're surrounded by ferns, the trees like soldiers standing at attention. Perfect for hiding a body. The thought tears at my insides.

I stand still, rooted to the spot.

He swears under his breath and approaches me, grabbing my elbow. Tugging, he pulls me into an area with flattened grass. "It's right there. Promise me you won't freak out."

He holds back a bush, indicating I should step through. Blood splatters the leaves as though something stumbled through it, mortally wounded. Blinking rapidly, I move forward.

"*Come on,*" he roars. "We don't have all day."

Against my better judgment, I obey.

And I gasp at the horrific sight.

THIRTY-SEVEN
AMBER

A dead buck lies on its side. The feathered head of a crossbow bolt pokes through its chest. I'm not familiar with deer anatomy, but it looks like it pierced its heart.

"You killed it?" I ask, surprised by the dismay in my voice.

"Yeah. I got him a few minutes ago."

Fred stoops beside the deer and drops the crossbow with his quiver of arrows. I chew my lip. "Wow, Fred... that's...great."

He gives me a smile that stops short of his eyes. "This is enough meat to feed us for a couple of weeks, but we have to process the carcass now."

"What do you need me to do?"

"Help me process the deer."

Fred drags the arrow from the hide, and I turn away, grimacing. "I'm not the best person for this."

"Well, I couldn't find your husband, and I doubt the kids have the stomach for this."

Fred unsheathes his knife and gets to work. I wince, stopping myself from wringing my hands. *Get over it, Amber.* I can't help it. I'm squeamish. A brief reel from my favorite chef comes to mind. In the video, she demonstrated how to prepare a spatchcocked chicken. I could barely tolerate the scissors snapping through twig-like bones as I cut around the spine. A full-body shudder runs through me.

"Can't we…uh, drag it to camp and do it there?"

"Bad idea," he says, aiming the knife at the deer's sternum. "It's better to take care of this at the kill site. I want to avoid attracting bears to where we're sleeping."

Makes sense. Bears have extremely sensitive noses, or so I've heard. The blood-scented air will attract them to this location. Panic wells in my throat. Great, now I'm worried about wild animals.

"What if a bear finds us?"

Fred pats the mace canister hanging from his backpack. "But it's useless if it charges us."

"Good to know."

"If you see one, don't run. They're just as fast as a race-horse, downhill and uphill. Don't climb trees. They'll come after you. You can shout as long as it's not shrill. Anything that sounds like prey will encourage them to attack." He bends over to make the first cut, and straightens. "I think it depends on which bear it is. If it's brown or grizzly, you're supposed to fight. If it's black, you play dead. Or is it the other way around?"

He shrugs and returns to his task. I avert my gaze as Fred carves up the deer. It's a gory process that only interests me because there will eventually be steaks. My mouth floods with saliva. Suddenly, I'm ravenous.

Fred finishes stripping the skin and slings the deer's flanks over my shoulder. Weighed down by meat, I follow the game trail back to the cabin. David swears when I stumble into camp. He jogs to my side.

"Holy crap. Is that deer?"

"Part of it, yeah. Where's your dad?"

"I'll get him."

David helps me unload the flanks, placing them on a pile of wood, and takes off. Nicole sets up a makeshift pallet with firewood. By the time we've hauled everything to camp, Scott and Cameron have returned. Everybody is ecstatic, especially my husband, who has never gone so many days without meat. There's a lot of back-slapping and high fives. David starts a fire as Cameron sharpens sticks for roasting. Before long, cooking meat scents the air with its ambrosial smell. Fat slips off steaks, evaporating in the flames with a pleasant hiss. I'm counting down the seconds until I can shove it down my throat.

The guys lay logs across each other in a pyramid with an opening. David cuts the meat into strips for jerky. There's one knife, so we take turns. Once it's built, Fred hangs the ribbons of muscle inside the hut. We work tirelessly until the whole deer is processed. Then Fred adds the finishing touch—a severed deer head. It perches on the smokehouse like an effigy for a horned god. Fred carefully transfers glowing charcoals inside the pyramid and sets a log over them.

"All right. I reckon we can eat," says Fred, bouncing on his feet.

I grab my stick. Steam wafts from the charred skin. I risk a burned tongue and sink my teeth into the savory perfection. I could cry at how good it tastes. Everybody's quiet except for the sounds of tearing flesh and swallowing. Cameron moans, juice dribbling down his chin.

"Best steak I've ever had."

Scott licks his fingers. "If we had salt, it'd be perfect."

David tears into his meal as Nicole takes a bite, frowning. "Why does yours look so weird, Uncle Fred?"

Fred plucks at the dark red meat. "It's the deer's heart."

Nicole's eyes widen. "Why?"

"I always eat the heart of every kill."

Creepy. Especially since that frosty delivery seems aimed at Scott. It's hard to miss Fred's budding frustration with his brother, who keeps taking credit for everything he's done. I wonder if that's their dynamic. David wipes his mouth with the back of his hand as tapping fills the air. I glance at my husband, who knocks the handle of the bloodstained knife against a hollowed can.

"I'd like to make a toast to the man of the hour," announces Cameron with a nod toward Fred. "Fred. If you could all join me and er—lift your sticks."

Everybody follows suit. Scott's lip quirks, but he complies.

NOT A NORMAL FAMILY 261

"When my wife told me you were coming on the trip, I wasn't happy. I thought, damn, another Maxwell to deal with? I didn't know you that well. I had no idea that you would save our lives. Fred, each of us owes you a deep debt. Not just for finding the cabin and shooting the deer, but making these fires, night after night, and never complaining about it. You're an amazing guy and I'm so glad that you're here. Without you, I don't think we would've survived. Cheers."

We clack our sticks together and lower them.

"Thanks, Uncle Fred," chimes Nicole. "You're the best."

David leans over and gives Fred, who seems touched by the attention, a fist bump. I'm swept by the wave of gratitude for the food. I hug Fred, whispering an apology in his ear. I'll make it up to him when we're home. It was stupid of me to doubt him.

Fred soaks in the admiration, two pink patches burning his cheeks. "Thank you, guys. That means a lot."

"We're sorry for doubting you, right, Scott? Where is he?" Cameron wheels around to face Scott, who wears a constipated expression, and slaps his back. "Come on, man. Congratulate your brother."

"Congrats," he murmurs.

Fred's gentle laughter ripples the air, landing like a whip on Scott's face. My ex-husband twists his stick and squeezes. Cameron and Fred's banter keeps adding fuel to the fire. My heart hammers as I watch Scott's mood transform from indifference to red-faced fury. I glance at Cameron, but he's focused on Fred.

"We'll throw a party in your honor. I'm serious. Maybe I can even book you gigs. My startup has a few events coming up. Would you be interested?"

Fred's eyes light up. "Yeah."

"I'll talk to my event coordinator as soon as we're back," says Cameron. "Do you have a website?"

"I do," Fred blurts, reaching for his phone before he seems to remember our situation. "I'll text you when we—"

The stick in Scott's clenched fists breaks, the sound as ominous as a limb snapping. A primitive warning blazes in my head as Cameron leans toward him, frowning.

"What's wrong?"

"He. Didn't. Save us." Scott hurls the broken stick in the fire, throwing Fred a black look. "We don't need *you* to survive."

A humorless smile spreads across Fred's lips. "Whose meat did you just finish eating?"

"They're sucking up to you right now because they think you're valuable, but if we were home they'd call you a psycho for your creepy hobby." Scott points at me, stirring the hot coals in my chest.

"Stop acting like a bullying jerk," I snarl. "I have zero issues with hunting. People did it all the time before we got complacent with prepackaged meat."

Scott sucks grease from his thumb, chuckling. "Yeah, well, disemboweling small critters and displaying them has nothing to do with hunting."

My stomach drops. I gape at his brother, expecting him to react with rage, but his wounded face storms with hurt.

"That was one time," he whispers.

Scott stares at him silently.

"I went to therapy," says Fred in a louder voice.

"That's part of the problem." Scott throws the bone he's picked clean. It rolls and hits the base of the bloodstained logs we used to carve the deer. "All that therapist does is validate every screwed-up thing you do."

Not again. "Scott."

"Shut up, Amber. You never saw what he did to animals when he was a kid. One morning, our stepmom woke up to find squirrels lined up with their guts ripped out. The psycho confessed. He'd done it because he wanted to scare her into leaving. Dad didn't let him hunt after that incident."

"You just can't help yourself," Fred explodes, shooting upright. "Anything to humiliate the black sheep of the family. Being Dad's favorite wasn't enough. You have to push me down like I've been pushed my whole life."

Scott tosses a handful of leaves into the campfire, his tone sour. "You think I'm the favorite? You're all Dad talks about. He guilted me into bringing you here."

Cameron straightens and clears his throat. "Guys. This is a stupid argument."

"Not to me," says Scott.

Cameron sighs heavily. "Why do you have to be like this?"

"Because you're praising him like he's Jesus for stumbling on a freaking cabin. Do you think I couldn't have done that? Or shot a deer? Dad took me hunting, too. I can do everything he's done."

The nerve of this man. "You're right, Scott. I have *tons* of participation trophies in my office at home. I'll mail you one as soon as we're out of here."

"Shut the hell up, Amber."

Cameron bristles. "I'm tired of you being rude to my wife."

"Yeah, well, I'm sick of everyone here." Scott draws his legs up and stands, a thread of warning in his voice. "You're all a bunch of losers."

Everybody but Nicole and I laughs. My stomach tenses as a cloud settles on Scott's shoulders. His mouth dips into a deeper frown.

Fred gets up, hands on his hips. "You know, Scott. All my life, people have been saying that I'm lucky to have a brother. I keep waiting for this brotherly connection to kick in. It never has. Know why? Because *you're* an asshole."

Scott balls his fists. "You're no Dalai Lama, either. You're hiding something."

"*So are you*. You're pretending everything's okay, even though Laura told me you lost your job!"

Oh God. Shut up, Fred.

Scott flinches. "Why would Laura tell you anything?"

I know why, but Scott doesn't. I'm guessing he's still in the dark. If Fred tells him, he'll figure out I lied, and all hell will break loose. *Don't look at Fred.* I'm terrified that my expression will galvanize him to confess. I try to hold off, but the temptation is too strong.

Don't do it, Fred. Please.

Fred's eyes sparkle with savage laughter as he lays down the anvil. "Because I've been sleeping with your wife."

Nicole makes a pained sound. David swears loudly. I brace myself for the explosion, but Scott chuckles.

"Did you hear me? I'm sleeping with your wife."

Scott glowers at Fred, his mouth twisting. "What's wrong with you? Can't we have one dinner without you going nuts? Are you off your meds again?"

Fred reaches into his jacket pocket and produces a pill bottle, rattling its contents. "I haven't missed a day."

Scott's lip curls. "Then you should fire your psychiatrist."

"Guys," interjects Cameron. "Come on."

"He's cracking stupid jokes about my dead wife, and you're taking *his* side?"

Cameron wets his lips, but says nothing. Fred seems dangerously off-kilter. A vein pulses on his forehead. "She loves me, you know. She said it the second time I was with her."

Cameron rubs his face. "For God's sake, Fred."

To my horror, Fred points me out. *"Amber knows about us."*

Scott laughs, waving him off.

Fred's stare impales me. "Tell him, Amber. Tell Scott what you saw at the movie theater."

A stone sinks into my stomach. It's too quiet. Like the silence after a coffin is lowered into the ground. Scott cocks his head. His intense glare roams my face, as though studying my reaction. Cameron's dark eyes flash a gentle warning, but it's no use. Scott can always tell when I'm lying.

I swallow hard, my pulse pounding. "It's true. I-I saw them making out in the Majestic Bay Theatre a month ago."

Scott's smirk wilts.

Heat claims my cheeks. "I'm sorry, Scott."

Fred shifts from one foot to another, the slight movement enough to break Scott's paralysis. He grabs Fred by his jacket and slams him into a tree trunk. "What did you do to her, you disgusting *freak*?"

Scott shakes him with the unhinged rage of a sleep-deprived parent toward their screaming toddler. Fred shoves him off with a snarl. Scott launches at him with a vicious sock to his gut. Fred drops, moaning. Cameron jumps in between them.

"This is not the time. *Stop.* I know how you feel, but we need to focus on getting out of here." Cameron staggers with Scott's rough shove, but he doesn't back off. "*Hey.* Look at me, not him. She made a mistake. She was probably drunk, right? That doesn't mean she didn't love you. It's not like they were having an ongoing thing."

"We've been having an affair for months," Fred brags, wiping blood from the corner of his mouth. "I see her twice a week while you're at CrossFit."

Oh hell.

Anguish twists Scott's face. My pulse races as I watch my ex absorb the news. I thought I'd be elated to see him suffer, but honestly…this brings back horrible memories. I replay how I burst into tears at the urgent care clinic. If Scott never understood the humiliation of a married woman asking for a full panel of STD tests, he does now.

Scott's shoulders curl forward. I almost think he'll slump off, defeated. Then he elbows Cameron out of the way and lunges at Fred, who darts to the side. Scott feints to the left, grabs Fred's shirt, and hurls his brother into the campfire.

Nicole and I scream, but luckily, Fred stumbles out of the flames in a shower of red sparks. Screaming, he bats at his leg. Scott launches at Fred with a running jump-kick that flattens him. They thrash on the ground. Cameron seizes Scott by his middle, but he's barely able to hold on to his thrashing limbs. It's hard to discern what he's shouting, but one word stands out:

"Deadbeat."

"Careful, Scott. You're jobless," quips Fred as he rolls up his sleeves. "Soon it'll be *you* asking Daddy for handouts."

"At least I won't be a boring hack who screws his brother's wife."

"Right," Fred laughs.

"Your music *sucks*. It sounds like Creed."

Fred shrugs. "Your wife loves my music."

Oh Jesus.

Scott breaks free of Cameron, snarling. Cameron manages to seize his shirt. He yanks Scott backward, pinning him in a headlock. Cameron's furious gaze lands on Fred. "Knock it off, damn it! You're not helping."

"What did you do to Laura?" Scott bellows, still fighting off Cameron. "You must've tricked her. Blackmailed her into touching you. She would never do it."

"I take care of her. You don't. She looks depressed when she's with you. She told me I treated her better than you. She talked about leaving you." Fred's faint smile holds sadness as he turns away from Scott, his voice thickening. "She sees me like nobody else does. That's why I-I've been so upset...I love her."

Big mistake, Fred.

My clenched teeth chatter as Scott points at him, his voice taut and low. "You killed her."

Fred shakes his head.

"I knew it. Oh God. It was *you*. You sick son of a—*you* did this. She turned you down, didn't she? Then you threw her down the mountain."

"No, that's not what happened!"

Scott tears out of Cameron's hold. He collides with his brother like a boulder. They both go down, but Scott is up in a flash. He straddles his brother's waist. Seizes Fred's throat and squeezes. I scream at him to stop. Everybody does, but Scott ignores us. His fingers whiten on Fred, who begins to sputter. Fred gouges Scott's hands with his nails, but nothing can shake him out of his rage.

Cameron yanks him off Fred.

Coughing, Fred props himself to a seated position. As Cameron leans over, his hand on Fred's back, Scott grabs something from the fire. Fred's knife. Scott makes a violent movement. Cameron screams just as the blade enters Fred's chest.

THIRTY-EIGHT
THE PAST

A dish shatters.

I guess Dad's fighting with his new girlfriend. That's different. Usually he does everything in his power to avoid fights. Colorful curse words echo through the vent near the door. I log out of my computer and head downstairs. Clutching my empty cup, I descend the stairs into the kitchen, where a short, plump woman kneels on the tiles, pushing together shards of porcelain into a pile.

"Where's Dad?"

"Hey. Nice to see you out of your room. I think he's in his office—*ow*. Shoot. I nicked myself." She clutches her hand with a pained hiss as blood oozes from a cut. "Do you happen to know where—"

"Bandages are in the butler's pantry."

By her wide-eyed expression, I realize she has no idea what that means. Sighing, I put my mug down and fetch them. She waits, chewing on her lip. I set the first aid box on the counter.

"Thank you. I'm a bit of a wuss when it comes to blood." She takes some gauze, pressing it over the wound. "So gross."

"Didn't your mom teach you not to pick up sharp things with your hands?"

"Yeah, I know." She makes an exaggerated wince as she wraps it in a bandage. "Um...can you also get the dustpan? Please?"

I grab the broom and sweep up the mess as she holds the dustpan. Once it's in the trash, she pats my shoulder with her uninjured hand. "Thanks."

This girl gives me damsel in distress vibes, which is not my dad's type. He goes for very controlling, high-strung women who are all about themselves. I can't wait to find out what fresh hell she has planned for me.

My lip curls in a sneer. I head for the fridge, but she intercepts me with a plate covered with foil.

I grasp the warm plate. "What's this?"

"French toast," she says, lighting up with an infectious grin. "I heard it's your favorite."

"Are you eating with me?"

"I thought we could have breakfast together."

My jaw tenses. Staying out of sight is how I manage living with Dad. Mostly, we pretend the other doesn't exist.

That's my preferred level of contact, but my dad's girl-friend is family-oriented. She keeps forcing us into the same room.

But I love French toast. My stomach growls at the scent of eggs fried to perfection. I sit at the kitchen table, where there's already a glass of orange juice and a jar of maple syrup. Tearing off the foil, I gaze at the fat slices of bread and strips of bacon. Powdered sugar dusts the surface. She's topped it with raspberries and thick wads of butter.

I frown at her. "Is this a bribe?"

"It's breakfast. Eat."

I shovel it down my throat. She sets down a mug of tea in front of me. Green. Steeped just how I like it. As far as bribes go, this isn't bad. She's putting in the effort. Why, though?

"How is it?" she asks with a sly glance.

"It's crap. I've had better at Denny's."

She rolls her eyes, still smiling. "I can tell by the way you're devouring it."

"Doesn't mean anything. I'm hungry."

"Well, there's bacon in the skillet." She gets up, helping herself. "Want some?"

"Don't bother. It's charred."

She lets out a resigned sigh. "Okay. I guess I'll finish it by myself. Unless you're willing to take some off my hands."

I nod, irritated. "Whatever."

She waddles over, dropping three pieces on my plate. As I demolish them, she sips her coffee, looking up from her phone to beam at me. Why is she always in a good mood? I've been pushing her for weeks, acting out, hoping she'll drop this act, but my insults roll off her shoulders like rain. Is she brain-dead? Or is she the type that internalizes her rage until it's too much?

"There's more French toast. I made a huge batch and put them in the freezer, so all you have to do is pop them in the toaster." An easy smile plays on her lips. "You're just like Cam. Both of you inhale your food like it'll run off."

You don't know what you're talking about.

I glide my fork in the maple syrup and suck the juice from the tines.

"So I thought that you and I should go somewhere today. You like books, right? I figured we could visit that indie bookstore in Capitol Hill and hit Ivar's for lunch. Then, maybe, an alt-rock show in Fremont."

That sounds perfect, which makes me suspicious. I finish the last of the bacon, annoyed at this stupid woman, who thinks she can swoop in and win me over with a snap of her fingers.

"Why would I do *any* of that with you?"

"Well...I moved in. We're going to be in each other's lives. We should get to know one another. Want a refill on that tea?"

"What are you, my butler?"

A bright flush invades her pale cheeks. "I'll take that as a no."

"And I'd rather kill myself with a thousand paper cuts than 'get to know you.' I have *zero* interest in you. Besides, I won't be around for much longer."

She looks stricken.

"I didn't mean it *that* way," I grumble, stabbing three raspberries with my fork. "When I graduate, I'm going to a college far away."

"Oh. I'm sorry to hear that. Can I be nosy and ask you why?"

I consider telling her, but why bother? She won't believe me, like everybody else. "Look, thanks for the food and the pep talk, or whatever this is, but I'm not buying this routine. You don't give a damn about me. I don't care about you."

"I care about you."

My chest burns at the lie. If by some miracle she's a decent person, which is impossible, she'll take off the second she figures out my dad. He invented fake backstories. Lied through his teeth about my upbringing. She has no idea I killed her two predecessors. Once she finds out, she'll leave and never think twice about either of us.

"You can talk to me," she says, a question shimmering in her eyes. "I'm not your dad's proxy. I don't report what you say to him."

True. She could've ratted on me about the rude things I've said, but she hasn't. She's going for the long con.

"He doesn't care about me."

Her hand glides over mine and squeezes. It feels nice. "I promise you, he does. And so do I."

I shake her off, immediately missing her warmth. "I don't believe you."

"I grill him about you all the time. He said that becoming an author is your dream. He told me that you love Ivar's and you're into alternative rock and that you hate museums. He mentioned you don't have your driver's permit yet, which is crazy. You're sixteen. We need to get you on the road. If you don't want to hang out, let's make a trip to the DMV."

My grip fumbles on the fork. It clatters on the table as I sit there, digesting her words. I've wanted a learner's permit since I turned sixteen, but my controlling jerk of a father would never let me. I'd give anything to gain my independence, assuming this isn't a trick.

"What do you want?"

"Your gratitude," she grunts, giving my shoulder a playful flick. "An adjustment to your tone, perhaps? Maybe you could respond to 'good morning' with less snark?"

I open my mouth to agree before I come to my senses. What am I, an idiot? She's lying.

"Okay, how about this? Thank you, future stepmom, for barging in my life and bringing your annoying daughter to live with us. Fixing me breakfast *totally* makes up for the huge inconvenience that is your existence."

"Why are you so difficult?"

"Because I see through this cheap attempt to flatter me."

Her chiding enrages me, and the lively twinkle in her gaze is like gasoline on fire. "This isn't flattery. Cooking is my love language. And for the record, it wasn't cheap. I got those raspberries from the farmer's market."

Big whoop. "The last one he was with did that, too. You're all the same."

"I'm not like them. I promise."

"Your promises are worthless to me."

I stand up, knocking my chair over. Then I throw my dish in the sink. It shatters.

"Hey. Those are from Pottery Barn!"

I shoot her a twisted smile. "Oops."

She stands, hands on her hips. "Apologize right now, or you're punished."

Good. She's finally acting in a way that makes sense. Let's see what she picks. Locking me in the basement? Taking away my food? What's in store for me? I sneer and wait, challenging her to go through it.

She points upstairs, her arm trembling. "Go to your room."

Really? That's what you're going with?

I snort, marching upstairs. My feet pound the steps. I charge inside and slam the door. Meadow, asleep in her dog bed, startles awake. I pace my bedroom, fuming. If she thinks I'll let her take control, she's mistaken.

I won't be her victim. I'll be her nightmare.

THIRTY-NINE
THE PRESENT

Fred is dead.

A knife sticks out from his chest, and his eyes stare at the heavens. I make a show of hand wringing and screaming like the others, but I couldn't care less.

Fred sucks. Nobody likes him, but he's tolerated because he's family. The self-indulgent jerk is wrapped up in his feelings. He doesn't realize that his actions affect other people, and he's extremely annoying. If I had to listen to another drawn-out story about his glory days in college, I would've lost my mind.

Every time I'm forced into a room with him, it's an effort not to tell him to shut up. He's such a narcissist. He can't go one minute without inserting his unsolicited opinion, which is often wrong, and he belches. Constantly. It's revolting. I'll be at the dinner table with him, looking at him dead in the eye, and he'll let it rip. No self-awareness.

Sleeping with another man's wife—strike one. Betraying your brother—strike two. Acting like a disgusting slob—strike three. Fred was begging to die.

I pat his pockets, pretending that I'm trying to shake him awake. I slip into his pocket. I grab something small and flexible. A guitar pick. *Fantastic*. He'll never ruin another family gathering with that noise he calls "music." I walk away, giving the body one last glance. He's gone, just like his horrible girlfriend. I hope there is an afterlife so he can reflect on his poor choices.

I replay his widened gaze when the knife sank into his chest. It reminded me of the mug shot of Brock Turner, the college kid who got a slap on the wrist for attempted rape. Men like him are used to getting what they want. They're always surprised by the order of the universe turning against them.

Just like my next victim will be. They won't see it coming.

FORTY
AMBER

Am I next?

Scott stands over his brother's body, his face glistening. He squeezes his eyes shut. He winces when he opens them, as though hoping his horrible mistake might vanish. Strange noises stream from his mouth—pleading whimpers and loud swearing. He slaps his head with violent swings of his bloody hand.

Cameron tried to revive Fred, but he's gone. Unlike with Laura, there is no funeral. Nobody dares float the suggestion. All I do is watch, openmouthed. Cameron palms my back, the weight of his hand pitting me with nausea. I don't know why. I've vomited everything in my stomach.

"You okay?" he asks.

My trembling lips part with a burst of mirthless laughter. "My ex-husband is a murderer. We're lost. We're never getting home."

"We will. We'll figure it out."

"He killed Nicole's uncle right in front of her."

My only consolation is that Nicole is safe, but I don't know for how long. She attempts to approach Fred, but David pulls her hard against his body.

"Dad," she whispers in a tear-smothered voice. "What did you do?"

Fear knots inside me as his gaze flicks to our daughter.

"Nothing," he declares in an oddly composed tone. "I-I didn't mean to."

"But you murdered him," says David.

Scott rounds on me, screaming. "This is *your* damned fault. You let me invite Fred to this trip without a warning."

"I'm sorry—*I let you?*" I say, hardening ruthlessly. "You told me he was coming. You decided that. Not me. And I couldn't tell you about the affair on the morning of this disastrous vacation."

Spittle flies from Scott's mouth as he jabs a finger in my face. "You had months to come clean about what was going on."

"I wasn't sure if I should tell you. If you'd even believe me." I cut across his protests. "No, I'm sorry Scott, but you can't blame me for what you did to him. That is one hundred percent on you."

"I get it. You wanted to give me a taste of my medicine." Scott hurls his arm out, bellowing. "You *want* me to break. You want me to lose my mind and kill my brother!"

Cameron hisses at me to drop it, so I shut my mouth. I grab Nicole by the elbow and yank her from her father. Scott beats his own skull. Then he screams, smashing his fist into a tree. Over and over, he pummels the bark.

I drag Nicole to Cameron and David, whose tense expressions mirror each other. We huddle by the fire. Nicole sobs into her hands, looking just as upset as when she learned her classmate, Erica, had died by suicide. David reassures her with a hand on her back as Cameron's gentle whisper floats over the group.

"Everybody be quiet. Don't talk to him. Don't reason with him. Give him an hour to cool off, okay? He has the knife and that damned crossbow. There might be more things lying around. I don't want anybody going near him. Especially you, Amber."

"Dad's gone crazy," Nicole says, her widened eyes tracking Scott as he sits down and rocks back and forth. "He killed Uncle Fred."

"He didn't mean to," David murmurs.

I replay the blade plunging into Fred's chest, shuddering. It looked like Scott meant it, but before this trip, Scott didn't have a violent bone in his body. Sure, he could be intense, but he wasn't *evil*. Losing his job, the infidelity, getting the whole family lost, and Laura's death—they must've shattered his fragile ego. The shell protecting his sanity broke. He must've been fighting to keep the madness inside.

Maybe I *have* to believe that.

It's too easy to blame the extreme circumstances. So far, everybody who betrayed Scott has ended up dead. I just have to keep him at arm's length. We'll organize watches. I won't bat an eyelash until Scott is in handcuffs.

Scott gets up, wiping his face. He grabs the axe—*damn it*— and swings it at a tree.

"He's distracted," I whisper. "We should leave right now."

Nicole shakes her head, whimpering. "He's still my dad."

"He's dangerous," Cameron mutters, his voice kind but firm. "I know you love him, but he's straight up lost his mind. I don't trust him with you anymore."

"Me neither, Nicky."

Nicole gulps, tears running down her cheeks. Staring at the ground, she nods.

Cameron's doubtful gaze snaps to Scott, who is hard at work, digging a shallow grave with his bare hands. "Where should we go?"

My throat thickens. "It doesn't matter. As long as it's away from him."

"Pack our stuff," he says, standing slowly. "Do it discreetly. I'll distract him."

"Cameron, I don't know about that—"

The corner of his mouth quirks. "Don't worry. I know what to say."

I dash into the cabin to pack our things. It takes less than a minute. All our worldly possessions fit in my bag. After a moment's hesitation, I grab Laura's diary from where I wedged it in the firewood. A pang hits my stomach. I'd almost completely forgotten about the damned diary. One line sticks with me: *I'm sure the sanctimonious prude can't wait to dish on my affair, which is ironic considering the skeletons in* her *family's closet.*

My mind whirls. Skeletons? My parents are the most normal people. My upbringing was very typical. Middle-class. The worst about my folks is that my dad occasionally brags about cheating on his taxes. Mom is sometimes careless with separating her garbage from recycling.

I toss the book on the floor. I can't entertain these thoughts for another second. Laura isn't trustworthy. I shouldn't put so much stock in a diary written by a spiteful woman. Grabbing my pack, I head outside.

Smoke drifts from the dying fire, which nobody seems to care about keeping alive. My insides squirm as I step around Fred's partially concealed body. Fred was the only one who'd mastered building a bow drill fire. What the hell are we going to do without him? As Scott drags pine branches over the corpse, David warms his hands on the smoldering coals.

I tap David's head. He stands and follows me.

"Where's Nicole?"

"Bathroom," he whispers, with a nervous look at Scott. "Are you sure he'll let us leave?"

"He doesn't have a choice. Where the hell is your dad?"

He bites his lip. "He went to the river to fill up on water."

Well, he picked a fine time to disappear. He's supposed to be watching Scott. "Okay," I grind out. "Go get Nicole."

I pat his back, and he jumps into the forest like a deer. I scan for more items we can use. Rope. Fistfuls of deer jerky. I stuff my bag to the brim with food, glancing over my shoulder. The campground is deserted. I clench my jaw to stifle my whimper.

Bear mace. Now.

Shaking, I rip open my bag. My hand plunges into its depths, searching for a cold cylinder. An enraged roar erupts from the corner. Fumbling with the zipper, I glance up. I meet Scott's manic gaze through a plume of smoke. Ice twists around my heart.

He clutches a black book. His other hand holds an axe. He's headed right for me, and then it dawns on me.

I'm alone. With a murderer.

FORTY-ONE
THE PAST

"Will she be okay?"

Tears thicken my throat as Amber's round face breaks into a warm smile, and she nods.

"She'll be fine." She strokes Meadow, who lies across the black leather, her head on Amber's knee. "She purged it out."

An hour ago, Meadow got into the holiday chocolate. She demolished several bars before Nicole burst into my room, screaming about the dog.

I wipe my streaming cheeks. "I must've called every vet in King County. I can't believe there aren't *any* twenty-four/seven vets."

"Staffing issues," Amber murmurs, scratching Meadow behind her ears. "But it's all right. We took care of it."

The bottle of peroxide Amber used to induce vomiting sits on the table. I'm in awe of her. She knew what to do. When she walked in on us freaking out, she strolled into the bathroom, fetched the bottle, and squirted a dropper in Meadow's mouth. Five minutes later, Meadow heaved brown liquid all over the kitchen floor. It soaked through Amber's pants, much to my father's disgust. She didn't seem to mind. She picked up Meadow, sat with her on the couch, and wiped her snout with a wet rag, singing to my dog in a babyish voice.

I rub my forehead. "She'll really be fine?"

"Oh yeah. She's just sleeping it off."

Amber slides off the couch, giving Meadow a belly scratch. Meadow's golden tail thumps the leather as she raises her head, as though wondering where her pillow went.

"I'm taking a shower." Amber checks her watch, yawning. "I can't believe it's three in the morning. You should get to bed."

"I-I don't want to leave her." I feel like I've suffered several heart attacks in an hour. "I'm sorry about the barf all over your jeans."

"I'll throw them in the wash. No big deal."

"It is to me."

Amber's brows knit. Then she wraps her arms around me. Something shifts in my chest as I hug her. My eyes shut and I tremble.

Amber rubs my back. "We'll take her to the vet tomorrow, first thing. Okay?"

"Okay," I choke out.

"You'll drive. Your test is next week, right?"

I nod.

"And you have a game on Saturday?"

"Yeah," I croak. "Are you coming?"

"Of course."

Amber pulls away, beaming. She bustles off to the linen closet and returns with blankets and a pillow. Then she makes a bed on the couch, drags the sheet to my neck, and kisses my head.

"Goodnight. Love you."

I mumble a response as she flicks the light switch, bathing me in darkness. As Amber climbs the staircase, Meadow's snores rattle the air.

I used to believe that her kindness was a ruse, but she comes to my games. And she's engaged. She isn't one of those moms that stays buried in her phone. More than once, I've looked over at the stands to see her upright, screaming. She follows through with her promises. Teaches me how to drive. Every day, she rides in the passenger seat as we navigate Seattle's insanely complicated grid. I know I'll pass with flying colors.

Life is much better with her around. I hadn't thought about it, but it's true. I've never had a parent like Amber. She does so many things to make me feel special. It never comes across as an act. When she helps me with homework, fixes me a snack, or saves my dog, it's because she cares. Like I'm her son. It feels good. I am so grateful to have her in my life.

I keep thinking something will happen, and she'll turn into a world-class jerk like Dad's other girlfriends. But she hasn't. The more time passes, the less cheesy her I-love-you's sound.

And the more I want to say it back.

FORTY-TWO
AMBER

My ex is about to kill me.

Scott seems undecided. He holds the axe, his right arm trembling. I hold my hands up to block an attack that may or may not come as he babbles in half-formed sentences, waving Laura's diary in my face.

I'm not listening. I can't hear him. My throttled heartbeat drowns out Scott's rant, and then he screams so hard my ears ache.

"Look at it!"

He shakes the book open to a page filled with her looping handwriting. My breathing hitches. I stare at the first paragraph in which she blames me for everything.

"Oh. Did you…did you read it?"

"*Of course I did,*" he shouts, flecks of spit landing on my face. "It was on my backpack, outside."

"How did it get there?"

"How the hell should I know? I saw it, opened it, and *bam*. Laura's motive for sleeping with Fred."

"I'm so sorry."

"*Shut your fat mouth*. I'm not falling for that crap anymore. One of you left this where I'd find it. It can't be Fred because he's..." His voice breaks and the axe drops a fraction. "It was Cameron or that freak son of his. They killed my wife and stole her diary. I knew it. I knew it and you—screw you, Amber—you were *wrong*."

Words fumble from my lips as I digest that. Once again, this sounds like a desperate attempt to deflect blame. I can't trust anything he says. I rub the sides of my head, mind reeling.

"So you found this on your backpack?"

"That's what I said."

"And you think my husband or David planted it?" I swallow hard, doing my best to sound calm and reasonable. "What for?"

"To torture me," he bursts, his eyes brightening with that crazed gleam. "This whole thing has been about me."

"You mean...the trip?"

"*Yes*. For God's sake, keep up."

"I'm sorry," I whisper, eyeing the axe. "I'm stressed out, I guess. I don't know what you're talking about."

"You had a part in this." His accusatory gaze narrows as he points the axe at me. "How could you not know your husband's a psycho? You can't. So that means *you* did this to me."

This is not heading in a good direction.

I laugh, or try to, but it's like I'm choking on air. "Scott, take a minute to reflect on what you're saying. You're emotional right now."

"Stop gaslighting me."

A stab of anger pierces through my panic because this idiot wouldn't know gaslighting if it bit him in his over-sized biceps. *Don't talk back. Agree with everything.*

"You *know* me. You lived with me for seven years. I used to be your wife. How many times did I take you to the chiro-practor when you got injured from CrossFit?"

Scott shakes his head. "That was a long time ago."

I lick my lips, seized by a sudden idea. "I-I was too proud to work on our marriage. You're right. I gave up on us. I shouldn't have, but I was hurt. What you did shattered me. I couldn't look at you without feeling completely devastated. Getting away was the only way I knew how to heal. I'm sorry. I screwed up." I grasp Scott's wrist, the one holding the diary. "Leaving you was the biggest mistake of my life. If I hadn't, none of this would've happened." There's still a strong chance he'll swing that axe. I stam-mer, grasping for straws. "A-and I married Cameron because I...I just wanted your attention."

He stares at me, blinking. Slowly, his eyes flood with emotion. Then he releases a pained sigh.

"I know...I'm sorry. Can you forgive me?"

His body stiffens. "It doesn't matter anyway."

"We can fix the thing with Fred." The *thing* being his murder. "You won't go to jail if we get our stories straight."

"Y-you would do that for me?"

No. "Yes. You're Nicole's father. Nobody can replace you." I dial it down, worried I'm coming off too accommodating, but Scott seems to buy it. "And I don't blame you for being angry at Fred. You're a good person. You were...overwhelmed."

Scott's axe lowers a fraction. "I'm not a killer."

"Of course not."

He flings aside the diary, turning his palm to hold my hand. "If we were together, I wouldn't be—I wouldn't—"

"Let me help you. I'll make up for what I put you through. I'll support whatever story you give the police about Fred."

He nods, stepping closer. "And you'll divorce Cameron. You'll come back to me."

"Yeah, sure," I whisper, my throat tightening. "We'll be a family again."

He lets go of the axe. It drops and hits the ground, blade first. He palms his face and shakes with a dry sob. "Amber, I didn't mean to do this. I swear."

"I know," I say, feeling sick. "It's okay."

It's not, but I pretend like Fred's murder is a tiny blip in the timeline of his mistakes. I take his shoulders, and his watery gaze collides with mine.

Scott manages a tremulous smile. "All I wanted was a second chance. I still love you."

Oh boy. I don't feel the same.

He throws his arms around me. I force myself to relax as he falls apart in an explosion of grief. He squeezes me in a bear hug, whispering an apology in the shell of my ear. I wince. It feels wrong. His hands rub up and down my *excessively overweight* body. His lids flutter. Then he leans in, angling his head for a kiss.

I cringe.

Then a shovel cracks over Scott's skull.

Scott drops to the ground, moaning.

My husband stands over him, shovel in hand. He tosses it aside and grabs Scott by the scruff of his collar and drags him across the forest floor, unmoved by Scott's pained moans.

"Took you long enough," I snap, following Cameron as he dumps Scott at the base of a large tree. "You were supposed to be watching him."

"Sorry."

I bristle. "He was about to kiss me."

If Scott making a move on me shocks Cameron, he doesn't show it. His lips twist into a cynical grin as he props Scott against the tree, pinning him there with a boot to his chest.

"I saw that." Cameron's smirk flashes in his direction. "Not your finest hour, is it?"

My spine tingles with unease. "He could've killed me."

"Yeah, but he didn't. You played him real good. Blaming everything on yourself. Making him think you were getting back together. I admire you so much, Amber. It's been a joy watching your claws come out."

I take a deep, hitching breath, parsing through Cameron's words. My fingers close around Laura's diary. I study the leather cover. How did it get here? Laura must've brought it on the hike, which meant someone took it. I sway, hit by a wave of queasiness. How long has it been riding in someone's backpack?

"I need to get the kids home. We have to get them out of here."

Cameron hauls Scott upright. "Sharing a kid with this grade-A moron must be tough. You're legally required to keep in touch with him. It's a hellish existence. I see you struggle. Every time he sends a text. Or calls. Whenever he makes a stupid joke at your expense. A normal person would've lost it a while ago."

He produces a coil of black nylon rope I've never seen before, pressing Scott against the tree. He winds it around the trunk, tightening it on Scott's chest. He winces.

I blink, coming back to life. "Where'd you find that rope?"

"I got it from my truck."

I stare at him, not amused. "Cam, we need to leave. What are you doing?"

"Tying him." Cameron secures a knot on Scott's chest, pulling so hard that his head jerks with the movement. "Should've done it after he wasted his brother, but I wanted to watch him unravel."

I rub my forehead, disturbed by his attitude. Cameron steps back. He smiles as though admiring his handiwork.

"The kids are by the river. Should we go?"

I gape at the faintly stirring Scott, and then Cameron, who is acting strange. Why is he pretending like this isn't a big deal? "We can't. He'll die. Or get eviscerated by a bear."

Cameron crosses his arms. "And?"

My mind whirls at his dry response. "And I'm not okay with that."

"Why not? Nicole would be better off without this pathetic excuse for a father."

"Yeah, but I can't kill him."

"Why not?"

A low wail rumbles from Scott. He lifts his head and opens his eyes, scanning his surroundings. Then he glances down at his bindings. He yanks at the ropes, his muscles bulging.

"We can't leave him strapped to a tree. It could be days before we can send help. He'll die for sure." Judging by Cameron's blank expression, he couldn't care less. I don't blame him, but still. "If we do this, it's no different than stabbing him in the chest."

"He's responsible for the week from hell. He deserves it."

"The police will handle the punishment."

"Cops don't give a damn about justice."

"Cam, you're freaking me out."

Cameron's frustration boils over in a hoarse yell. Then he grabs me. His powerful hand cinches my wrist as he pulls, dragging me away from Scott. My foot connects with Laura's diary, and it tumbles into a bed of leaves. He frog-marches me past trees as Scott begs for us to return. His desperate pleas unleash something inside me. I try to twist out of Cameron's grip, but he's stronger and shows no signs of relenting.

"What has gotten into you? Let go of me!"

"David," he bellows when we stumble into the empty campground. "We're leaving."

He scans the trees, swearing when nobody approaches. Then he shoves my hands together. He wraps a bundle of rope around them. I realize what he's doing too late. A shriek tears from my throat as he fists the rope, the fibers tearing into my skin. He drags me to a tree and ties me to it.

"Let me go!"

"I'm so sorry about this, but I can't trust you to stay put. I'm going to look for the kids. I'll be back."

He kisses the top of my head and vanishes. Cameron's upset. He's under a lot of stress. That must be it. Sometimes we do crazy things to protect the people we love. Like bind them to a tree. I'd accept that if it wasn't the only blazing red flag. The diary. Minutes ago, Scott waved it in my face, hollering.

Skeletons in her family's closet.

She didn't mean my family. She meant *Cameron*. But his family has nothing horrible in their past. His mom and dad are divorced. Big deal. It's not like they *killed* anyone. Have they? She made it sound like they have huge problems. Some of the criminal variety. *Skeletons*—was she talking about David's biological mother?

Who else could it be?

A sick feeling stabs my plunging stomach. As though on cue, Scott's hysterical screams blast my ear. He begs an unknown assailant to stop. I wrench at the rope binding my wrists, gritting my teeth. I yank out one arm.

There's time. I can still save him.

Another high-pitched wail pierces my heart, followed by a pained moan. His tortured sobbing dissolves into soft pleas, and then…nothing.

FORTY-FOUR
AMBER

Scott is gone.

I freed myself, but I was too late. Slashed ropes. Blood. I pick up the frayed pieces, studying the crimson stains. Specks of bright red sprinkle the ferns below the tree. Someone cut him loose. The marks are too clean. Does that mean he's dead? No, there would be a body. I plaster a shaky hand to my forehead, unable to take it in.

Nicole. I left her with David. I crash through the underbrush, shouting her name. Stumbling back into camp, I gape at the spot where Fred lay, which is now a tangle of branches.

"Nicole? *David.* Where are you?"

A low moan reverberates inside the cabin.

A man's voice. Scott? A flicker of apprehension courses through me. I sprint toward the door and yank it open. A curtain of light spills over a shivering Scott, who's curled up on the floor. A bloody gash from his abdomen seeps blood into his filthy T-shirt. Nylon rope binds his hands. His feet, too.

"What happened?"

He blows out his cheeks, grimacing. "David cut me free. The knife nicked me."

I inhale a quick breath. "Is Nicole with him?"

"I-I don't know. When you guys left, I kept screaming until someone approached. It was David, holding a knife. Christ, I was so scared. I thought he was going to gut me, but he let me go. Told me to run, so I did...until I—"

His wet blue eyes meet mine, widening.

A body moves behind me. My stomach tenses as metal digs into my back. Cold metal juts into my spine as I turn around, gasping at the sight of my captor.

FORTY-FIVE
THE PAST

It's my seventeenth birthday.

This is the most elaborate party I've ever had. My dad saw no point in celebrating them, but Amber is festive. We rode bikes to Magnuson Park, followed by a picnic. I swear, Amber puts in more effort for me than her daughter. I think because I worship the ground she walks on, and Nicole is such a brat. She's the epitome of teenage and entitled. I can't stand her, but I try to get along for Amber's sake.

Nicole faces Lake Washington, standing barefoot on a shore filled with pebbles. She hurls rocks at the lapping waves, frowning when they sink.

"You're doing it wrong."

I pick up a flat rock, toss it, and it bounces on the water twice before disappearing. Nicole glares at me with burning eyes. "Are you cool with our parents getting married?"

I have nightmares about them breaking up, so yeah. Shrugging, I choose another rock. My answer seems to placate Nicole, whose head gestures toward my dad with a taut jerk.

"What's his deal?"

I chew on my tongue before answering. "What do you mean?"

She crosses her arms, a snide tone entering her voice. "He's a simp for my mom. He's trying too hard. It's very cringe."

She's referring to the moment we rolled up in our bikes. Dad had been waiting for us at a picnic table, which had balloons tied to it like I'm a five-year-old. He stood, a big, fake grin stretching his broad face, talking about how he got a double-layered, salted caramel cake from Larsens, my favorite bakery, while Amber was in earshot. I'm glad someone else sees through it.

"He's like that with all his girlfriends."

"Why don't you like him?"

"I have my reasons."

She presses her lips into a thin line. "Should I be worried for my mom?"

I shake my head, the question eating at me. He's not abusive toward his partners. His son, on the other hand?

"He's a flying monkey," I tell Nicole.

"Like...from *The Wizard of Oz*?"

I nod. "That's what my therapist calls him. It's a psychology term. It means he does the bidding of a narcissist."

"Are you calling my mom a narcissist?"

"No...never mind."

I won't elaborate. Opening up to Nicole is a mistake. The truth will not set me free. It will exile me. For the first time in my life, I'm happy. I can't ruin it.

Her forehead wrinkles. "Flying monkey. That makes no sense."

"It would if you cracked open a book once in a while."

She whirls around, her hair catching the light like shimmering gold. Her pink mouth curves. "You mean those doorstoppers on your bookshelf?"

My chest burns. "Stop going in my room."

She removes the sunglasses from her face with a flourish, her eyes dazzling against her pale skin. "I don't take orders from a guy who thinks he's Bill Shakespeare."

"It's *William*."

She grabs my shoulder, her touch burning through my shirt. "Bill is short for William, dummy."

"What do I have to do to make you leave me alone?"

She blows in my ear.

I hiss and shrug her off me. Her laughter rakes my back as I turn away from her, eager to put distance between us. She gets on my nerves almost as often as my father.

Dad tosses a tennis ball to Meadow, who races after the green blur. Like everything else, he never showed an interest in my dog until Amber. He lobs the ball at Amber, who takes over, and then he strides over to me.

"Having fun?" he asks.

"Do you care?"

He gives me a vicious side-eye. "I have a good thing going with Amber. You're not screwing this up for me."

"Oh, I'm not?"

"No. You won't."

Luckily for my dad, I have no intention of harming his latest squeeze. Saying I like Amber would be a massive understatement. She's the mother I never had. Still, I flash my father a cheeky grin.

"What makes you so sure?"

"You like her, too. You're happy, but that can change in an instant."

My heart hammers. "What do you mean?"

"If you want our new family to survive, you will *behave*. You will never tell her what you did. The moment you do, she walks out of our lives."

I swallow hard.

He gives me a stiff nod and wanders back, beaming at Amber. He's right. Coming clean isn't an option. I catch myself wanting to do terrible things, but I don't because it'll hurt Amber. She'll treat me like a monster, the way the others did. That would kill me.

I can't lose her.

I just can't. I'll hold off for as long as possible, but disaster is inevitable. It's like the smell of ozone before rain falls. It's coming.

FORTY-SIX
AMBER

"Cameron?"

At least, I think it's him. He's wearing my husband's clothing and his mouth curls in his Han Solo smirk, but I don't recognize him. His gaze is flat. He points a gun at me.

I study the nozzle, searching for orange paint, anything to prove this is a sick prank.

"Cameron?" I whisper, ignoring the pressure on my chest. "Where did you get that?"

It's not the most important question—and he knows it. What's he going to do to me? My mind refuses to go there.

"From my truck," he says in a low, unhurried cadence. "I took it off Scott when everybody was distracted with the deer. I put it in the truck for safekeeping. It's a rental. Parked a half-mile from here. I didn't want to use the gun. I tried to look for the knife on Fred's body. I thought it'd be poetic if I killed Scott with the same blade that took his brother's life, but I couldn't find it."

My pulse spikes. He has a way out of here? His casual delivery suggests it's no big deal. He planned this. My stomach clenches as I search for an escape, but Cameron blocks the door.

"Why do you have a car?"

"I'll need it when I drive out of here. I've known where we are the entire time."

"*What?*"

"I knew it," Scott bursts, struggling to free himself. "He's a *psychopath*. He's *after* me. He's been messing with me since the beginning. He killed Laura."

"W-what?" I feel like a broken record, still stuck on the fact that my amazing husband is threatening me. "Is he telling the truth?"

Cameron smiles an apologetic grin. "For once in his miserable life."

Laughter threatens to bubble from my throat, but I tamp it down. I gape at him, more and more alert. My mind gallops ahead.

"I planned this whole thing. Built the cabin weeks ago, knowing that I would lead us to it. I let Scott take us the wrong way for miles. I wanted…to observe him closely as I ripped him apart."

A danger sign flashes in my mind. "Why?"

"Because he killed my fiancée."

I whirl at Scott, who gapes at him. "You did?"

He shakes his head. "I don't know what the hell he's talking about."

Cameron skewers him with a vicious glare. The arm holding the gun swings, aiming at Scott. "That scar on your leg. Is it healed?"

Scott holds his hands up, trembling. "W-what?"

"I said, did you heal from the accident that killed my fiancée?"

Recognition seems to dawn on Scott's face as he breathes in deeply. "I didn't...I—"

"Lie to me one more damn time."

"Fine. Yes, I was in an accident. I was near Snoqualmie, on this long, woodsy road. It was dark. I was turning left. I noticed this swerving white car." Tears sparkle in his beseeching blue gaze. "I turned left. I thought she'd stop. She jerked her steering wheel to avoid me and flipped, smashing into a tree. I lost control and slammed into a ditch. Messed up my leg. I got out but she was dead, so I-I took off."

I shake my head. "You're a disgusting coward."

"I had to, Amber. I had a few drinks. It would've been horrible for us. Hit-and-runs are misdemeanors. A felony DUI with my driving record already being a mess? I would've lost my job. Amber, please. Believe me. She was dead. Why ruin another life? It makes no sense."

"Because there's no justice in that," I hiss, balling my clenched fists. "Because you're a reckless idiot that *deserves* to get the book thrown at him."

"It's not my fault. I'm telling you, she was *drunk*. I-I swear —" Scott shuts up as Cameron raises the gun to his eye level.

"The next morning, two officers showed up at my door. They informed me that my fiancée's car was wrapped around a tree. They needed me to identify the body. Imagine seeing the love of your life decimated beyond recognition. It was so...awful." Cameron's mouth twists, a muscle quivering in his jaw. "I salvaged the dash camera. That's how I found you. The police told me there was nothing they could do. You're under no obligation to stop unless you're in the car accident. And because my fiancée's toxicology screen was positive for benzodi-azepines, they said they wouldn't pursue criminal charges. Everybody told me to let it go, but I couldn't. How could I? I was supposed to plan a wedding...not a funeral. My fiancée was dead. Killed by a man who suffered no conse-quences. Look at him. He doesn't even know her damn name."

Scott mutters something indistinct, and Cameron fires the gun. The sound zips up my spine. Blood explodes from Scott's thigh. Cameron's roar is like a dragon as he bends over, shoving the gun in Scott's face.

"*Kim*. Her name was Kim."

I dive toward Scott to staunch the bleeding, folding my palms over the gushing wound. Cameron drags me back with an enraged shout. I elbow him off and clamp my fingers over Scott's thigh. Cameron seizes my collar and hurls me against the wall.

"Don't touch him."

"But he'll bleed out."

"I don't care," he growls, his mouth an inch from my face. "He destroyed my life. You're either with me, or you're against me. What's it going to be, wife?"

I swallow hard, trying to block out Scott's sobbing. What should I do? Keep talking? Stall him? I'll never overpower Cameron. God, I hope the kids are safe.

"What happened after the police told you they wouldn't charge him with anything?"

Cameron pulls back, frowning. "I spiraled for a while. It was a horrible time. I became obsessed with him. I looked him up. Learned you were divorced. I made sure we bumped into each other. At first, you were a means to make him suffer. I just wanted to mess with him. Once we started dating, I figured out that he wasn't over you, so I stepped up my efforts. I thought marrying you would soothe me. I wanted to move on. I wanted to love my new wife, but I couldn't stop thinking about Kim. What would she think if she saw me, rubbing elbows with her killer? So I shared the dashcam footage with Scott's boss. Threatened to post it on social media. They fired him. That was fun, but still not enough."

"Look, I'm sorry, okay?" Scott stammers through clenched teeth, his bound hands struggling to stem the blood flow. "I apologize to the deepest depths of my freaking soul, but it was an *accident*."

"Once Amber told me about this vacation, I realized I could get justice for Kim. It took a few trips back and forth to build the cabin. I rented a car and left it nearby. When you told me Fred was coming with us, I was ecstatic. This was a chance to destroy *three* Maxwells. And I barely did anything. All I had to do was let Scott screw up. He forced his wife to eat psychedelic mushrooms, despite everyone telling them not to." Cameron's mouth pulls into a sour grin as he gives Scott a thumbs-up. "Couldn't have done this without you."

Appalled, I exchange a horrified glance with Scott. "Did you push her off that cliff?" Scott grinds out.

"Maybe I did. Or maybe I didn't have to. *You* did all the work for me. You're an easy man to manipulate, Scott. A gentle nudge here and there, and you walk in the wrong direction." Cameron taps his temple, smirking. "Not much going on up there."

"*You* sabotaged the food."

Cameron nods. "It was an opportunity to divide you and the others. It worked. You blamed it on Fred."

"You're sick," says Scott hoarsely. "You made me stab him."

"I lightly fanned the flames. You stuck that knife in his chest. I bet another suggestion from me would make you murder Amber, too. You are a spineless coward who can't accept responsibility for anything. You deserve to die."

"Oh yeah? Well, I didn't come out here planning to *kill* anyone!"

"But you did," Cameron says with relish. "You killed your wife. Your brother. If I weren't here, your daughter would've died, too."

Scott breaks down into loud tears, slipping in his blood as he struggles to stay upright. Spittle dribbles down his chin. The gleam in his eyes hardens. Scott draws rattling breaths as he whispers, "What will you do with Amber?"

"Nothing." Cameron slides an arm around my waist. "She hates you as much as I do. We'll go back in the woods, collect the kids, and stumble upon a truck with the keys inside. Once we reach a ranger station to send help, you'll already be dead."

Nausea pits my stomach with every sickening word. The fact he'd assume I'd be okay with this speaks to his shaky grip on reality. How will he explain the gunshot wound?

I step away from Cameron. "No."

His head swings at me, his brow quirked. "No?"

I ignore Scott's sharp *"Amber,"* as my chest swells like a bullfrog. "No, we're not skipping off into the sunset after you murder my ex."

Scott lets out a pained groan.

"I'll never—*ever*—forgive you for doing this to David and Nicole. They could've died. We were starving. Dehydrated. They could've drowned in that river or poisoned themselves. What the hell? You thought I'd give you a pass for all of this?"

"Amber, for God's sake," Scott begs, his voice cracking. "Stop talking."

Cameron holds my gaze, the silence suffocating. He doesn't look anywhere but my eyes, and that sends a shock down my spine. "I see. You're picking him."

I swallow, willing myself not to tremble. "I-I'm not, but I can't let you kill him."

"Don't," Scott pleads. "You're making things worse."

Cameron squares his shoulders, facing me fully. "How will you stop me?"

My heart hammers at the disturbing ease of that question. "Cameron, please. I know he's awful. I lived with him for years, but you can't do this. Think about it—how will you explain his death?"

"We'll tell them he was overcome with remorse after ending his brother's life and took his own."

"No," I blurt, ignoring Scott's disapproving hiss. "You're taking us to the truck and we're leaving."

"That won't work for me."

"Amber, *shut the hell up*. He's made up his mind. Just go." A tear slips down Scott's cheek. "He's right. I deserve this."

I can't believe what I'm hearing. "Nobody *else* has to die, for God's sake!"

"Ignore her. Shoot me."

Cameron grabs Scott's hair and wrenches, exposing his flushed neck. Cameron lowers the gun over his skin. I seize a splintered piece of firewood. I swing. It crashes into my husband's face. The gun drops. Cameron falls to the side, swearing.

I head for the door, but Cameron is faster.

He grasps me in a brutal hold. He throws me on the floor, my shoulder connecting painfully with the earth. Suddenly, he's on top of me, his cold hands wrapped around my esophagus. He squeezes. Lights pop in my vision. I'm dying. The last thing I'll hear is my ex begging my husband to spare my life.

There's a footstep and a *zwip*.

His fingers loosen their grip. He rolls off me, clutching at the arrow piercing his throat. Behind him, a shadow moves into the light.

FORTY-SEVEN

THE PAST

Nicole bursts into my room without knocking. She has an annoying habit of barging through doors and interrupting me, but I like that she's not scared of me. She gets in my face regularly. Nicole throws my diary on my bed.

"What is this, a fictional serial killer memoir you're writing?"

I push my chair away from the desk, where I'm supposed to be rewriting my *Into the Wild* essay. The teacher took offense that I didn't find it a compelling story. I still don't understand why I should care about that privileged idiot. Sometimes he reminds me of Nicole, who doesn't appreciate how lucky she is.

I click my tongue. "Nice of you to go through my things."

"Well?"

"Well, what?"

She huffs. "Is it real?"

I sigh. "How much of it did you read?"

"All of it," she says, not betraying a hint of shame. "You're a talented writer. You could get into a good grad school with those essays."

I smile wryly. "Thanks."

Nicole falls on my bed, her cornsilk-blond hair spilling over my duvet. She picks up my diary, thumbs to a page in the middle, and gives voice to my private thoughts. "My mother was my first victim. I hate that word for her, but that's what the police and my father insist on using."

I bite my lip, heart pounding wildly.

"I did a background check on you. It's funny what twenty dollars will tell you about someone." Nicole shuts the diary, and my pulse skyrockets. "Is this *true*? Did you really...kill your *mom*?"

"She...she was abusive. It was self-defense. She was killing me, a little bit every day, just like—" I break off before realizing she knows about Kim, too. "Like my dad's ex."

"I know," she whispers, softening. "I read everything."

"You shouldn't have."

"It was a great read, especially once I combined it with your rap sheet. Five glowing stars."

I cross the room and shut the door, whispering. "You can't tell Mom about this."

"Why not?"

I turn, a knot forming in my throat. "She'll panic. She'll hate me like you do right now. I'm not a threat to any of you, okay? I was punished. I did my time. My psychologists told me…that I have…a problem. Writing helps me. It purges my thoughts before they get out of hand."

"I won't rat on you."

I sink into my chair, winded. "Blackmail?"

"Nah. You don't have anything I want."

And yet, she studies me like she *does* want something. Her stare tracks me up and down. She sets the diary aside and sits upright, hands clasped in her lap. "Do you feel bad about it?"

"Sort of. I know it wasn't right." I rub the back of my neck, my pulse erratic. "It's hard to explain. I'm not proud of the way I am."

She bounces off the bed and stands behind me, her fingers brushing the top of my hair.

"What are you doing?"

"Hugging you," she says, sliding her arms around me. "You did nothing wrong."

My eyes burn. Great, I'm about to cry in front of a girl. I slide my hand over hers.

"Why are you nice to me?"

"Shouldn't I be?"

I shake my head. "No. I'm evil. I should be kicked out of here and forced to live in a group home with other violent kids."

"Is that what you want?"

I don't speak.

"David...I know what it's like to be angry."

"Not this angry."

She lowers until her curtain of blond gossamer touches my cheek, and the smell of her invades my nose. My heart pounds. I'm not supposed to feel like this.

"You're not a bad guy," she whispers in a husky voice that makes me blush. "You're one of a kind."

"Yeah. I sure am."

"They were hurting you. You defended yourself. That's a *good* thing." She squeezes me again. "And I don't care what you've done in the past. It doesn't matter. I want you here."

She heads to the door.

I wipe my face. "Nicole?"

Beaming, she turns around.

"I love you."

She blushes, her pink lips parting with shock. She doesn't say it back. Of course not. I don't deserve these people. I'm a freak. I turn toward my computer, cheeks smoldering, and then her hand glides over my shoulder. She bends over and kisses my cheek, showering me with sparks. Then she pulls away, red-faced.

"Love you, too."

She dashes out of my room.

Well, that was unexpected but…awesome. She accepts me, but will Mom? I just don't know. Taking that leap is too scary. If I have to hide who I am for the rest of my life, so be it.

I grab the diary on my bed and flip to the next blank page. Then I slide it over my desk and start writing.

In case I get caught:

Mom,

I'm sorry I killed Dad.

Hurting you wasn't my intention. I only want to protect you from the monster my father truly is. I don't think I can convince you. You swallow his good-guy BS. I don't blame you, though. Most believe he's a saint. You have never doubted me…not once, but I can't risk losing you. You and Nicole are the only people who care about me. I hope you'll still love me after you find out what I've done.

Trust me when I say he deserved it. They all *deserved it.*

FORTY-EIGHT
AMBER

David lowers the crossbow. He tosses it aside and rushes to me, his knees hitting the ground. He palms my head.

"Are you hurt?"

I cough, rubbing my neck. "No."

"We found help. They're on their way."

A mountain of relief crumbles inside me. *Thank God.* "Where's Nicole?"

She emerges through the doorway, her thin frame trembling. Her widened gaze takes in Cameron, and then her father. She utters a frantic sound and rips off her jacket.

"Dad, you're bleeding. What happened?"

Scott grimaces. "Your stepdad shot me."

She ties a tourniquet around Scott's leg. "You'll be okay. An ambulance is coming."

"I'm *fine*. Just get me the hell out of here."

With her help, Scott limps outside. My attention snaps to Cameron, who sits against the wall. He holds his neck. He makes an odd, whistling noise as he breathes, the arrow protruding from his throat. It looks excruciating. A stream of blood trickles down his shirt.

I crawl toward him, but David's arm catches me across the chest. "He's too dangerous."

"But he's in pain."

"Help is coming. Let them deal with it." David grabs my arm and moves me away from Cameron. "I found a truck parked nearby with the keys inside. Nicole and I drove it until we got a signal. We called nine-one-one and high-tailed it back. I was supposed to collect everyone and meet her at the car, but...I ran into Scott."

"Your dad tied him to the tree. It's a long story."

"I know," he says, in a voice thick with tears. "Sorry."

"For what? You saved me. I'm so proud of you."

His head hangs. "You shouldn't be. I'm a monster, just like him."

"Why would you say that?"

"Because...I killed my mom. And Kim."

David's head bumps in Cameron's direction, winding me, and then he tells me everything. He describes the abuse, and how his dad stood by and enabled it. Then his sins stack up like bricks. He caved in his mother's head with a rosewood ornament. He slipped drugs in Kim's wine, and she died that evening in a violent car wreck. When we reach the part with his father inventing backstories, he can barely choke out the words.

"I should've warned you about Dad, but I really like living with you. I was afraid…you would leave. Without you, I have nothing. I'm stuck with him. But I still don't understand what happened. He was happy with you. I knew Dad had this vendetta with Scott, but I had no idea it was this serious."

My mouth drops open as I digest that. It's a lot to take in. The parts that involve Cameron's additional betrayal hit me hard, especially the abuse. It explains David's wild behavior in the beginning. I suspected Cameron was downplaying his first wife's relationship with David, but I never looked into it.

I push the damp hair off David's face. "Thank you for telling me."

He nods, looking like he might be sick. "I know you'll never be able to forgive me, but for what's it worth, I'm sorry. I didn't know he'd do this. Please believe me."

"I believe you."

"I did so many bad things, Mom. I stole Laura's diary. It was in her backpack. I read it."

A weak smile trembles on my lips. "I did, too."

"But—"

I cup his face. "You're still my son. I'm not giving up on you."

"But I have a compulsion," he says fervently. "Sometimes I want to hurt people."

"Did you hurt anybody on the trip?" I ask.

"Well, no, but—"

"Then it sounds like you're controlling it."

His eyes widen. "Y-you don't care? I admit to killing my mom, and you're cool with that?"

"I'm not thrilled, but I'm glad you told me the truth."

Honestly, I'm devastated. My life is falling apart for a second time. I need a shower, a cheeseburger, and a long nap. I can't process that David killed his abusers because I'm furious with Cameron.

"Your dad is the one I'm angry with, honey. He lied about everything. He put us all in danger. I can't forgive that."

"When he goes to jail, what happens to me?"

"We're a family. We stay together, no matter what."

David's watery gaze spills over before he tackles me in a hug, his fingers digging deep into my back. A siren's wail drifts into the cabin, reminding me that my marriage is over. I cling to my stepson, crying.

THEY RUSH US TO A HOSPITAL.

All of us, including Fred. As it turns out, he's *not* dead. Doctors zoom him into surgery, along with Cameron, whom I have yet to face. I'm not sure if I want to see him again. Facing my husband's betrayal is too difficult. He's the one who checked Fred's pulse and declared him dead, and we believed him because…who would lie about that?

Two days later, I sit at Scott's bedside as Nicole and David sleep in chairs. Scott stares at the ceiling, his wrists shackled to the bed. He sobbed with relief when paramedics pulled an unresponsive Fred onto a stretcher, but I'll never forget his knife sinking into Fred's chest.

The police interviewed us. To my surprise, Scott fessed up to stabbing Fred, which means he'll probably get a few years in prison. Nicole wanted us to lie, but Scott shot that down.

"You know what I keep thinking about?" Scott croaks, breaking the rapt silence. "Whenever we're in the same room, I'll have to explain to people that tensions are high because I stabbed my brother who slept with my wife, who was killed by my ex-wife's husband, whose fiancée died in a car accident that I witnessed."

I smile, fighting a bizarre urge to laugh. "So true. Christmas will be awkward."

Scott's baleful gaze centers on me. "We'll never be whole again."

"Yes, we will. Give it time—okay, a lot of time—but Fred will forgive you. He's not exactly innocent." I swipe through my phone's gallery, sighing when I find a photo of Laura. "The rest of it, you'll have to atone for."

"Will Nicole forgive me?"

I smile at him, nodding. "We're still a family, even when we're not together."

His arm jerks against the restraint. "Yeah, but I screwed things up."

I touch his shoulder. "Then let's promise to do better."

His face flushes. "How?"

I lean back, glancing out the window. "Well, we can start by being kinder to each other."

Scott got five years.

I'm glad he's going away. Honestly, I need more distance from him. I attended his sentencing with Nicole, who sobbed into a tissue as the bailiff hauled her father to prison. She visits him often. Since his release from the hospital, Scott and I haven't talked except to exchange a few pleasantries. I don't hate him anymore, but there's still a long way to go before I'll tolerate his presence without grinding my teeth. He put me through too much. Hopefully, he'll reflect on his behavior and come out as a better person. I have to believe that *some* people are capable of change.

As for Cameron, he can rot in prison for eternity. He pled down to attempted murder in the first degree for shooting Scott. They couldn't get him for Laura because of insufficient evidence. He got life with the possibility of parole. The last time I saw him was in the courtroom. His cold gray eyes met mine as the judge read out his sentence. He's contacted me a few times from prison, but I never accepted his calls and after a few months, he stopped trying. But the other day, a postcard arrived with his handwriting:

> *There's something I need to tell you.*
> *Call me.*
> *- Cam*

I threw it in the trash. I'm not interested in whatever he has to say. David and I deserve to move on without the shadow of Cameron looming over us. That's what we've been doing in the past twelve months.

My slippers smack the vinyl floors as I head outside in my robe, peeking out of the three-story townhome I moved us into a month after Cameron's trial ended. Living in the home we used to share was too painful. My heart hammers as I fit the key into the box and turn. The lid falls, revealing a stack of letters. The chill bites my fingers as I cycle through junk, searching for postcards from my ex-husband. As I reach the last envelope, my body stiffens.

My shoulder hits the door. It flies open. I close it and race upstairs, where the kids are having breakfast. David's hand drops from Nicole's.

"What is it, Mom?"

I wave the envelope. "It's from UW."

His fork clatters on the plate as he stares at the mail in my hand. He's been expecting this for weeks, obsessively checking the mailbox. Nicole was accepted to UW, and they're dead set on attending the same college.

I slide it in front of him.

"It's small," he whispers, still not reaching for it. "Does that mean I've been rejected?"

"It's the same size as mine," Nicole says.

"Yeah, but I think yours was thicker. There was more padding."

"David, just open it." I slide my hand over his upper back. "I know UW is your first choice, but there are other schools. If you're not accepted, it's not the end of the world."

He swallows hard. "Right."

Nicole shakes his shoulder. "Open it."

He takes the envelope like it's a live bomb, fingering the seal. He rips it. A letter slides out. He unfolds it, gnawing his lip. His eyes dart from side to side.

"Well?"

He folds the letter. His gaze lifts, meeting mine. Then his face breaks into a boyish smile.

"I'm in!"

Nicole squeals and dives into his arms, nearly knocking him off the chair. He laughs. She kisses him. He scoops her in his embrace. My stomach flips as I watch them, struck by a memory of Cameron. I try not to dwell on our failed marriage, but sometimes I miss him. At least, the part of him that wasn't homicidal.

I did everything I could to discourage Nicole and David's relationship. Two teenagers dating under one roof is a disaster, but they're great to each other. They've respected my rules. Since the divorce was finalized, there's no reason to keep them apart.

I pull David into a big hug. "I'm excited for you. You're going to have a blast at UW. I'm proud of you."

"Thanks, Mom."

I disengage from him. "This is a good thing. You can stop looking so shell-shocked."

"I can't believe it. I'm so lucky."

"Luck has nothing to do with it. You worked hard. You both did." I hug Nicole, whose eyes gleam with happy tears. "We'll go out tonight and celebrate. Any ideas on where?"

"What about Canlis?"

David's dry chuckle echoes in the kitchen. "Sure, if you don't mind waiting six months for a table."

Nicole pulls away from me and shoves David. "All right. You suggest something."

"Ivar's," he says.

"We went there last week."

"And? It has the best views of Lake Union. It's not expensive. It has that cute outdoor patio. It has seagulls ripping french fries out of your hand. What more could you want?"

Nicole scoffs. "Less wildlife, maybe? Better food?"

His mouth curves. "I'm partial to the ambience."

I raise my voice, cutting into their banter. "How about you make a list of a few places, and I'll pick."

David gives me a thumbs-up, and I stagger upstairs to change. As I walk past Nicole's room, I spot wet towels on the bed. I gather them, gritting my teeth. I've told her so many times not to do that. I straighten, balling the damp fabric in my arms. Her room is such a mess. Papers on the floor. Sheets spilling off the mattress. Empty wrappers on the vanity. A seltzer can tips over the partly open dresser drawer, its contents dripping inside.

I grab the handle, preparing to shut it. My gaze wanders over a guitar pick and a pink sparkling case stuffed inside. I gasp, backing away from it like it's a viper. My pulse skyrockets. I wipe my face, inhaling uneven breaths.

What's Laura's cell doing in Nicole's drawer?

It can't be what I think it is. It just can't. I seize it, flipping it to the black screen. I slide my thumb over the power button. It boots up. I read her messages, finding multiple heartbreaking texts from Scott. I check her photo album, scrolling down to the latest image. I select it. It's a photo of Laura's corpse, taken by someone standing above her. A tear trembling on my lid falls, sliding down my cheek.

Oh my God.

Why does Nicole have this?

Nausea pits my stomach as I cycle through a myriad of possibilities. My daughter has a dead woman's phone. Someone my ex murdered. Laura's phone shouldn't be in her possession. How did it end up here?

Their laughter drifts upstairs. I swallow hard and call out loudly, "*Nicole*. I'm in your room. Get up here *now*!"

Her footsteps race up the stairs. She's still riding the high of David's acceptance to UW until her blue gaze lands on the pink case digging into my palm. Blood siphons from her face as she whispers, "Mom, I can explain—"

"You need to turn yourself in."

FIFTY

NICOLE

Yes, I killed Laura.

I killed my classmate Erica. I never got to kill Cameron. I would've finished off Fred in the hospital, but getting away with it would've been impossible.

Do I feel remorse?

Yes and no. I'm not sorry because I read that disgusting diary. Laura was a monster. She hurt my dad. Cheating is one of the worst things you can do to a person. I know. I watched my mother struggle with what my father did for years. And it's not like I didn't give Laura plenty of chances to break things off with Fred. I confronted her several times, but if anything, the idiot dug in her heels. Laura deserved that broken neck. So did Fred, but he's lucky. He survived, healed up, and joined an eighties cover band. Apparently, he plays at venues around Seattle. I'm not too disappointed. With Fred alive, my dad gets out soon.

Unfortunately, I'm not getting out for…a while. After Mom turned me in, the police searched my room and found my trophies. Now they're investigating Erica's death as a homicide, and it probably won't end well for me. Broke my mother's heart. I do feel bad about that. I never imagined that helping my parents would cause them so much pain. So I'm sorry for that. I'm sorry that I won't get to go to college with David. I'm sorry we'll never move into an apartment after freshman year, like we talked about. I'm sorry that I love my parents too much.

Erica died because she threatened to tell everyone at school what we saw when we walked in on Fred and Laura at Dad's house. I couldn't have that, so I lured her to the rooftop of the Science building and…gave her a push. Erica had serious emotional problems. It was only a matter of time before she jumped.

David saw me shove Laura. He was furious with me. Once I explained myself, he agreed to keep it a secret. Then he folded like a deck of cards once Mom got involved.

Honestly, it's fine. Things aren't so bad here. Mom and David visit me every week. So will Dad, once he gets out. I found a college that'll give me a bachelor's degree in prison. I'm happy that David didn't get into any trouble. Someone has to keep an eye on Mom.

She has a boyfriend.

Todd. He's an accountant. After Cameron and my father, I guess she needed to go for the safest, dullest man she could find, and overcorrected in that department. I can't complain. He seems like a good guy. David's been through his belongings, searched through his browser history, texts on his phone, etc. He's squeaky clean.

My compulsion to kill is gone. Whenever I feel off, I talk to my therapist. Or I hug Mom and the healing light from her compassion warms me. I am so grateful David's with Mom. Between her and David, I feel so blessed to have this perfectly imperfect family.

So Todd better watch himself.

Because David loves my mom, too…and he'll do anything for her.

ACKNOWLEDGMENTS

This book was partly inspired by a mushroom trip gone wrong. Thank you, Washington, for your hauntingly beautiful forests. There is no better setting for this book. Thanks also goes to my surrogate family in the PNW, my furbabies, and my soulmate. Kevin, I love you so much.

Jess, Kat, and Jaime—you are the real deal. Your continued friendship and support through all these years has meant the world to me. Thank you Bettye Underwood and Christine LePorte for editing this book. Props goes to my betas for helping me tighten the plot. Credit goes to Kevin McGrath for the incredible cover. You will always be my favorite designer. To Eliette and Rene, my French translation team, you're amazing!

ALSO BY RACHEL HARGROVE

Thrillers

Not a Normal Family

The Maid

Sick Girl

My Sister's Lies

Contemporary Romance *as Blair LeBlanc

The Guarded Heart

ABOUT THE AUTHOR

Rachel Hargrove is from Montreal, Canada. She earned a BA in English and Comparative Literature at San Jose State University and worked as a data analyst in a biotechnology company. When she turned 26, she left her career in tech to write fiction full-time. Rachel now lives in Seattle.

Rachel's debut psychological thriller *Sick Girl*, was released in March 2018. She is represented by Jill Marsal of Marsal Lyon Literary Agency. Rachel can be reached at admin@rachelhargrove.com